What Others Saying about M

"This portrayal of Mary, mother of the Messiah, takes you inside her head and heart, allowing you to breathe the air of Hebrew family, food, and worship. Her much-repeated prayer, *O God who sees me*, may well become your own. True to the scriptural account, this story puts flesh on the bones of history. *Yeshua lives!*"

—*Eleanor Gustafson*
Author, *The Stones*

"Diana Wallis Taylor takes the reader into the everyday life of Mary, the mother of Jesus. We experience the wonder, the hardships, and the heartache right along with her. I love how close to Scripture this narrative is! As well as historically accurate. I've done a lot of research of the Roman era, and this novel's depiction of the society, the settings, and the interactions are true to reality, as best we can recreate it. This is truly a book readers will have a hard time putting down."

—*Lena Nelson Dooley*
ECPA and CBA bestselling and multi-award-winning author,
The Gold Digger and *A Heart's Gift*

DIANA WALLIS TAYLOR

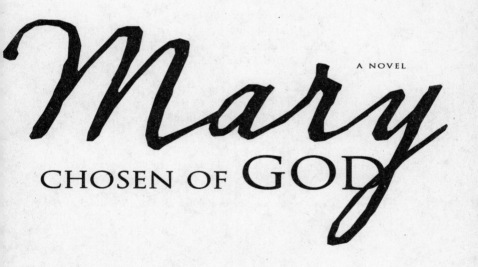

A NOVEL

Mary

CHOSEN OF GOD

WHITAKER
HOUSE

All un-italicized Scripture quotations and paraphrases are taken from either the King James Version of the Holy Bible or the *New King James Version*, © 1979, 1980, 1982, 1984 by Thomas Nelson, Inc. Used by permission. All rights reserved. All unmarked italicized Scripture quotations are taken from *The Complete Jewish Bible*, © 1998 by David H. Stern. Published by Jewish New Testament Publications, Inc. Used by permission. All rights reserved. Scripture quotation marked (NLT) is taken from the *Holy Bible, New Living Translation*, © 1996, 2004, 2007. Used by permission of Tyndale House Publishers, Inc., Carol Stream, Illinois 60188. All rights reserved.

MARY, CHOSEN OF GOD

Diana Wallis Taylor
www.dianawallistaylor.com

ISBN: 978-1-62911-748-5
eBook ISBN: 978-1-62911-749-2
Printed in the United States of America
© 2016 by Diana Wallis Taylor

Whitaker House
1030 Hunt Valley Circle
New Kensington, PA 15068
www.whitakerhouse.com

Library of Congress Cataloging-in-Publication Data (Pending)

1 2 3 4 5 6 7 8 9 10 11 LLJ 23 22 21 20 19 18 17 16

She is clothed with strength and dignity, and she laughs without fear of the future. When she speaks, her words are wise, and she gives instructions with kindness.... "There are many virtuous and capable women in the world, but you surpass them all!"

Proverbs 31: 25–26, 29 NLT

ONE

*W*ith a sigh, Mary paused to sit on a nearby rock and tie the leather strap again. Her sandals had been new a year ago, but the rough roads and hillsides of Nazareth had taken their toll. For a moment, she sat quietly looking around her, listening to the song of the birds calling to each other from the fig trees. A gentle breeze brushed a lock of hair protruding from under her mantle, and she smiled. It was when she was alone, with the hills of Nazareth around her, that she felt Adonai closest to her. She prayed as she walked, and his presence was like a warm cloak around her shoulders.

Remembering that she was on an errand for her father, she chided herself for stopping so long. She adjusted her mantle to protect her face from the unrelenting heat of the month of Av. The vintage had begun and workers were in the vineyards stripping the ripe fruit from the vines. She watched them for a moment and then, with a sense of anticipation, started for the shop of the local carpenter.

Jacob skillfully moved the bow drill back and forth with his hands, intent on boring a hole in a cartwheel. She stood quietly until he became aware of her presence and looked up. He smiled and put the tool down.

"Ah, Mary. What can I do for you today?"

"The donkey got loose again and when my father tried to catch him he kicked up his heels at our wooden bench and broke it. He is not a very good donkey."

"And your father wants the bench repaired?"

She nodded.

"Tell him I will come and look at it this afternoon." His eyes twinkled as he suppressed a smile. "When I see how much damage that beast has done, I'll know how long it will take to repair it. Have your parents ever considered replacing that donkey with one a little more mild-tempered?"

She laughed then. "No, we have had the donkey since it was a colt. Abba says the animal works well with the plow, but when he gets loose, he kicks his feet up and trots around the yard, making a great deal of noise."

Jacob stroked his beard and shrugged. "Ah well, it is your donkey."

Mary looked around the shop. Jacob was alone. There was no sign of Joseph and her heart sank.

Seeing her disappointment, Jacob answered the unspoken question. "Joseph has gone to Sepphoris where there is much building going on, and he can earn good wages. He is making frames for the brick makers." Then he added kindly, "He promised to be back in time for Hanukkah."

Four months? It would seem forever. She would miss the wonderful stories he always took time to share with her. When she was curious about the tools he and his father used in the shop, Joseph explained their various uses to her.

It seemed so natural to spend time in the carpenter's shop, for she and Joseph had known each other since they were children. Mary looked up to him as the brother she'd never had.

She thanked Jacob for telling her, and as she made her way back home, she thought back to the day when Joseph was called upon to recite in their small synagogue. He had turned twelve, and in the eyes of the law, he was now a man. Standing confidently with his *tallit*, the prayer shawl, covering his head, he'd begun to recite the *Shema*: "Hear, Isra'el! ADONAI our God, ADONAI is one;

and you are to love ADONAI *your God with all your heart, all your being and all your resources....*"

His voice was already beginning to deepen. Half the girls in the village who watched through the lattice separating the women in the synagogue murmured among themselves. He was very handsome. Mary had heard the other young girls talking about how they hoped their fathers would choose him for their husband in the years to come, yet he seemed oblivious to their devotion.

Mary and her parents, Heli and Anna, had been invited along with most of the village to the home of Jacob and Rachel for his special birthday celebration. He had smiled directly at her as she entered with her parents and something touched her heart that day. Joseph was still like a big brother, but what was different? As she watched him laughing and talking with the other young men of the village, she wondered at the strange new emotion that filled her. Why did she suddenly feel shy near him? He was only Joseph, her friend, wasn't he?

One day Mary teased him and asked whom he would choose to marry from the girls in their village. He had winked at her and replied solemnly, "Why, I'm waiting for you, Mary."

The Joseph she knew now was tall and strong, his arms muscular from the work in his father's shop. His dark eyes held a light when he smiled, and Joseph smiled often. He seemed so content with the life God had chosen for him. Now as she walked and recalled his words, she blushed, as she had that day two years before.

Joseph helped his father in the shop and was polite to the young women who paraded by, as they found one excuse after another to talk to him. Mary, busy with more household tasks now that she was fourteen, only stopped by occasionally, still wondering at the butterflies fluttering in her chest when she saw him. He would turn and nod to her, put his tools down and, over a cup of water, take time to talk. Sometimes they discussed the Torah and she listened intently. He seemed so wise to her.

Now, as she walked slowly along the road, Joseph's face came to mind as it seemed to so many times lately; those laughing eyes of his seemed to see into her heart. Why, when she thought of Joseph, did the day seem brighter? Suddenly she paused in the middle of the road. *Joseph!* Like the bud of a flower gently opening to the sun, something awakened in her soul. She looked up at the heavens, her heart filled with joy. Wrapping her arms around herself, she cried out, "Oh God Who Sees Me, may your name be praised." Why had she not seen it before? It was not Joseph the big brother she wanted. It was Joseph the man. She spread her arms and whirled around, drawing the curious stare of a farmer in the nearby field. She stopped quickly, and feeling the heat of embarrassment in her face, hurried home.

When she entered the small courtyard, her parents paused in their conversation.

Heli smiled, making little crinkles by his eyes. "Ah, daughter, it is good you have returned. Your mother and I were just, ah, talking."

She looked from one to another, questions forming in her mind.

"You are now fourteen and it is time to consider seeking a husband for you."

Anna nodded. "There are several eligible young men in the village. I have seen them turn to watch you walk by. Any day now we should have offers for your hand."

Her father nodded sagely. "Of course as our only daughter, and the most beautiful girl in the village, we will need to choose wisely." A slight smile played around his lips.

Mary, savoring the knowledge that had filled her only moments before, wanted to cry out to them, *Please, let it be Joseph.*

She hesitated, then, "Do you have someone in mind, Abba?"

He stroked his beard. "Perhaps, daughter, perhaps. Now tell me what the carpenter had to say."

She related Jacob's words, then, with her thoughts tumbling about, helped her mother with their evening meal. Her mother had made a stew of brown lentils, onions, barley, leeks, and mustard greens in olive oil, cooked until the barley turned golden. The aroma made Mary realize how hungry she was. She cut a large cucumber into cubes and added olives from the crock in the storage room, then mixed in some sprigs of finely chopped dill and sprinkled it with small chunks of goat cheese. Then bread and a few dates were placed on the table and the family gathered around it while Heli blessed the Most High for providing their food.

After the remnants of the meal had been gathered up and their wooden platters cleaned, her father made sure the night candle was burning. Mary bid her parents good night and went up the narrow stairs to the roof of their small house. During the warmer months her parents let her spread her pallet there and it was pleasant having the space to herself. Mary was glad their home was more secluded, separated from the neighbors on either side by enclosures for livestock. Due to the rocky terrain, most of the houses including her own were constructed of fieldstone with smaller rocks placed in the cracks and then smeared with clay for insulation.

The sun was slipping down behind the hills as she knelt in the gathering dusk and looked up at the first star of the evening. Waiting quietly, she felt the presence of Ha'Shem and she began to recite her evening prayers: "Praised are you, Adonai, our God, Ruler of the universe, who closes my eyes in sleep, my eyelids in slumber. May it be your will, Adonai, my God and the God of my ancestors, to lie me down in peace and then to raise me up in peace. Let no disturbing thoughts upset me, no evil dreams nor troubling fantasies. May my bed be complete and whole in your sight. Grant me light so that I do not sleep the sleep of death, for it is you who illumines and enlightens. Praised are you, Adonai, whose majesty gives light to the universe."

Then, as she prepared for sleep, she looked up at the heavens and another prayer rose from her soul. "Oh God Who Sees, hear my heart. Joseph can have his pick of the young women of Nazareth. Perhaps he has already chosen one." At the thought, her heart began to beat faster. "Oh, Ha'Shem, may your will be done." She bowed her head and gave her wishes into the keeping of her God. She had been brought up to be obedient to her parents and would abide by their wishes, but her heart sang, *Joseph, Joseph.*

TWO

*T*he months passed with unbearable slowness. Mary thought it strange her parents said no more about a betrothal, even when one father actually came with his son, a shy, gangling youth. Thankfully, and to Mary's great relief, her parents kindly refused the offer. She marked the time as the month of Cheshvan moved into Kislev and the village prepared for the celebration of Hanukkah.

It was Mary's favorite time of the year, and while it was a holy time, it was a Jewish festival that did not require the men of the family to journey to Jerusalem. On the twenty-fifth of Kislev, they would begin the eight days of celebration.

Mary loved seeing the lighted *menorahs* that glowed from windows and courtyards of nearby homes as each family lit first a *shammash*, the servant or helper candle, and then one more candle each night until at the end of the eight days all the candles were lit. Her mother made sure the candles were placed in the *menorah* from right to left, but lit from left to right.

The first night of Hanukkah, a half hour before sundown, Mary and her father stood by and watched Anna light the *shammash*, and the first candle of Hanukkah as Heli intoned three prayers:

"Blessed are you, Ha'Shem our God, King of the universe, who has sanctified us by his Commandments, and has commanded us to kindle the lights of Hanukkah.

"Blessed are you, Ha'Shem our God, King of the universe, who wrought miracles for our fathers, in days of old, at this season.

"Blessed are you, Ha'Shem our God, King of the universe, who has kept us alive, and has preserved us, and enabled us to reach this time."

After the candles were lit and her father had recited the blessings, Mary and her mother joined him in singing.

"These lights we kindle upon the miracles, the wonders, the salvations, and the battles which you performed for our forefathers in those days at this season through your holy priests. During all the days of Hanukkah these lights are sacred, and we are not permitted to make ordinary use of them, but look at them in order to express thanks and praise to your great name for your miracles, your wonders, your salvations."

And another song.

"Oh mighty Rock of my salvation, to praise you is a delight. Restore my house of prayer and there we will bring a thanksgiving offering. When you will have prepared the slaughter of the blaspheming foe, then I shall complete with a song of hymn, the dedication of the altar."

At the end of the day, Mary's parents were careful to only burn the candles for one half hour after dark and then snuff them out.

The second day of Hanukkah, the main rains began, and the streets became thick and muddy. The women had to be careful going to the village well for water and Mary returned with the hem of her tunic muddy each time. Today she ignored the mud, her attention fixed on the conversation at the well.

"Joseph has returned from Sepphoris," a girl named Judith announced knowingly.

The young women tittered among themselves.

"I hear he did well there."

"And, I heard he is seeking a wife," another added.

Judith turned to Mary. "You and Joseph are friends. Has he mentioned anyone?"

Mary shrugged and kept her back to Judith, pretending to concentrate on drawing her water. When the girl asked again, she shrugged and kept her face averted so they would not see the flame that lit her cheeks. Why didn't Joseph let her know he was back? She sighed. She was only a friend to him. He was probably busy getting ready to select his bride. She hurried home, trying to think of an excuse to go to the carpenter shop the next day. Perhaps he would tell her whom he had chosen.

That evening, after the lighting of the candles and prayers, she still had not thought of a reasonable excuse. With her new knowledge, her heart skipped and shyness enveloped her just at the thought of talking to him. Would he see in her eyes how she felt? Would he think she was just another lovesick girl in the village who hoped to influence him toward marriage?

Her thoughts were interrupted by a knock at their gate. She peered from the doorway of the house as Heli went to open it. She heard a familiar voice, and there stood Joseph and Jacob.

Mary's heart beat so loudly, she was sure everyone could hear it. Joseph had come with his father and it could only mean one thing. It was the moment she had prayed for so fervently. Surely her parents would accept Joseph.

Jacob bowed his head solemnly. "Peace be upon this house."

Her father stepped back to let the two men enter. "Welcome, Jacob. Welcome, Joseph. Please enter our humble home. It is well with you?"

Jacob nodded. "It is well."

The two fathers discussed the health of the flocks and herds and the carpentry trade as Joseph held his hands behind his back, patiently waiting for the usual preliminaries to be over. From time to time he glanced at Mary who shyly cast her eyes down.

When Joseph and his father had partaken of some wine and fresh bread, Jacob cleared his throat. "We have come on a most important matter. As you know, my son Joseph has been working these last months in the city of Sepphoris, carefully saving his wages. Added to what he had already saved, he feels that now he is in a position to offer a fair bride price for a wife. We have chosen Mary and pray that you will find the sum acceptable."

Joseph reached in his tunic and brought forth a leather bag. He opened it and spread the silver coins on the low table. Mary heard her mother gasp and her father's eyes grew large.

"This is indeed a very acceptable bride price." He scrutinized Joseph. "It has taken a long time to gather this."

Joseph nodded slowly. "I wanted the bride price to be worthy of Mary. We have known each other since we were children, but we are no longer children. I would make her my wife."

Heli stroked his beard, then turned to Mary. "Well, daughter, he is agreeable to you?"

Mary blinked. Her father was asking her? As she nodded slowly, Heli looked from Mary to Joseph and with a smile and a twinkle in his eyes, nodded his head. "This will be a good match, Jacob. The bride price is worthy of our Mary. We will inform the village elders and the betrothal ceremony will take place at noon tomorrow, before the ceremonies of Hanukkah begin. Shall the wedding take place after the barley harvest?"

Jacob and Joseph stood and bowed to her father. Jacob stroked his beard. "It shall be as you say." As they turned to go, Joseph gave Mary the briefest of smiles and a lift of his chin.

When they had gone, Mary turned to her parents. "I knew you were thinking of making marriage plans for me. I hoped it would be Joseph."

Heli chuckled. "Are we blind, daughter? Could we not see how it was with the two of you? Joseph has been working hard for you and you alone."

Anna waved a hand in the air. "Now that you men have settled things, we have a betrothal ceremony to plan. You must see the rabbi in the morning, and then...."

Mary's father rolled his eyes. "Ah, so it begins."

THREE

*M*ary knelt by her pallet, now placed inside the house due to the weather. She missed being able to look up and see the stars. As she listened to the soft snores of her parents, she felt she couldn't contain her happiness. The *Shtar Tena'im*, the "Document of Conditions," had been signed, signifying that the *shidukhim* had been agreed to. Joseph took the cup of wine, declaring his love to be so strong for Mary that he would shed his life's blood, if necessary, to protect her life. He handed the cup to Mary, and waited, his eyes asking the question: will she place her trust and hope in his love for her? She sipped from the cup, joining her life to his. She handed the cup back to him, and he spoke confidently, "I will build a home for us onto my father's house. I look forward to sharing this cup anew with you, this cup of joy, on our wedding day."

As her mother, Anna, and Joseph's mother, Rachel, broke the traditional plates at the joyous betrothal ceremony, the local women smiled and nodded their heads.

"It is a love match," they whispered to one another.

Mary thought of how many times in her village a girl married someone from a distant family or another village, without knowing her groom until the wedding day. She would not have to wait until the wedding day to view her bridegroom for the first time. It would be her beloved Joseph.

As she prayed by her pallet, Mary felt the familiar warmth of the presence of Ha'Shem and lifted her praise from the joy filling her heart. Suddenly she ceased praying, aware of a strange silence. The hair on the back of her neck rose up and she looked around. She waited in the stillness, listening.

A soft light began to glow and then, suddenly, standing before her was a being so magnificent and powerful that she fell on her face, her heart pounding.

The voice was gentle but strong as the being spoke. "Greetings, favored woman! The LORD is with you."

Favored woman?

Was this an angel? Speaking to her? Mary slowly sat back on her heels, her mind sorting out what this could mean, and she looked up with fear and expectation as the glorious being spoke again.

"Don't be afraid, Mary," the angel told her, "for you have found favor with God! You will conceive and give birth to a son, and you will name him Yeshua. He will be very great and will be called the son of the Most High. The Lord God will give him the throne of his ancestor David, and he will reign over Israel forever, his Kingdom will never end."

Mary stared at the angel. *What type of a greeting is this? I am favored with God? I shall have a son before I am married?* She gathered her courage to speak to the angel.

"But how can this happen? I am a virgin."

The angel appeared to understand her honest bewilderment for there was no guile in her.

"The Holy Spirit will come upon you, and the power of the Most High will overshadow you. This child to be born will be holy, and he will be called the son of God."

As Mary shook her head in wonder, the angel smiled. "What's more, your relative Elizabeth has become pregnant in her old age. People used to say she was barren, but she is now in her sixth month. For nothing is impossible with God."

The Most High had sent his angel to tell her this astounding news. What could she do but be obedient to his will for her as well?

She bowed her head and said, "I am the Lord's servant. May everything you have said about me come true."

The angel reached out and touched her shoulder with the gentleness of a butterfly alighting, yet she felt strength flowing through her body. In the next moment the angel was gone.

Mary looked around at her parents, expecting to see them looking at her wide-eyed, but they slept peacefully. They had not seen the angel. A night bird resumed singing and all was still. Had she been dreaming? She looked toward the window. *I am to bear God's son? The long-awaited Messiah?* Tears rolled down her cheeks as she contemplated the awesome responsibility God had entrusted to her. For centuries her people had prayed for the Messiah to come. Every Jewish mother hoped that she would be the one to bear him.

Then she realized—the father of this child could not be an earthly man, it would have to be Adonai. A child with a human father could not be the son of God, for he would carry the sin of Adam. She put her hands to her face and bowed her head on her knees.

Then more troubling thoughts came. What would her parents say? What would Joseph say if this were true? Would the village consider it Joseph's child? Would Joseph accuse her of being unfaithful or believe her and still agree to the marriage? And what about Elizabeth? Was she truly with child after all these years of being barren? If God could give Elizabeth a child in her old age, as the angel said, nothing is impossible with God.

She must go to Elizabeth, but how? It was a long journey, past Hebron. Would her parents even allow her to make such a trip? She could only pray. *O God Who Sees Me, you have ordained this. Make a way to get to Elizabeth. She would understand. She would help me.*

When she sat back she tentatively placed her hands on her flat stomach. When would this happen? When would she know? Even as the questions chased themselves in her mind, she finally lay down on her pallet and as the words *I have been chosen…chosen* ran through her mind, she felt herself falling into a deep sleep.

FOUR

$\mathcal{M}$ary stared unseeing at the wall of the courtyard. The weather had cleared for a day and she stood breathing the air freshened with the scent of rain. With her woman's time due in less than two weeks, she considered her dilemma. If it came, she would know the scene with the angel was just a dream. If it did not, then the words of the angel were true and if it were true, how would she explain all this to her parents? She'd always been truthful, but would they believe such a strange story? Would they think that she and Joseph had not waited for their marriage ceremony to consummate the marriage?

Go to Elizabeth.

The words were clear in her mind. If what the angel told her was true about Elizabeth, then she, Mary, was to be...the mother of God's son, the promised Messiah. Suddenly dizzy, she sank down on their wooden bench.

"Mary!" Her mother stood in front of her, holding a broom. "Mary, are you daydreaming again? There is work to do." She waved a hand in the air. "I don't understand you. These last few days all you do is daydream. I speak to you and you do not answer. What is happening?"

Mary rose quickly. "Forgive me Ima, I was thinking about... Joseph." That was indeed truthful. How would she tell him? She had a short time. If she waited too long her mother would know something was wrong. Then she would have to tell them…and Joseph.

Anna smiled. "That is natural, Mary, but we have work to do. Feed the chickens and check for eggs. The rains will begin again soon."

Mary nodded, glad to have something to keep her mind occupied.

Go to Elizabeth.

Ha'Shem wanted her to go to her cousin Elizabeth. Her heart began to beat erratically. Would Abba allow her to go? It was a five-day journey just to Jerusalem, and if Elizabeth's husband, Zechariah, had finished his priestly duties, they would have returned to their home in Juttah, which was even farther, past Hebron. She looked up toward the heavens.

Oh God Who Sees Me, you have chosen me to carry your son. Just as your angel said, nothing is too hard for you. May your name be praised. If you wish me to go, please make a way for me to travel to Elizabeth.

Mary put the broom aside and approached her mother. "Ima, I was indeed thinking of Joseph, but also of a strange dream I had. That is what has been on my mind. Ha'Shem spoke to my heart and told me I am to visit our cousin Elizabeth. In my dream she needed me."

Anna continued kneading the bread dough for a moment, then paused and studied her daughter's face. "You want to go to visit Elizabeth? Impossible, child." She frowned and regarded Mary with raised eyebrows. "A dream? I know the Most High speaks to us in dreams, but why would he suggest such a journey to a young woman, and one betrothed at that?"

Mary continued to look up at her mother, willing her to understand. Anna shook her head. "You say Ha'Shem told you in a dream?" Anna sighed heavily and planted floured hands on her hips. "Tell me this dream."

"It was an angel, sent by the Most High. He told me that Elizabeth is in her sixth month with child and I was to go to her."

Mary continued to look up expectantly as her mother contemplated her words.

"Ach, Elizabeth with child? Impossible! She has been barren for years and is past the age of childbearing." Anna dismissed the idea with a wave of her hand.

"It was very real," Mary persisted.

"Of course I would wish to know if such a miracle has happened, but why would Ha'Shem send you?"

"Who am I to question the way of the Most High? I'm sure he will protect me, Ima."

"He also does not want us to make foolish decisions." She sighed heavily. "We will speak to your father about this dream. He must decide."

She sought some way to convince her mother. "Perhaps there is a caravan I could join?"

Anna raised her eyebrows. "That is more foolishness. It would not be proper to go on such a journey before your marriage."

Mary looked up into her mother's face. "If Ha'Shem wants me to go to Elizabeth, he will make a way."

"Enough of this talk. Your father will not let you go." Her mother shook her head vehemently. "Dream or no dream. It is impossible." She began kneading the dough again.

Mary continued to pray as she helped her mother prepare their dinner. Soon her father would be coming in from the field and would be hungry. What would he say to her strange request?

When Heli returned home, Anna served him grilled tilapia coated with a mixture of vinegar, honey, garlic, and olive oil. Mary put together a bitter herbs salad with watercress, grapes, walnuts, and dill. Then she placed a basket of fresh bread and a bowl of olive oil on their small table. It was one of Anna's best meals. Perhaps this might work in her favor. A good dinner could put her father in a favorable mood.

Her father eyed the feast with obvious pleasure. Mary was glad her mother was a creative cook, using carefully what she had to work with. For a simple family they ate well.

Heli looked up at the anxious faces of his wife and daughter and stroked his beard. "There is a special occasion I should know about?"

Anna shrugged. "I found fresh fish in the marketplace this morning. It was reasonable."

Heli nodded. "Ahhh."

After the washing of hands, Heli bowed his head and began the first of the blessings on the food. *"Baruch atah Adonai, Eloheinu melekh ha'olam, ha'motzi Lechem min ha'arets.* Blessed are you, Lord our God, King of the universe, who brings bread forth from the earth."

When Heli had been served, Mary and her mother joined him. Though it was the custom for the man of the house to eat first and then the women, Mary was glad her father did not like to eat alone.

Mary watched her father and glanced hopefully at her mother.

Anna sighed heavily. "My husband, Mary tells me she has had a dream about her cousin Elizabeth and feels that she is to visit her. I told her she could not make such a trip alone."

Heli's hand paused in midair with a morsel of bread. "A dream?" He scrutinized Mary's face. "You had a dream about Elizabeth? And what did you dream, daughter?"

Mary sent up a silent prayer. "An angel told me she was with child, in her sixth month, and that nothing is impossible with God."

Anna shook her head. "The dream couldn't have been true. Elizabeth and her husband are past the age of childbearing. They have been married over twenty years and she was not young when they married. They...." her voice trailed off, and she looked at her husband.

Heli was silent a long moment. "Mary has always been a truthful daughter. She has never told us of such a thing before. If Elizabeth is with child, this is truly a miracle. Perhaps Mary's dream is a sign. If the Most High sent his angel on such a mission, who are we to question his ways? We must learn if this wondrous thing has happened to our relatives."

"Then you would let Mary, our only child, make such a journey? I am afraid for her!"

"I do not feel afraid, Ima," Mary broke in. "I believe Elizabeth needs me and Ha'Shem is telling me to go."

Heli nodded, his face thoughtful. "Then you must honor the dream and obey what the Most High has ordained."

He pulled on his beard. "Arrangements must be made. I must find out who is traveling that way." Suddenly his eyebrows rose. "I remember now. Only this morning, Omar, the potter, said that now the days of Hanukkah are over, he and his family are leaving to travel to Hebron for the wedding of his brother's son. We have only weeks before the spring rains begin. I will inquire if they are willing to take Mary with them."

"But, my husband, Elizabeth's home is past Hebron, her journey would be over one hundred and twenty miles. How will Mary get to Juttah?"

"Perhaps Omar can be persuaded to see Mary to Juttah and then return to Hebron."

Anna shook her head and clasped her hands together. "I don't know...." she murmured over and over.

Mary silently thanked Ha'Shem for the answer to her prayer. He would get her to Juttah somehow.

After their meal, Heli rose, and ignoring the anxious face of his wife, murmured, "I will speak to the potter," and hurried out the gate. When he had gone, her mother shook her head and covered her face with her hands. Then, gaining her composure again, she faced Mary, sighing heavily. "Will you have time to arrive in Juttah?"

She knew what her mother was asking. She could not travel if it was her time of women and she was unclean. She gave her mother a bright smile. "I will have time, Ima."

Less than an hour later, Heli returned. Mary hurried to him, eager to hear his news.

"You have spoken to Omar?"

"Yes, I have, and since his wife, daughter, and young son will be traveling with him, you would be properly chaperoned. You can help care for the boy."

"Then he is willing, Abba?"

"He is willing. But you must be ready to leave at first light, when the day is still cool." He put a hand on her shoulder. "I am reluctant to let you go. You are my only daughter and you are still young. But we must trust the dream. Omar is a good man. He will watch over you. When they are ready to come back to Nazareth, you can return home with them."

Mary could only smile up at her father. "Thank you, Abba. I will be careful." Only she knew the other part of the dream. What lay ahead was unknown, yet she sensed her stay with Elizabeth would be more than a couple of weeks. And after that? She gave an involuntary shudder. She could only depend on Ha'Shem for strength to face the ordeal ahead.

FIVE

*M*ary perched on the end of the small cart next to the potter's daughter, Huldah, adjusted her shawl, and then reached out for the small traveling bag she had prepared. Anna handed it to her along with another bag holding some bread and cheese and a goatskin bag of water for the journey. Mary would have to buy other provisions on the way. Her father handed the potter a small bag of shekels for Mary's care. Mary knew how much it must have cost him, and for a moment a twinge of guilt assailed her conscience.

Just then a figure came striding toward them. It was Joseph. "I just heard of your journey. Did you not wish to say goodbye?" His handsome face was clouded with concern and he frowned. "I do not understand why you must travel such a distance at this time."

"Oh Joseph, there was no time to speak with you." She slipped down from the cart and took him aside to tell him of her dream about Elizabeth.

He listened quietly then spread his hands. "So then, you must go. If your father has allowed this, then there is little I can say. For your cousin's sake, I pray the dream is true." He gave her a hopeful smile. "By the time you return, the extra room will be added to my parent's home...for us."

His eyes caressed her face. "Go with our God, my Mary. I shall be eager for your return."

"I too, Joseph. I will think of you every day." She longed to fling herself in his arms and pour out all she was holding in her heart but knew their customs forbade that kind of physical contact, at least in public, until their marriage. Would he feel the same about her when she returned? How would he react to her story of the angel's words? *Oh Ha'Shem, what a terrible magnificent burden you have bestowed on your maidservant.* She wrapped her arms around herself instead and poured her love and longing into her eyes. He held out his hand and in his palm was a small carving of a bird.

"To think of me while you are gone."

She took it gently and smiled. "It is beautiful, Joseph. I shall treasure it."

He lifted her back up on the cart then took a deep breath and stepped back, his dark eyes never leaving her face. "That is good."

Omar's wife Timnah settled their young son, Jethro, in the cart and then climbed up beside her husband. Mary glanced at Huldah, a plain girl, slender to the point of being thin, with sad eyes and dark hair straight as straw. The village women had clicked their tongues and cast sympathetic glances at Timnah…a daughter nineteen and unmarried. Such a shame. It was assumed that Huldah would be living with her parents all her life, with no family of her own.

With a jerk, the cart began to move forward. Mary waved and then watched her parents and Joseph become small figures in the distance. The village roads were uneven, and Mary and Huldah were jostled as the cart moved slowly over the ruts left by the rains. Omar growled to Timnah that he would be glad to reach the Roman road that at least was kept in reasonable repair.

Joining other families traveling to Jerusalem, their group became large enough that Mary felt they were fairly safe from robbers. They traveled by day and at night camped by the side of the road. Small fires were built as the women prepared meals for hungry children and husbands.

Mary and Huldah helped with the serving and cleaning up. A young man in their group began playing a *kinnor*, a small harp. As he played, people became quiet to listen as the soothing sounds wafted through the camp. Finally, when all was still except for the hooting of an owl seeking his dinner, the family wrapped themselves in their cloaks and prepared for sleep, with women and children on the inside of the circle and men on the outside for protection. Morning would come too soon, and with it another day of travel.

The two girls talked occasionally through the long hours on the road. "Are you excited about being married?" Huldah asked. "You are so fortunate to be marrying someone you know."

"Yes, I am glad it is Joseph."

"How can you bear to leave him?"

"It is still our time of betrothal. He has work to do. I will miss him, but I have something I also must do."

"Your cousin? Why must you visit her now?"

Mary hesitated. "She needs me." It didn't answer the question, but it was all she could say to this curious girl.

Sensing Mary did not want to talk, Huldah became quiet and turned to look at the scenery.

Whenever they stopped to rest, Omar tended to the donkey and the women stretched their legs. Jethro occupied himself with chasing butterflies or looking for interesting bugs among the rocks.

That evening as they were preparing for sleep, Huldah whispered. "My parents are talking about a cousin in Hebron. I've never met him." She sighed softly. "I think the reason we are going to Hebron is to speak to his family."

"I thought you were going for a wedding," Mary whispered back.

Huldah paused and there was a catch in her voice. "There has been no mention of a bride. I am thinking that the wedding will be my own."

Mary opened her mouth to respond. Her heart ached for Huldah, and she whispered back. "Why wouldn't your parents tell you if this was the reason?"

There was a loud "Ahem," from the direction of Omar. The girls hushed immediately but Mary reached out for Huldah's hand in the darkness and squeezed it as they settled down to go to sleep. As the other girl slept, Mary looked up at the stars. Life seemed so simple in Nazareth. Yet now she was traveling over one hundred miles to a town near Hebron to see a relative she saw only occasionally in Jerusalem at Passover. How would Zechariah and Elizabeth receive the news of her condition? Yet if what the angel said about Elizabeth were true, they, of all people, would understand. She needed the older woman's wisdom on this great miracle she could not as yet share with her own mother.

Oh God Who Sees Me, grant me your peace. I am frightened of what is to come. I am your handmaiden. I must trust your plan, but there is so much I don't understand.

As she finished her evening prayer, a small breeze came up, cooling the air and ruffling her hair like a caress. It seemed to whisper, *Rest, beloved of the Lord.* Her anxious thoughts quieted, and she closed her eyes.

SIX

The most direct way to Jerusalem was over many mountains and through Samaria, but it was known that the Samaritans closed their inns to those traveling to Jerusalem. The route was also stony and difficult. The caravan avoided the Samaritan route for both reasons.

Mary's caravan traveled over the steep path to the south of Nazareth and then joined a familiar route eastward to the Jordan River. The road built by the Romans was smoother and took them to the Jordan Valley. Mountains loomed on either side, but they didn't have to traverse those. They followed the Roman road sixty miles to the town of Jericho where the group was able to find lodging for the night in a caravansary. Omar purchased fresh hay for the donkey, and they were directed to shelter in one of the open rooms off the main courtyard set aside for travelers. The noise and smell of the camels from another caravan was overwhelming but the straw in their shelter was clean. Omar decided they would stay for two days to rest the animals and replenish their supplies. Mary learned that Timnah was expecting another child, and Omar, contrary to his gruff nature, appeared to want to take more time for her sake.

Mary sympathized with Timnah. How difficult it must be to travel when one is several months into a pregnancy. Then she thought of her own journey home. How far along would she be, and how would she manage to get home to Nazareth? If Omar returned home after the wedding, would she be ready to go with him? She reached into the bag of her possessions and took out the carved bird that Joseph had given her. As she ran her fingers over the surface, she thought of the time and love that had gone into its creation. Oh Joseph. How she missed him.

Huldah looked at the bird. "Oh, it is so pretty. May I hold it?"

Mary placed it in her hand. Huldah turned it this way and that. "I remember Joseph handing you something but I didn't see what it was. This is very beautiful." She sighed. "It must be wonderful to have someone love you that much."

"Perhaps one day love will come to you," Mary said softly, retrieving her treasure and placing it back with her things. She glanced down at Jethro and breathed a sigh of relief. He was asleep. Small boys were rough on things, and he would have wanted to hold it, too.

A short time later, Jethro woke and stretched. He sat up and watched the scenery for a while, but soon tired of riding in the cart.

"I want to walk. I don't like riding in the cart all the time," he announced. Omar grumbled, but stopped the cart so Mary and Huldah could walk with him. Jethro was full of questions.

"Why are you going with us to Hebron?"

"To see an elderly cousin who needs me."

"Why didn't your parents come too?"

"They have things to do in Nazareth. It was not a good time for them to travel."

After several more questions, Mary was relieved when his attention was caught by a flock of birds winging their way over the hills. When they at last returned to the cart, Mary occupied Jethro's attention by telling him stories, the stories of ancient prophets of Israel as her father had told them to her over the years when she was younger. Jethro listened eagerly. Mary caught Timnah's eye and sensed a silent thank you from the weary mother.

The next part of their journey, the Jericho Road, was the most difficult. Robbers lay in wait for unsuspecting travelers who traveled alone or in too small a group. Mary knew Omar had been concerned about their safety, for she heard him speaking about it to Timnah, his voice low, yet loud enough for Mary and Huldah to understand.

"We must find others to travel with on the Jericho Road. If we travel alone, we could be robbed or worse. I will ask around to see who is continuing on to Jerusalem."

When he returned to their shelter in the caravansary, he was exultant. "A contingency of soldiers is traveling to Jerusalem. They came in last night and will travel with us. Two other families are going also."

Roman soldiers were not a welcome sight among her people, yet she knew Omar and the others would welcome the protection the soldiers provided. The soldiers, for their part, wished to have nothing to do with the Jews, but it was their job to keep the peace and they wanted no clash with local bandits.

Mary's anxiety about their safety abated as she silently thanked Ha'Shem for his provision.

The road from Jericho was steep as they headed up toward the Holy City of Jerusalem. The soldiers rode to the head of the group but as they passed they glanced at Mary and Huldah. Their crude comments caused the girls to look away and pretend they didn't hear. Mary knew the Romans disliked her people, but the emperor had decreed they were to be left alone to follow their religion. Nevertheless, there was a story that was passed among the villagers in Nazareth of a young woman getting water alone who was caught and harassed. Two soldiers were drunk, and there was no officer with them. They dragged the girl to an alley where they ravished her. The unfortunate girl was hysterical and so shamed that her family had no choice but to send her to relatives as far away as possible and arrange a hasty marriage with a less-than-desirable prospect. The priests and the villagers had made such uproar that the two soldiers were quickly disciplined and sent to another post.

Mary knew that Omar heard the comments the soldiers flung at the cart, but he kept his eyes locked straight ahead. He would not speak to the soldiers lest he bring trouble on his family.

There were no further incidents with the soldiers, and Mary trusted in the gentle presence of the Most High, reminding her that she was under his protection. She was carrying his son and the thought came to her that nothing would happen to deter her from carrying out the mission he had given her. It suddenly gave her confidence.

When at last they could view the city of Jerusalem, the walls seemed to shimmer in the afternoon sun, almost blinding travelers with the glare. Mary had been there with her parents for Passover and still marveled at the enormity of the sprawling center of Jewish life. The Temple rose like a benevolent giant in the center of the city. She looked around her as Omar led them down one narrow street after another until finally stopping at a home on the far edge of the city with a small courtyard. The family and Mary waited while the potter knocked firmly on the gate. After a few moments an elderly man opened the gate and peered at them.

"Yes? What can I do for you?"

"You are Jether?"

The man nodded.

"I am Omar, son of your brother Abijah. We are traveling to Hebron and ask for shelter for the night."

The old man brightened. "Ah, welcome, welcome. Enter my humble home. I will tell my good wife Enid you are here." He nodded his head several times. "It is good to see family."

A woman nearly the age of her husband hurried out, wiping her hands on the cloth tucked around her waist.

"I was making a vegetable stew. Come in and partake with us."

Omar introduced his family and explained how Mary was traveling with them. She was welcomed warmly also.

Jether studied her a moment. "This has been a long journey for you. Are you not sorrowful to be so far from your parents?"

"I go to help a cousin, my lord. She is with child and needs me."

Enid waved a hand. "Surely there are midwives in Juttah? The Most High must send a girl on such a long journey?"

Omar, knowing about her dream, stepped in. "If God directs us, should we not be obedient?"

The elderly couple at looked each other and Jether shrugged. "Our God knows his way."

After a meal of stew, fresh bread, and fruit, Mary, Huldah, and Jethro were relegated to the roof to sleep. It reminded Mary of her own rooftop at home and for a moment she wished she were back with her parents and that all was as it had been before the angel's amazing pronouncement.

She could not turn back time; she knew she had no choice but to finish this road the Lord had placed her on. Her stomach was still flat, but sometimes, rising in the morning, she felt a touch of nausea. She did her best to hide it. She could not have Timnah asking questions. When she prayed, the nausea left her.

Shortly after Huldah and Jethro had gone to sleep, she rose to her knees, and silently cried out her fears as well as her praise to Ha'Shem.

Oh God Who Sees Me, who am I that I have been chosen to carry your son? May Elizabeth understand this great thing that has happened to me. Show me what I must do. Help me to be worthy of this child I bear. So much burdens my mind and heart and there is no one that I can speak to about it. I feel so alone, yet you are with me. You are my joy and strength.

When she had poured out her heart to her God, she sat back on her heels and felt a wave of weariness wash over her. Cautiously, she lifted her cloak and without disturbing the other two sleepers, slipped under it and closed her eyes.

The next morning they left Jerusalem, and thanks to the generosity of Omar's family, they were loaded with more bread, cheese, date cakes, and nuts. Their goatskin flasks were filled with fresh water.

They bid goodbye to their hosts and wound again through the narrow streets to the city gates. It was nearly eighteen miles to Hebron.

The sun beat down on them as the cart moved slowly through the countryside. Mary and Huldah, riding on the back of the cart again, watched the great city slowly disappear in the shimmering rays of the sun.

Mary had approached Timnah about the wedding they were going to and asked if they knew the bride and groom.

Timnah was strangely hesitant in her response. Glancing over at her daughter. "We know the groom, my husband's nephew. I hear he is a nice young man. It will be a good wedding." She turned away and busied herself with preparing bread and fruit for their dinner.

When they stopped at midday for Timnah to walk into a clump of trees for her needs, Mary and Huldah also took advantage of the stop, then walked quietly in the nearby fields. "Why are your parents so hesitant to talk about the wedding? Weddings in Nazareth are happy occasions."

"Because it is true. I am beginning to suspect who the bride is to be. Why else would they not talk about it?" Huldah hesitated, tears forming in her eyes, then blurted. "Omar is not my father. My real father died when I was only five. My mother married Omar but he has never been fond of me. I don't know why. I…I have not had an offer of marriage, and I think this is his way of getting me off his hands. I'm afraid my husband will be old and ugly. Who else would take a plain girl like me, past the age of marriage?"

Mary put her arms around Huldah. "The Most High cares for you, Huldah. He alone can bring beauty from ashes. I'm sure your groom will turn out to be someone wonderful."

Omar called them and as they returned to the cart, Huldah sighed. "Thank you, Mary, you are kind, but I am not expecting anything. If I don't expect anything I will not be disappointed. Is that not true?"

"He is a God of miracles, Huldah. Nothing is impossible with him." And Mary realized she was reminding herself.

SEVEN

They approached Hebron, known as the "Town of Four," since it was situated between four hills. Passing through the abundant vineyards for which Hebron was known, the group entered the town and the marketplace with its arched roofs and maze of alleys. Numerous shops sold dried fruits, fresh vegetables, breads, carvings and bowls of olivewood, pottery, and assorted woven fabrics. As the cart moved along, Mary listened to the cries of the vendors as the smell of pungent spices and fish wafted on the breeze.

She remembered one of the stories Joseph told her. Here was the cave of Machpelah, where the patriarchs, Abraham, Isaac and Jacob and their wives were buried. She had never been to Hebron, and never expected to be there again once she was married and settled down in Nazareth. Then the thoughts came again, striking her subconscious like darts. Would she be married in Nazareth? Would Joseph still take her to wife when she returned? She thought of what the villagers would say behind her back, of the shame brought on her family and Joseph's if they didn't believe her story. Sorrow overwhelmed her and it was all she could do to appear calm as if she was taking in the scenery.

Huldah, subdued for the journey from Jerusalem to Hebron, rarely spoke, her face the picture of abject misery. When the cart came to a stop in front of one of the homes, they all got down and stood behind Omar as he knocked on the gate.

A woman opened it. "This is Omar's sister-in-law, Kenzia," Huldah whispered to Mary.

Kenzia waved them into the courtyard. "Welcome. We are glad you arrived safely." Her long face and deep-set eyes that darted to and fro, taking in the group, belied her cheery words. She especially scrutinized Mary and Huldah. A brief light of approval fell on Mary.

"This is your daughter?"

Omar cleared his throat and pulled on his beard. "That is Mary. She is traveling with us on her way to relatives in Juttah. She is already betrothed." He turned to Huldah. "This is my daughter."

Kenzia's face changed immediately as she took in Huldah's straight hair, eyes set too close together and sad face. She inclined her head for them to follow her, then, without a word turned on her heel and returned to the house.

As they sat on a rug in the shade of a tree, Kenzia brought them diluted wine, cheese, and a wooden platter of grapes. She studied Huldah again and shook her head.

"Your brother and nephew are delivering some pots that were ordered. They shall return shortly. With your long journey, we have dispensed with the year of betrothal as agreed. The wedding will take place tomorrow."

Mary sat near Huldah and wondered what she would do in the same situation. Secure in her parent's love, she had never doubted that they would arrange a good marriage for her. They had known of Joseph's feelings and kept her for him. It had all been so wonderful and she had been wrapped securely in their love and Joseph's, at least until the visit from the angel. All had changed and now she felt more than ever that she needed the advice and comfort of Elizabeth.

She turned to Kenzia. "It is important that I get to Juttah as soon as possible. Do you know of a caravan going that way?"

"My husband will know. Asa keeps up with what is happening in the town." She shook her head. "How is it that a young girl, and betrothed, is allowed to travel such a distance alone?"

Mary knew she could not tell this woman of the dream and especially not of the angel. "It is a matter of great importance. My cousin needs me."

Kenzia sniffed, obviously desiring more information. She studied Mary and raised her eyebrows, pressing her lips firmly together.

Omar turned to Mary. "I promised your father I would make arrangements for you to get to Juttah. You will leave the matter to me."

Instantly contrite, Mary murmured, "Of course, you are right. Forgive me for my impatience."

Omar, somewhat mollified, pulled on his beard. Then he turned to Huldah. "Since you are still unmarried, I have made a contract of betrothal to Gershom, son of my brother, Asa."

Huldah regarded him with tear-filled eyes. "Could you not have told me? Why was this done in secret?"

Omar's eyes narrowed with anger. "It is not your place to question what I do!"

Huldah turned to her mother for comfort, but Timnah only shook her head and was silent.

At that moment there was the sound of voices. Asa and his son had arrived at last.

Mary watched the two men enter the courtyard and caught her breath. While the younger man was not unpleasing to the eye, he leaned on the arm of his father and seemed to be looking over the heads of the small group gathered before him as he tapped the ground ahead of him with a walking stick.

With the innocence of a child, Jethro observed the young man and announced, "He can't see. Gershom is blind!"

EIGHT

*M*ary put an arm around Huldah, whose lower lip was trembling. She murmured just low enough for Mary's ears. "This is my husband-to-be? A blind man?"

Gershom tapped his way to a bench and sat down. "We have guests, Father?"

Asa put a hand on his shoulder. "I have arranged for a bride for you. The stepdaughter of my brother Omar."

"Let me see her."

Mary puzzled at the term. How could he see Huldah if he was blind? Omar took Huldah by the hand and half-pulled her over to the bench, seating her beside Gershom. "Her name is Huldah."

The young man smiled. "Do not be afraid. I see with my hands." He reached out and gently explored her face with his fingers. Huldah closed her eyes, enduring the strange scrutiny. When Gershom had finished, he chuckled. "You are very pretty."

Huldah's eyes flew open to see him smiling. "You...you think I am pretty?" She observed him more closely as did Mary. He was not ugly or old. He had a pleasing, even handsome face.

She hesitated and then blurted, "How did you lose your sight, Gershom?"

"A fever, when I was six years old. I am used to it now. I even help my father make pottery."

Mary looked across the courtyard to a shed where a potter's wheel stood along with shelves of newly cured pots. So Asa was a potter like his brother.

42

Mary turned back to Kenzia, who seemed to relax a little. Her mouth was no longer pursed in disapproval. She was looking at her only son with an expression akin to relief. Omar also looked relieved, perhaps anticipating more resistance from Huldah. The two young people were speaking quietly together, and Huldah's face had lost its pinched look.

Asa stroked his beard. "She is presentable, my son?"

"Yes, Father. She is presentable."

"Huldah, you will marry him?" It was more a statement than a question.

She glanced at Omar and her chin lifted slightly as she answered. "I will marry him." Then she gently laid her hand on Gershom's.

~

The last of the guests had gone. It was a small wedding. The rabbi seemed to be in a hurry, but observed all the protocols. A glass, wrapped in a cloth was placed in Gershom's hands and he crushed it under his foot. To Huldah's surprise, her mother produced her own wedding dress that had been wrapped carefully and hidden among their things. Mary's heart grieved that Huldah would have no seven-day marriage celebration. Omar was in a hurry to return to Nazareth. He had done his duty by his stepdaughter and that was that.

As the two young people spoke the words of the betrothal and wedding prayers, Huldah's voice was strong and Mary knew she had made up her mind to make the best of the situation. At least Gershom appeared to be a kind young man, perhaps, in his blindness, glad to have a wife. Mary glanced at Kenzia and wondered how Huldah would fare with her new mother-in-law. Huldah's mother had tears in her eyes. She and Huldah had talked quietly in the corner of the courtyard, and Timnah had embraced her daughter. Mary wondered if they would see each other again. Her parents had come here for a purpose, and Mary suspected they would not soon be back.

Jethro was everywhere at once. Everything interested him, a bug crawling across the dirt, the chickens, and especially the goat. With the hasty preparations for the wedding, no one had paid much attention to a small boy until there was a loud noise from the goat pen, and Omar had to haul his son out quickly by the scruff of his neck.

"I only wanted to talk to him," Jethro protested.

Asa chuckled. "I should have warned you about the he-goat. He isn't very friendly."

Jethro was plunked down in a corner of the courtyard on the dirt where, after a stern warning from his father, he sat abjectly.

After the wedding, Mary, Jethro, and his parents slept on pallets in the courtyard for Huldah and Gershom were given the privacy of the roof for their wedding night under the *chuppah*, and Kenzia waited at the foot of the stairs for the bloody linen sheet, proof of Huldah's virginity, which Timnah received from her daughter. Kenzia displayed it for her husband to see. The bride chosen for his son was indeed a virgin. He nodded his acceptance.

Long after the others slept, Mary lay awake listening to the muffled voices from the rooftop and thought of Joseph. What would it be like for them, if he were still willing to marry her? They would have to wait until after the birth of this God-ordained child, but what new bride had her wedding night after the birth of a child? A widow perhaps? But she was not a widow nor had she ever lain with a man. She knew with a certainty that a baby grew within her, but when had it happened? The thoughts moved around in her head until she cried out in silent prayer to Ha'Shem. Once again, a sense of peace covered her, lulling her to sleep.

NINE

Omar and Timnah prepared to return to Nazareth and Asa made arrangements with another family to take Mary on the short journey to Juttah and her cousin Elizabeth.

As the new bride and groom came down the stairs, Gershom was smiling and Huldah kept her head down modestly. She took his arm and gently led him to the wooden bench to sit and then turned to face her parents. She listened silently while Omar mumbled a hasty goodbye with his final instructions.

"You will be all right. I have done my part and provided you with a husband. Do not give your new family any reason to be sorry."

Huldah only nodded, then turned to her young brother. Jethro looked up at her, a tear running down one cheek.

"Will I ever see you again, Huldah?"

She bent down and hugged him as he clung to her. "One day, Jethro. Perhaps one day. Be a good boy for Ima."

Then Huldah faced her mother. The two women embraced. Timnah drew herself up, and Mary could see she was struggling to reign in her emotions. "I have taught you how to keep a good house. Be obedient to your husband and your mother-in-law."

Mary felt they were not the words Timnah wanted to say, but Omar was impatient to be going. Timnah climbed up into the cart beside her husband, her eyes wet with unshed tears. Jethro got in the back of the cart, his face the picture of sadness. He slowly waved to Mary. "I will miss your stories, Mary."

"I'll be back to Nazareth soon, Jethro."

"I will tell your parents you are safe and you will make arrangements on your own to return to Nazareth," Omar called over his shoulder, then urged the donkey on.

Mary and the family of Asa waved as the cart moved down the road and then Asa closed the gate.

Gershom had risen, and tapping with his cane, followed the sound of voices. "Huldah?" She touched his arm and he placed it protectively around her. She whispered something in his ear, and he nodded as she stepped aside with Mary.

"I will be all right, Mary," Huldah murmured softly. "He was gentle and will be kind to me. I believe I will learn to care for him."

"That is good. I wish you happiness Huldah, in every way. May you bear a son for your husband."

The two young women embraced and Mary went to gather her things to go with Asa. They were to meet one of the priests, Jonah, and his wife, Chloe, who would accompany her to Juttah. Jonah had finished his service at the Temple and they had only stopped a night to see relatives in Hebron. She was told they were in a hurry to return home.

Mary also wanted to be on her way, but at the same time wondered what she would say to Elizabeth. Was her cousin truly with child after all these years? She would soon know.

It was a good hour's walk from Hebron to Juttah. Jonah and Chloe walked quickly, and Mary struggled to keep up with them.

"You are going to visit your cousin in Juttah?"

"Yes, do you know Elizabeth and her husband, Zechariah?"

The man and his wife exchanged startled looks. Jonah stopped. "Have you then heard of the miracle bestowed on them by the Most High?"

Mary's heart began to beat faster. Was it true then? She took a deep breath and said, "I have been told she is with child."

Chloe shook her head. "Yes. She was barren, past childbearing age. Zechariah must have beheld a wondrous vision, for ever since he returned from his service in the Temple, he has been unable to speak."

"He cannot speak?"

"Not a word," Chloe assured her.

What strange situation would she find when she reached the home of her cousin? Mary could only go on the knowledge that Ha'Shem had sent her. He would help her face whatever was ahead.

When the trio reached the small town of Juttah, the couple saw her to the door of Zechariah and Elizabeth's home and hurried on their way.

Mary stood at the door, feeling quite alone and frightened, yet excited. Perhaps she had not come all this way for a dream. Gathering her courage, she knocked.

"I'm coming; give me a moment."

Elizabeth opened the door. "Yes?"

Mary smiled at her. "Elizabeth, it is your cousin, Mary. I bring you greetings from my mother and father in Nazareth." She glanced down at Elizabeth's belly, indeed great with child. So it was true! *Oh Adonai, what great gift have you given me?*

Elizabeth beckoned Mary to enter, then suddenly clutched her belly and her eyes widened in wonder. Raising her hands in praise she cried out, "You are favored by God above all other women, and your child is destined for God's mightiest praise. What an honor this is, that the mother of my Lord should visit me. When you came in and greeted me, the instant I heard your voice, my baby leaped within me for joy! You believed that God would do what he said; that is why he has given you this wonderful blessing."

Overcome with emotion, Mary felt the presence of the Lord as words rose from deep within her soul, pouring forth like a waterfall of joy.

"Oh, how I praise the Lord. How I rejoice in God my savior! For he took notice of his lowly servant girl, and now generation after generation forever shall call me blessed of God.

"For he, the mighty Holy One, has done great things to me. His mercy goes on from generation to generation, to all who reverence him. How powerful is his mighty arm! How he scatters the proud and haughty ones! He has torn princes from their thrones and exalted the lowly. He has satisfied the hungry hearts and sent the rich away with empty hands.

"And how he has helped his servant, Israel. He has not forgotten his promise to be merciful. For he promised our forefathers— Abraham and his children—to be merciful to them forever."

Realizing that she had prophesied for the first time in her life, Mary could only shake her head with amazement as Elizabeth gathered her into her arms.

"Oh Mary, how is it that your parents allowed you to make such a journey? Do they know of this great miracle bestowed on Zechariah and me? How did they know to send you to me?"

"It was the angel that appeared to me and revealed God's plan. I heard the voice of the Most High in my spirit telling me to come here."

"Then your parents don't know of this miraculous child you are to bear?"

Mary hung her head. "No, and neither does Joseph, my betrothed. I don't know what faces me when I return. He will know the child is not his, but will he believe my story? If he renounces me...." Her words trailed off as she contemplated the penalty that could be her fate.

"The Most High will give you courage and go before you. If he has given you this great honor, he will see it come to pass."

"Oh Elizabeth, Joseph must believe the angel's words. He's a good and kind man. We have known each other since we were children. I was so joyful when he asked my parents for me. Now I don't know what will happen."

"God will take care of Joseph, Mary. Believe that." Elizabeth suddenly remembered her duties. "You must be hungry. Our evening meal is almost ready and Zechariah will return home soon. Would you like to help me?"

Mary nodded, glad for something to do.

Elizabeth had just set the pot of lentil stew on the table when Zechariah opened the door. He paused for a moment, obviously startled to see Mary.

"We have a guest, husband. My young cousin, Mary, has come to help me in my final months. You remember her? She is the daughter of Heli and my cousin Anna. She knows you cannot speak. Oh my husband, just as the Most High has blessed us with the miracle of a child in our old age, so he has blessed Mary with a wondrous gift. She has seen a vision of an angel, who not only told her I was to bear a child in my old age, but who told her she is to bear the long-awaited Messiah!"

Mary expected Zechariah to look at her with skepticism, but his eyes watered with tears as he raised his hands in silent praise to the Most High. He placed a hand on Mary's shoulder and nodded, his face filled with joy. Then he motioned to himself, making signs with his hands.

Then Mary knew. "You saw an angel also?"

Pleased that she understood, Zechariah nodded vigorously looking from one to the other anxiously.

Elizabeth put her hand on her husband's arm. "Oh Zechariah, I knew something had happened when you were at the Temple but you couldn't tell me. Did he tell you I would have a child?"

Zechariah nodded and patted his chest, pointing to himself then cradled his hands as if holding a baby.

"A boy? I would have a son?"

Zechariah beamed and nodded again.

Elizabeth clasped her hands and cried, "Not only has the Most High taken away the shame of my barrenness, but I will honor my husband and give birth to a son!"

Zechariah made eating motions with one hand and looked questioningly at his wife.

"Yes, husband. Our meal is ready. Let us bless the Most High and acknowledge the One who provides sustenance for us."

Since Zechariah could not speak the words of the prayers out loud, the women bowed their heads as his lips moved in silence. When he looked up, they began their meal. After the meal, Zechariah opened his mouth to say the *Birkat Hamazon*, the long prayer at the end of their meal that offered thanks to God for his provision and care.

Once again, Zechariah's lips moved silently but Mary spoke the words in her heart that she had heard from the time she was a young child, "Blessed are you, LORD, our God, Master of the universe, who nourishes the whole world in goodness, with grace, kindness, and compassion. He gives bread to all flesh, for his mercy endures forever. And through his great goodness we have never lacked, nor will we lack food forever, for the sake of his great name. For he is God, who nourishes and sustains all, and does good to all, and prepares food for all his creatures which he created. Blessed are you, LORD, who nourishes all...."

The Most High God was Master of the universe. He would sustain her and prepare the way for the great gift he had bestowed on her. Yet, in her heart, the future was still uncertain. What would her return to Nazareth hold for her?

TEN

The days moved quickly as the almond trees bore their fruit and the women stored them away for cooking. Soon the flax harvest would occupy the men and women of Juttah. It was also when Elizabeth's child was due.

Mary's days were filled with the ordinary activities of family life, drawing water from the local well, baking bread, preparing meals, and observing the Sabbath. She helped wash their clothes and take care of the animals as Elizabeth's pregnancy progressed and those tasks grew more difficult for her.

This day they prepared for the Sabbath, baking extra bread and making dishes that would not have to be heated, since no cooking fires burned in a Kosher Jewish home on the Sabbath. Mary cut up cucumbers and combined them in a bowl with coarsely chopped olives and crumbled goat cheese. This would go in a pottery crock with finely chopped dill. Fish had been purchased from the marketplace for the *gefilte*, or stuffed fish. The day before, Mary and Elizabeth soaked a bowl of figs for several hours and then drained and chopped them. Mary mixed the figs with nuts and cinnamon and then baked the rounds in the clay oven in the courtyard until they were dry. Some fig cakes were taken out for meals and the rest were stored in a stone crock and sealed. What was left after this evening's meal would also be kept in a crock in the coolness of the storage room that had thick stone walls to keep out the heat.

Elizabeth wiped her brow and smiled at Mary. "The babe moves often. I feel the time will be soon."

Mary put an arm around her cousin and helped her to a bench under the shade of the mulberry tree in the corner of the small courtyard. Elizabeth's forehead was wet with perspiration and Mary frowned. "Should we call the midwife?"

Elizabeth smiled. "No. My pains have not yet begun. Ha'Shem will let me know when it is time."

When it is time. What will be the circumstances of my time? Her unique situation troubled her occasionally and she sought the comfort of her God daily, praying for her family, for Joseph and the confrontation that was to come. Yet the peace of the Most High God sustained her…carried her, assuring her and giving her strength. She glanced down at her belly, which was no longer flat. The roundness of pregnancy was making itself visible. Mary knew the women of the village were observing her covertly, knowing she was betrothed to a man in Nazareth. As the month of Adar drew to an end and Mary's pregnancy became a possibility, she noticed them murmuring among themselves as she passed by. She could only pretend she didn't see them or hear the words that were sometimes said purposely in her hearing.

"Is she with child?"

"I heard she is betrothed but the marriage ceremony has not taken place."

"Well, may the Most High forgive me, but I heard…."

And so it began. Would it be worse in Nazareth when she returned? Since Joseph was not the father, what would he do? He could divorce her if he didn't believe her story about the angel. On and on the thoughts flew through her mind. She sighed heavily. She'd put it off while waiting for Elizabeth's child to be born, but the reality was that she must make arrangements to return to Nazareth.

She had stayed with Elizabeth and Zechariah through the Feast of Purim when they celebrated the saving of her people by the great Queen Esther.

The Sabbath eve began. Two loaves of *challah* bread were placed on the table and covered with an embroidered cloth. Mary poured wine into the cup for *kiddush*.

Zechariah hurried in from the fields with an eye on the approaching sunset. Elizabeth sighed with relief and pulled her shawl over her head to light the Sabbath candles. She moved her hands slowly over the flames and then closed her eyes, covering them with her hands as she prayed aloud, "Blessed are you, LORD, our God, Sovereign of the universe, who has sanctified us with his commandments and commanded us to light the candles of *Shabbat*."

She opened her eyes and Mary murmured "Amen" with her.

It was the moment when a father blessed his sons and daughters and then turned to his wife to recite the words of chapter 31 of the book of Proverbs, *"An excellent wife, who can find? For her worth is far above rubies…."* Yet Zechariah could only gaze warmly at Elizabeth without words.

Then Zechariah held up the cup of wine, diverting Mary's attention from her thoughts. He recited the *kiddush* again, his eyes closed and his lips moving in silence. As usual, they had to watch his lips to know when the words had ended. Mary wondered if the Most High would ever allow Zechariah to speak again, and why his voice had been silenced in the first place. He could not tell them.

Elizabeth brought a small basin and they each took turns washing their hands, pouring it first over the top and bottom of the right hand and then the left hand.

This time Zechariah said his prayer silently then nodded to his wife who faithfully recited, "Blessed are you, LORD, our God,

King of the universe, who has sanctified us with his commandments and commanded us concerning washing of hands."

Mary in turn recited the prayer as she washed her hands. Then Zechariah uncovered the *challah* bread, and after his silent blessing, tore pieces of the bread and passed them to Elizabeth and Mary.

Mary sensed Elizabeth's weariness, and after the meal was not surprised that her cousin announced she was retiring for the night. Zechariah and Mary also retired to their respective sleeping mats. The sun had long since set and the Sabbath had begun. Just as Mary dozed off, she was awakened by a sharp cry.

ELEVEN

*E*lizabeth was clutching her belly and moaning. Her pains had begun.

Zechariah was also awake and looked at Mary, his eyes wide with alarm. She urged him toward the door. "Please, fetch the midwife. It is time." Mary smiled at Elizabeth. The Sabbath was an auspicious day for a miracle child to be born.

Phoebe, the local midwife, soon hurried into the house. She brought her bag of herbs and a birthing stool. Elizabeth was encouraged to stand so that the weight of the babe would naturally move it down to birth. The women of the neighborhood crowded in the house to see the birth of this child to a woman Elizabeth's age. Two of them held Elizabeth by the arms as she labored toward the birthing of her child.

To the surprise of the women, the baby slid out into the world in less than two hours.

Phoebe shook her head. "Considering that you are not a young woman, the Most High has gifted you with a short labor! Your husband is blessed, for you have a son!" She cleaned the baby gently and rubbed him with salt, then wrapped him tightly in swaddling cloths.

The neighbor women rejoiced as Mary carried the baby around the room so they could all admire him.

One woman murmured, "Baby Zechariah. He shall be called after his father."

Elizabeth spoke up quickly from her pallet where she was resting from the ordeal of birth. "Not so. He is to be called John."

The women murmured among themselves and one woman cast a puzzled glance at Elizabeth. "No one of your kindred is called by this name. We must ask his father."

Zechariah was called and his son was placed in his arms. Phoebe asked Zechariah how the baby was to be called. He motioned for a writing tablet, and when it was brought to him he held the baby with one arm and wrote, "His name is John."

As soon as he wrote the words, his tongue was loosened and he spoke out loud, praising the Most High for the gift of his son.

Elizabeth, Mary, and all who were in the room were astonished that his voice had suddenly been restored. The neighbors murmured among themselves as to what this could mean.

Zechariah, filled with the Holy Spirit, lifted one hand, held John in the crook of his arm, and began to prophesy.

"Blessed be the Lord God of Israel; for he has visited and redeemed his people, and has raised up a horn of salvation for us in the house of his servant, David; as he spoke by the mouth of his holy prophets, which have been since the world began; that we should be saved from our enemies, and from the hand of all that hate us; to perform the mercy promised to our fathers, and to remember his holy covenant; the oath which he swore to our father, Abraham, that he would grant unto us, that we being delivered out of the hand of our enemies might serve him without fear, in holiness and righteousness before him, all the days of our life. And you, child, shall be called the prophet of the Highest; for you shall go before the face of the Lord to prepare his ways; to give knowledge of salvation unto his people by the remission of their sins, through the tender mercy of our God; whereby the Dayspring from on high has visited us, to give light to them that sit in darkness and in the shadow of death, to guide our feet unto the way of peace."

When he finished speaking, his eyes still closed, there was a profound silence in the room. Neighbors stood in awe and with glances at Mary and Elizabeth, they quietly filed out of the house, and once in the yard, flew down the street like a flock of chickens to spread the word of the return of Zechariah's speech.

Mary was overcome with emotion, her heart beating rapidly, and tears of joy running down her cheeks. Phoebe took the baby from Zechariah and placed him gently in the arms of Elizabeth. She stood watching them for a long moment, and then gathered her things.

"In all the times I have helped deliver a child, never has there been a birth like this one. I don't understand the words Zechariah spoke, but this is a child that has been called by the Most High for great things." She addressed Zechariah and Elizabeth. "Blessings on you both." She turned to Mary, questions in her eyes as she glanced down at Mary's belly. "Will you be returning to Nazareth, or…?"

Mary left the last part of the question unanswered. "I am anxious to return to my parents and share the good news of the birth of John."

When she had gone, Zechariah smiled down at Mary. "You have had much to contend with for a young woman. We will pray for your trip home and what you must share with not only your parents, but also your betrothed. God will go before you." After kneeling down and sharing loving words with his wife, he caressed the head of his son and then rose.

"I will see what arrangements can be made for you to return to Nazareth, Mary."

He left the house and was gone for about two hours. When he returned, he wiped his brow. "The spring rains will begin soon. It is good you travel now."

"Were you able to find someone for me?"

"There is another priest and his wife who are traveling to Jerusalem. His lot has come up for service in the Temple. You may travel with them and the priestly group that is going that way. They will leave in two days' time."

"Thank you, Zechariah. I will be ready to go."

That evening Mary climbed up to the crowded space on the rooftop that Elizabeth and Zechariah used to store grain and other supplies. It had been her place of prayer where she could be alone. She folded a small blanket and knelt, looking up at the stars. She had been with Elizabeth and Zechariah three months. What must her parents be thinking, and Joseph, after Omar returned to Nazareth without her?

As she lifted her praise to the Most High, she thanked him for his great gift and the child to come. What would the child be like, a baby that was the son of God? Would he be different from all the other children in Nazareth? Would she be able to remain in Nazareth? As she gave herself to prayer, she was aware again of a presence with her, like wings surrounding and covering her.

She prayed for her parents and for Joseph and lifted her arms in worship to the One who had singled her out and made her the most blessed of women. She didn't know how long she prayed, but it seemed only moments, so real was the presence around her. It was almost nightfall when she finally came down from the roof. The long blast of the *shofar* long since signaled the end of the Sabbath.

Mary tended to her cousin and the baby for the next two days, allowing Elizabeth to get all the rest she could before Mary left and she would have to take up her household duties as well as tend her son.

"I'm sorry I will not be here for his circumcision ceremony, Elizabeth. He's going to be a sturdy boy."

"Do not let it concern you. It has been a joy to have you here with me. Adonai has plans for our sons, but we will not know what they are until the time comes. We can only trust the strength of our God to help us bring them up in the commandments of the law and teach them what they need to know as sons of Israel."

"You will have Zechariah, a priest, to teach your son. I do not know if I will even have a husband."

"You must have faith that Adonai goes before you and will direct your path. He would not have chosen you and given you this blessed task if he were not going to see you through. You can only trust him to prepare the way, both with your parents and with Joseph."

Mary sighed. "I am truly blessed among all women, and I do not understand why the Most High chose to do things this way, but he is sovereign and who are we to question his ways?"

Mary had cuddled little John and learned a few things about caring for a baby. She hoped it would stand her in good stead when her own time came. At least her mother would be with her, and she knew that Nazareth had a good midwife.

She lay down that night for the last time in the home of Zechariah and Elizabeth, and wondered what the next few weeks would hold.

In the morning, Mary wore a cloak that covered her so that none in their traveling party were aware of her pregnancy. Either the priest's wife had not heard about Mary from other women of the village or she was kind enough to not inquire. Most of the women of Juttah were still occupied talking about the miraculous birth of a son to a woman who was considered barren and past the age of childbearing.

When they reached Jerusalem, the city bustled with people. She marveled at the crowds that moved through the streets of the city and filled the marketplace. Vendors hawked their wares and she observed herds of goats and sheep being driven into the Temple by herdsmen. Their bleating and baaing filled the air. Perhaps they were for those who did not have a sheep or goat to sacrifice.

She watched carts pulled by mules and donkeys and groups of people carrying bundles on their shoulders, along with parents trying to keep track of small children as the mass of humanity streamed in and out of the city. Families arriving to visit relatives or visit the Temple, others leaving the city to return to their homes. A stream of camels carrying merchandise from far-away cities ambled along in single file, looking over those they passed with indolent eyes full of disdain.

After some inquiries by the leader of their group, Mary was entrusted to a caravan traveling past Nazareth. Once again Ha'Shem provided for her and there were several families traveling with the caravan—with some obvious questions about a young woman traveling alone.

"I'm returning to my family in Nazareth," she assured them, "I have been helping a cousin who has just given birth to a son." Finally, they agreed with the caravan master to watch over her on the journey.

She remembered how long the first trip took, and now it seemed even longer as she had to walk and there was no cart to ride if she wanted to rest. She prayed for strength and kept her eyes and heart on home.

TWELVE

When they neared the road leading down to Nazareth, a merchant traveling with the caravan approached the family who had taken Mary into their care.

"I understand this young woman is going to Nazareth," he said. "I have watched and seen that she is very weary. I do not wish to place you in an awkward position, but I have a daughter about her age, and would watch over her for the final journey to her home. I am taking leather goods to Nazareth. If she wishes, she may ride on the back of my cart the rest of the way. It is only a short distance to the town."

Mary looked at the man's face and saw only kindness and concern. She had been putting one foot in front of the other, tiredness a weight upon her body.

"Will you be all right, Mary? Your parents will not object?" her caretaker asked.

"As he says, it is only a short distance, and I am tired." She turned to the merchant. "Thank you for your kind offer. I will gladly accept."

The merchant helped her onto the back of the cart where she sat on the end with her legs dangling as she had done with Omar and his family. She thanked Ha'Shem for giving her a short rest. She would need her strength to meet her family.

As they traveled, Mary tried to push aside her anxious thoughts by remembering stories and prayers from Jewish Scripture and by thinking of home. She could not read, but like most women, had listened to the stories passed down from family to family and learned the Scriptures as she listened to the priest in the synagogue. She smiled, remembering how she and other children acted out the stories in the Scriptures for entertainment.

As she approached the familiar countryside of Nazareth, her heart lifted. Home. A small village, muddy in winter and dusty in summer, streets that ran haphazardly with only the outside walls of the courtyards visible to those passing by. Some of the houses so close together that in the summer, when families went up on the roof as a respite from the heat, they could talk to one another.

As Mary pictured her home and her parents, sudden anguish rose up in her heart. Nothing would ever be the same as when she left.

While she stayed with Elizabeth, Joseph had been adding a room for them onto the home of his parents. She envisioned him hauling the stones and carefully placing them. She could almost hear him singing to himself as he worked. She imagined him in the carpenter shop, helping his father and preparing the room for their marriage bed—all the time unaware of the terrible yet wonderful news she came to bring him.

When Mary did not return with Omar and his wife, her parents would assume she had stayed to help her cousin. It had been three months. Did they know that Elizabeth was truly with child? And how could she tell them the time of her return? She caught her breath as the town came into view, and felt the cold weight of apprehension in her chest. Because of her slender figure, the evidence of her pregnancy showed early. Instinctively she pulled her cloak tighter over her gently rounded belly.

Oh God Who Sees Me, she prayed silently. *Grant me the courage to carry out your plan and to face my parents and Joseph. Give them grace to believe me. They must believe me. Strengthen me, and help me*

*through these next few hours and days. I am your handmaiden, may
your will be done.*

As the cart entered the village, Mary wondered if the merchant
would be willing to take her to her home. She needed to gather
her thoughts before facing Joseph. To her chagrin, they passed the
carpenter shop and at the sound of the cart, Joseph looked up. His
face broke into a wondrous smile as he dropped his tools and hurried out to greet her.

"Mary, I thought you would never return. Omar said you
would make your own arrangements but I was sure something had
happened to you." He stood beaming up at her, his eyes filled with
love. Mary, resigned, stepped down from the cart.

He waved his thanks as the merchant moved on down the
street. As he took her hands, he began, "I finished the room...."
But his words sputtered to a stop when Mary's cloak fell open. He
glanced down and the light in his eyes was extinguished, replaced
by pain, then anger.

"What is this? Mary...." He jerked his hands from hers.

Tears came to her eyes as she felt his rejection. This was no
place to talk. As she sought the right words, she put a hand on
his arm. "Come to the home of my parents," she pleaded. "I have
something wonderful and glorious to tell you."

His brow furrowed and his face was as dark as the twilight
shadows as he gripped her arm and practically dragged her to her
house. Once or twice he opened his mouth to say something and
clamped it shut again, his jaw set in grim determination.

When they burst into her small family courtyard, her mother
gave a glad cry and ran to embrace Mary. "You are home at last.
We have been so worried, it has been so long...." She looked at
Joseph's stormy face and stepped back. "What is wrong?"

Joseph pulled Mary's cloak back and pointed to her belly. He
almost spit out the words. "My betrothed is with child, and I am
not the father!"

"Aieeee, Mary! What has happened? Were you accosted? I knew it was wrong to let you go so far. Who is the father of this child?" She turned to Joseph. "Then you and Mary did not dishonor your betrothal time?"

Mary put her hand up, interrupting. "Ima, Joseph, I have not dishonored our betrothal; it is God's child. A wondrous being appeared to me the night of our betrothal and told me that I had found favor with the Most High and that I had been chosen to bear the long-awaited Messiah. I was to call him Yeshua, and he would save his people from their sins. Then he told me even more astonishing news: my cousin Elizabeth, formerly barren, was with child and she was in her sixth month. He told me that nothing is impossible with God."

"An angel?" Joseph fairly spit out the word, his eyes flashing. "God's child? Tell us the truth, Mary, not some story about an angel. Who was the man?" Joseph's voice was bitter. "It is Mary who has dishonored our betrothal." His eyes were full of hurt and anguish. "There is nothing she can say. There will be no wedding. I cannot marry a stained woman carrying another man's child. I will decide what I must do." Then suddenly, spent with his emotions, Joseph's shoulders drooped. With tears in his eyes he shook his head. "I have loved you ever since I can remember, and you have done this." He turned and almost ran from the courtyard.

"Joseph!" Mary held her arms out to him, tears running down her cheeks, but he did not heed her cries.

Mary wiped her eyes on her cloak and took a deep breath as she slowly turned back to her mother. "When Abba comes I will tell you of Elizabeth and the wondrous thing that the Most High has done for me."

Anna covered her face with her hands and wept. Mary put her arms around her mother to comfort her, but when Anna took her hands away from her face, her eyes flashed with anger.

"How will we live down the shame? How could you do this to Joseph? To our family and his? We brought you up to be a virtuous woman. We never should have allowed you to journey so far from home. You are too young. I tried to tell your father but he insisted you were only following the word of Ha'Shem." She covered her face with her hands again.

Mary, weary from her long journey and the anguish of her heart, sat down on the small wooden bench and briefly remembered when she had gone to Joseph's father to repair it.

Anna stood for a moment, shaking her head, then came over and sat down by Mary.

"Your father is working the field assigned to us. He will return soon. I don't know what we will do. This will break your father's heart, daughter."

Mary looked earnestly at her mother's face. "When he hears my story he will realize that I am blessed among women."

Her mother's face registered indecision and sadness. "Oh Mary." She rose slowly. "You will be hungry after your long journey. I will bring you something to eat and then we will wait for your father."

⟿

Mary pulled her mantle forward to protect her eyes from the unrelenting sun. She wrapped her arms around herself. Her heart was in her throat. She knew her father loved her, but he would abide by the laws of the Torah. She was pregnant and not by her betrothed. Would he allow her to be stoned? Would he reluctantly take her to the elders? Would Joseph? And what about the words of the angel? Would Adonai allow his child to come to harm after all she had suffered? She had to trust in the task she had been given. Adonai would make a way, somehow....

THIRTEEN

News reached Heli quickly that his daughter had returned. As he entered the courtyard, he gave a glad cry and hurried over to embrace Mary.

"My daughter, you are safe. You have returned to us. May the Most High be praised! This is a happy occasion. Let us call Joseph and celebrate your return." Then he looked from Mary to the face of his wife. "What is wrong?"

Anna spread a hand toward Mary. "Our daughter is with child. It is not Joseph's."

Then Heli's eyes took in her rounded belly and his eyes widened. "What is this? Daughter, how did this happen?"

Mary breathed a silent prayer for wisdom and addressed her parents. "Please, Abba, Ima. I have something very unusual and wonderful to tell you. It is true Joseph is not the father. The Most High God is the father of my child."

Anna's eyes flashed. "What kind of a fable is this? Another dream like the one you used to go away? You have never lied to us. You have been a good daughter. What can you possibly tell us that we can believe now? That Joseph and the neighbors will believe?"

Heli held up a hand. "Wife, we have brought Mary up to be a virtuous young woman. There has to be an explanation. We can at least listen to what she has to say."

Mary smiled with relief. Her father was willing to listen to her. "Abba, I love Joseph and only Joseph. I would not dishonor him. This is what happened...." As she related the events of the night the angel appeared to her, her father listened with astonishment. She told him the words the angel spoke to her.

She paused, sensing the warmth of the Holy Spirit around her. "Oh Abba, Ima, it was more than I could understand. I asked the angel how this could be, for I am a virgin and have not known a man."

Her father's brows were knit together and he stroked his beard repeatedly. "What did this being tell you, then?"

"He said that the Holy Spirit would come upon me and that the power of the Most High would overshadow me so that the child I was to bear would be called the son of God."

Anna sniffed. "And you could not tell this to your father and me?"

"Oh, Ima, the angel then told me that our cousin Elizabeth, barren all these years and past the age of child-bearing, was with child and in her sixth month! That nothing was impossible with God. What could I do but submit to Adonai and do his will? You have taught me to obey God, and I am his handmaiden, a servant of the Most High. I told the angel that it would be as he had said. Then he was gone."

"So you told us you had a dream?"

"I thought the next morning that it must have been a dream, Abba. It seemed so strange and I was overwhelmed. But think of the Torah, Abba, does not every Jewish mother dream of giving birth to the Messiah? Yet Adonai opened my understanding. As I remember the Scripture from the Sabbath, does not the prophet Isaiah tell us that a virgin shall conceive and bear a son, and shall call his name Emmanuel? The Messiah cannot have an earthly father. He must be without the sin of our ancestor Adam."

Heli's eyes widened. "And you remembered this Scripture?"

She nodded. "Adonai must have brought it to my remembrance."

Her mother shook her head. "So you went to Elizabeth. You could not come to me?"

Mary put a hand on her mother's arm. "Ima, how could I tell you what I did not understand myself? All I could think of was that I'd had a dream about Elizabeth, and I had to go and see for myself. Don't you see? If Elizabeth was truly with child, then it was not just a dream, and it would come to pass as the angel told me."

"When did you know then?"

"When I greeted Elizabeth. Her first words to me were a blessing, and then she asked how it was that the mother of her Lord should come to her. And Ima, she was truly with child and in her sixth month as the angel said."

Anna clasped her hands. "So it is true then? It is a miracle."

"Yes, Ima, think of the story of our Father Abraham and Sarah and when they had Isaac. Was that not a miracle of God?"

Heli cleared his throat. "And how did Zechariah take all this? He is of the priestly class and has served in the Temple. Did he believe you?"

"It was when he was in the Temple that the angel appeared to him to tell him the prayers of he and Elizabeth were answered and Elizabeth would bear a son and they were to call his name John."

"John? There is no one in their family with that name." Her mother threw a questioning look at her husband.

"That is another miracle. When Zechariah did not believe the angel and questioned him, the angel said he would be mute until the child was born. When I got there he could not speak, not a word. Yet when the baby was born, he regained his voice and prophesied over the child."

Heli stood up suddenly and scratched his head. "This is a hard story to believe but I have watched your face as you spoke and I believe you are sincere. I cannot believe that you would make up such a story." He paused and looked toward the gate. "And what about Joseph? This is hard for a man. Have you told him this?"

Anna began wringing her hands again. "Oh, Heli, he brought Mary here and would not stay to listen. He was angry and hurt and rushed out of the courtyard like a man driven. I don't know what he will do."

"He can bring her before the elders and accuse her of adultery, Anna. Mary could be sentenced to be stoned for adultery if they will not believe her."

Her mother put her hands over her face and wept aloud. "Aieee! Not our Mary. He could not do such a thing."

Heli put a hand on her shoulder. "When a man has news such as this, and is angry enough, he may do that which he would never think to do otherwise. We can only wait to see what he decides. We must give Joseph time to think this through. In the morning we shall no doubt see Joseph again...and Jacob."

Anna rose slowly and turned toward the house. "I have a meal to prepare. It may be our last evening of peace before the village knows of all this. If they do not already know."

"Let me help you, Ima."

Anna paused, shaking her head. Then flinging her hands up, she nodded. As Mary followed, she glanced back at her father. He had sunk down on the bench, his face in his hands. His shoulders shook with silent tears.

FOURTEEN

*E*arly the next morning, it was obvious her parents had not slept. Their eyes were red and it was as if they had both aged ten years overnight. Anna went about her duties, putting bread and grapes on the table along with some goat cheese. Heli ate absentmindedly, staring at the gate from time to time.

Mary had spent most of the night on her knees beseeching God for Joseph and for her parents and the confrontation to come. She had finally fallen asleep, weary from the strain of the previous night's events, but at peace. It was in the hands of the God Who Sees.

Just as Mary was helping her mother put away the remains of their meal, there was a rapid knock on the gate. Mary almost jumped, and Heli, with heavy steps, went to open it.

"Peace be upon this house."

"And to you, Joseph. Welcome Jacob. Please enter."

Barely stopping to touch the *mezuzah* at the gatepost with a brief prayer, father and son entered the courtyard.

Jacob stood to one side, his face the picture of bewilderment. He spread his hands and shrugged as he looked at Heli and Anna.

Joseph hurried to Mary and took both her hands. "Forgive me, beloved. I was so angry and hurt, thinking that you had lain with another man and were with child. I was awake half the night trying to decide what to do. I didn't want to bring you before the elders. I could not do that. My father suggested I quietly obtain a writ of divorcement and you could go and stay with Elizabeth until the birth of the child...."

"You were going to give me a *get*, Joseph?" She bowed her head and would have withdrawn her hands but Joseph held them tightly.

"Yes, I had resolved to just put you away quietly, without notifying the elders, but then I had a dream." His eyes were wide with excitement and awe. "An angel appeared to me... I don't know if I was awake or sleeping, but he said to me, 'Joseph, son of David, do not fear to take Mary as your wife, for that which is conceived in her is of the Holy Spirit. And she shall bring forth a son and you shall call him Yeshua, *Salvation*, for he will save his people from their sins.'"

"Oh Joseph, the God Who Sees has heard my prayers and I am grateful with all my heart!"

"We will be married as soon as your parents can arrange it and you will come to our home and the room I have prepared for you."

Joseph looked around at the astonished parents who could only stare back, speechless.

Anna finally found her voice. "Joseph, you are saving Mary's life, and from great shame." Her practical mind took over. "You know that you will be ascribed as the child's father? And...."

Heli interrupted her. "It is not against the Torah, wife. It has happened, and they are considered married, so it will not be thought of as fornication. The villagers will only shake their heads that Mary and Joseph did not wait out their time of betrothal."

Jacob came forward. "I do not know how to see all this. Last night my son was angry and in anguish of spirit, vowing to put Mary away, and this morning he is a different man, ready to take Mary as his wife and claiming to have had this dream." He flung up his hands. "I am hard put to understand any of this and so is my wife." He turned to Joseph. "My son also has been an honest young man, not given to fantasies and has obeyed the commandments from his youth. For that reason and that reason alone, I will not fight the marriage nor go to the elders. I believe Joseph has had a revelation, for nothing else could change him from how he was last night to how he woke up this morning except a vision from the Most High, blessed be his name."

Heli nodded sagely. "That is wisdom. This will be between our families. There is no need to try to explain such a thing to the village! I will arrange for the *chuppah* and a rabbi to perform the marriage. Both of you, Mary and Joseph, will have to endure the gossip of the women and, Joseph, there will be comments from the men, but I believe you are able to overcome that in the strength of the Most High, blessed be his name."

Joseph smiled at Mary, the light of love sparkling in his eyes as he looked at her. "Let them say what they will. We know who the child's father is, and we have been blessed beyond my greatest dreams. Mary is to bear the long-awaited Messiah, and I have been given the honor of being an earthly father to God's son, along with the solemn responsibility to raise him."

Arrangements were discussed. The usual ceremony ending with the bride and groom consummating the wedding in the *chuppah* room was not to be carried out under the circumstances. Joseph would just come for his bride and walk her to his home. Rachel and Anna would prepare refreshments for the guests.

When Joseph and his father had gone, Mary turned to her parents.

"Adonai has gone before me and prepared the way. Only he could change Joseph's mind like that."

Anna looked at her husband. "I cannot pretend to understand any of this."

"Nor do I, Anna, but who are we to challenge the Most High? Does the God of the heavens not know his way?"

FIFTEEN

*M*ary woke early and stood to stare out over the village from her rooftop sanctuary. It was her wedding day, but not the day she had dreamed of only a short time before. She tried to hold back the tears that threatened to spill down her cheeks. There would be no official consummation of the marriage, and no bloody cloth to show that Mary was a virgin bride. She was pregnant now, and, in the eyes of the village, she was obviously no longer a virgin.

She sank to her knees and cried out, "Oh God Who Sees Me, give me the strength I need to go through this day. Thank you for showing my beloved Joseph whom this child belongs to. I hear the wagging tongues and see the pinched faces of disapproval. Even my close friends stay away from me." She looked up at the sky. "Their mothers think I am a bad example for their daughters."

She sighed heavily and gave herself to her morning prayers.

When she came down the steps, her mother met her with the white linen gown that was to be her wedding dress, enlarged to make room for her pregnancy. Anna said little as they waited for Joseph to come and claim her as his wife. Her father was also silent. He glanced at Mary and just shook his head.

It was the custom to parade the bride through the streets on the arm off her groom to the home of his parents as the villagers showered them with blessings. Mary dreaded this and found herself plucking at the shawl she wore over her dress. It could not hide what the entire village knew.

As they walked, Mary hoped to receive the good wishes of the neighbors and townsfolk, but expected the comments that fell along the way:

"I wonder why they did not fulfill the betrothal year?"

Another woman sniffed. "They certainly did not wait for the wedding night."

"Well, I heard from Rizpah, who told Zipporah. She was nearby when Mary returned from the home of her cousin. As you can see, she is obviously pregnant."

"Really? I thought Mary was so virtuous. I wonder how her parents reacted to the news."

"Well, you know, there was that other young couple a few years ago. When her parents found out she was pregnant, they turned her out of the house telling her husband to come and get her. There was only the briefest marriage ceremony."

"I heard the child died. Obviously the judgment of the Most High!"

"Aiee, what is this world coming to when a betrothed couple do not respect the customs!"

On and on it went. The words like arrows piercing her heart. What more would she have to bear for the task Adonai had given her? It was all she could do to smile bravely and keep her eyes on the road ahead. She glanced up hesitantly at Joseph from time to time and the villagers could not miss the devoted and loving looks he gave her in return.

Her hand was on Joseph's arm and as she tensed, he felt her faltering and covered her hand with his own. He was there, lending her his strength.

When they reached the home of Jacob and Rachel, Joseph's mother met them, her face grim, but only for a moment. Then she gushed over Mary as the mother of the groom did by custom, welcoming her to the family. Mary knew how hard it was for her.

Rachel turned to her guests and, with head high, graciously beckoned them to partake of the food that had been prepared. Other women of the village brought food and small gifts for the bride and groom. The men glanced smugly at Joseph, and some of the women gathered on the side, murmuring among themselves.

Joseph was surrounded by his peers and submitted to many jibes by those who couldn't resist making him aware of his position. He had been the young man in the village all the parents had looked upon approvingly as a person devoted to Adonai and to his parents.

"So Joseph, your bride was too tempting to wait?" This said with a smirk from a heavy-set youth with a full beard. He spoke loud enough for others to hear and was quickly shushed.

Mary knew there were other things the men said, but now they spoke in quieter voices, glancing her way from time to time with low chuckles.

Joseph did not respond. He merely smiled and shrugged. What could he say to them?

Mary did not fare much better. The village women felt the need to make sure she knew they did not approve as only women can do.

"You have a handsome groom, Mary. It must have been hard to resist him."

"Such a lovely celebration. And when is the baby to be born?"

"I'm sure that Anna and Rachel are pleased to have a grandchild, and so soon."

Mary sent up a prayer for them, letting the inner joy of the child she was to bear deflect the unkind words.

Even those who judged harshly had to note the gentleness and tenderness with which Joseph spoke to her during the celebration.

His love for her was like a shield as they moved about the court-yard greeting friends and neighbors.

When the last of the guests had finally gone, only Joseph and Mary and their parents remained.

Jacob took a deep breath and addressed them. "I have thought on this matter carefully and as I said earlier, I believe the best path to take is to say that Joseph is the baby's father. The village believes this and there is no need to try to explain, even to the elders, the story my son and Mary have told us. We as parents want to believe our children who have been raised to be honest and obedient. It is a hard thing to believe, but the only path for us to follow at this time. Do you agree, Heli?"

Mary's father pulled on his beard and sighed. "What you say is true. The village will not believe Mary's story. It is enough that Adonai has sent his angel to change the mind of Joseph. If he is willing to do this and save Mary from more shame, I will not stand in the way. Your words are wise and my wife and I agree."

Heli glanced at Anna, who shook her head from side to side in frustration. Her shoulders sank as she nodded. "It will be as you say, husband. It is best."

Rachel also agreed. "There must be no slip of the tongue to fuel the town gossip. Already rumors fly like leaves in the wind."

Heli then kissed Mary and clasped Joseph's hand. "You have a steep and rocky road to walk, Joseph, but from now on you walk it as my son. Take care of our Mary for us."

"I will take care of her and guard her with my life."

Anna embraced her daughter. "I will be with you as the time comes, Mary. Be a good wife and obey your mother-in-law as you serve in her house."

"I will, Ima." Mary embraced her mother and then her father and stepped back as she watched them turn and slowly walk out of the courtyard.

Rachel regarded Mary for a moment, and then surprisingly embraced her and smiled.

"Welcome, Mary. We always wanted a daughter and now we have one. Tomorrow we will begin to work together."

Mary's heart leaped. Rachel had always been kind to her, and her kindness did not waver now. It was a good sign. There was an awkward silence, and then Joseph turned to his bride. "Come, beloved." And as the evening star twinkled through the gathering shadows, he reached out his hand and led her to the room he had so carefully and lovingly built for them.

Mary entered the room and looked around. A woven hanging of a bird and flowers graced one wall. She knew Rachel was gifted with weaving and felt warmed by her contribution. The *chuppah* of soft, finely woven linen was held over the bed by four strong poles Joseph had lashed to the frame. A thick blanket topped fresh straw and hand-woven linen cloths covered two down-stuffed pillows. A small table stood beside the bed; on it stood a clay pot filled with a spray of vibrant blue lupine. Mary recognized a wool rug that lay on the earthen floor. She thought her mother had sold it in the marketplace.

"Oh Joseph, it is so beautiful." She paused and turned to him, not knowing what to do next.

He gathered her in his arms and kissed her tenderly. "Well, beloved, this is not how I imagined our wedding night. You are even more beautiful to me now, but I will not touch you in the manner of a new husband. You carry a special child, and Adonai has seen fit to choose me as his earthly father. I will guard and care for you both with all my heart to the best of my ability. We will meet our challenges together. Rest now, Mary, with me."

She put off her wedding clothes and shyly lay down in her simple shift, conscious of her growing belly. Joseph covered her with the blanket. He blew out the candle in the small niche in the wall and slipped in beside her, cradling her head on his arm. She was so weary after the struggle to keep herself together through this day.

Joseph murmured softly, "Rest. Beloved, I am here. I will always be here."

And feeling the steady beat of Joseph's heart, Mary sighed and fell asleep.

SIXTEEN

A rooster crowed from somewhere nearby and Mary opened her eyes. Joseph was tying the sash around his waist. He had put on his sandals and placed the *kippah* on the back of his head.

"Good morning. How did you sleep?"

"Too well. I should have been up earlier to help your mother with our breakfast. Why didn't you wake me?"

"Because, my Mary, you are beautiful even when you are sleeping and I didn't have the heart to disturb you." He came and helped her rise from the bed, pulling her into his arms. "A kiss from my bride?"

She kissed him and, with a shake of her head, propelled him toward the door. She needed to dress quickly. With a grin he closed the leather flap that served as a door and left her.

A few moments later she stepped into the courtyard as Rachel pulled a fresh loaf of bread from the clay oven. Its aroma reminded Mary she was hungry. She inclined her head toward Jacob who was sharpening a tool in the corner of the yard.

"I'm so sorry I overslept. What can I do to help, Mother Rachel?"

"You are entitled this one morning, Mary. You had a long day yesterday. Come, slice the cheese. We will send the bread and cheese with the men to the shop."

Mary did as she was told, grateful her new mother-in-law seemed in a companionable mood.

Later in the morning she worked under the fig trees, carrying cloths full of ripe fruit picked from the trees assigned to Jacob. Rachel and the other women of the village eagerly anticipated their share of plump figs, used in so many dishes. Mary especially looked forward once again to the fig cakes they would bake and store in the stone crocks.

Mary was in her fourth month of pregnancy and estimated that the child would be born sometime around the time of Sukkot and the first rains. She felt faint stirrings in her womb and marveled at the life that grew within her. At night she and Joseph whispered together about the child, sharing fears and hopes and wondering if, as God's son, he would be different from the other children. The prospect was exciting and at the same time frightening.

"Will he play with the other children?" Mary wondered one evening.

"I would think that since Adonai chose ordinary people to raise him that he wants him to grow up as an ordinary child."

"But Joseph, to what purpose? Will he eventually free us from the Roman rule or become a prophet?"

He laughed softly. "Beloved, perhaps Adonai wanted him to learn our ways so he would understand us."

"If he is the son of God, would he not already know us?"

"Adonai is sovereign. He can do as he pleases. He will show us what to do as he has shown us so far. We must trust that we will know all things in due time."

She gave a small gasp. "The child moves!"

She put Joseph's hand on her belly and could imagine his eyes widening in the dark. "So soon? He moves so soon?"

Another night she asked him, "I see the looks of the men. What do they say?"

"They suspect it is not my child but will not come out and ask me. One who was near when you returned home asked me why I was angry. I told them it was because you had been gone so long and had not told me about the child. It is the truth. Whether he shared it with the others I don't know." He sighed. "What does it matter, beloved, when *we* know who the child's Father is?"

She was silent a while. Then, "If the child was not growing within my body I would have believed it only a dream, the fantasy of a young girl. Yeshua is not a dream. I am anxious for his birth, yet fearful of being his mother."

She waited for Joseph's response but heard only soft snores instead.

SEVENTEEN

*M*ary missed working outside in the warmer weather for the clay stove filled the house with smoke along with the smells of cooking. Grain had to be ground on the small grinding wheel under a shelter because of the sporadic rains. In good weather, Mary loved the cool of the early morning, but now she wrapped her cloak around her more securely as she worked.

Her heart sang, not only for the love of her husband and how Adonai had worked it all out, but because her time was approaching. Her mother visited more frequently and she and Rachel helped Mary prepare the swaddling cloths she would need. Joseph had made a beautiful cradle out of olivewood that stood in the corner of their room. Yom HaTeruah, the day God descended at Mt. Sinai with the voice of a trumpet as his people were gathered to him, was approaching, but this year she would spend it with Joseph and his family.

Joseph and Jacob were working to repair the shelter over the animals, and the roof of the house was now used for storage instead of sleeping. Anticipating the muddiness of the dirt floor of the house when the first rains came, Joseph surprised his father by building a framework to put their straw pallets on for sleeping off the floor. Neighbors came to see it and wanted one made for them also. The added business kept father and son busy in the carpentry shop.

When the holy days of Yom HaTeruah and Rosh HaShannah arrived, Heli and Anna were invited to join the family for the celebration. It was a joyous time for Mary's family as friend and neighbors filled the synagogue for two days in the Hebrew month of Tishri to celebrate this feast, which always concluded with honey cakes and apples dipped in honey, symbolizing a sweet new year. Mary, with her taste for sweets, loved the dipped apples.

As her father embraced her, Mary was surprised at how thin he was since the last time she'd seen him. He carried a walking stick, which he leaned on from time to time, and had a small cough, which he sought to cover.

Mary looked at her mother with raised eyebrows.

Anna shrugged, "It is nothing. A small cough. It will get better."

Her mother's anxious looks at Heli every time he coughed belied her casual words, and Mary resolved to pray fervently for her father that night.

Rachel prepared saffron millet with raisins and walnuts from her small storehouse. Mary chopped the fresh coriander and leeks. Anna brought a dish made of squash with capers and mint. Lamb was a food seldom on their table for it was costly, but Rachel had found a reasonable piece at the butcher's stall in the marketplace. She cut it into chunks and slit the meat to insert small slivers of garlic. As it sizzled in the pot, she added onions, broth, coriander seeds, bay leaves and a cup of lentils. Along with fresh bread, baked that morning, Mary felt it was the best meal she had ever eaten. She was hungry a great deal of the time now.

"I do believe you are eating for two, beloved," Joseph teased her.

The men talked about the work in the carpenter shop, work in the fields, and the amount of crops harvested, and the women spoke of who had married in the village, and who was expecting a child. As the time came for the lighting of the evening candle, Anna and Heli took their leave.

"I will pray for Abba," Mary told her mother. "Adonai can bring healing to him."

Anna nodded, and after embracing Mary and wishing a good evening to Joseph and his family, Mary's parents made their way home.

⌇

Mary moved more slowly as the child grew.

"I feel like a great cow," she told her mother-in-law. She remembered Elizabeth murmuring one day as she bent over a grinding stone, making flour for their bread. Mary had taken over that task to relieve her. Now Mary knew how Elizabeth felt.

Rachel watched her daughter-in-law thoughtfully as the months went by. Always there seemed a question on her mind, but she did not ask it. Mary did everything she was asked to do. She was an obedient daughter-in-law and her willing heart gave Rachel nothing to complain about.

Mary and Joseph slept in the room Joseph had built, but sometimes Mary longed for the quiet place on the roof of her parent's home where she could be alone with Adonai and sense his presence. She was seldom allowed to be alone for Rachel was always there, watching over her. She insisted that the steps up to the roof were too much for Mary. "You have nothing to hold to, and what if you fell? Better to stay on level ground at this time."

Mary could only nod. She would have to go into the courtyard after everyone was asleep if she was to have time alone with Ha'Shem.

Anna came again that morning to see how Mary was.

"I feel the birth is imminent," she declared. She stayed as long as she could, but reluctantly returned to her tasks at home.

Just after she had gone, there was the sound of commotion from the village. The words "Roman soldiers!" were carried from house to house. Rachel and Mary stood in the gateway wondering what was happening. For Jews, the appearance of soldiers was something to fear. Joseph came hurrying down the street and strode past them into the small courtyard.

"This is impossible! Why must the emperor decree this now?" He waved his hands and paced back and forth. Suddenly aware of the startled faces of the women, he stopped ranting and looked at Mary, her pregnancy stretching the tunic she wore.

Rachel put a hand up. "Joseph! Stop pacing and tell us what is wrong. What has the emperor decreed?"

"It is a census. Each man must report with his family to the place of his house and lineage to register his household."

Rachel gasped. "You are of the house and lineage of David, Joseph. You must go to Bethlehem." She turned to Mary. "You cannot make the trip at this time. You could give birth along the way. I must go with you."

Joseph flung his hands up in exasperation. "Ima, the trip would be too hard for you and Abba needs you here. I will register all of us." He turned to Mary. "Are you able to do this? We have little choice."

"I will go, Joseph." Mary put a hand on his arm. "If you do not appear with your family we do not know what the soldiers will do. We must obey the emperor's decree or bring trouble on all of us."

"But your time is near. How can you travel that far, even on a donkey?"

Mary stood for a moment and suddenly felt the presence of Adonai, strengthening her and as the words of Scripture formed in her mind she turned to her father-in-law, and felt the joy bubble up from within.

"Father Jacob, what does the Scripture say about Bethlehem? From the prophet Micah?"

Jacob scratched his head, puzzled and frowning as he sought to remember the Scripture. The words came slowly, but as he spoke, his face suddenly lit with amazement as he recited the age-old

Scripture: *"But you, Beit-Lechem* [Bethlehem] *near Efrat, so small among the clans of Y'hudah, out of you will come forth to me the future ruler of Isra'el, whose origins are far in the past, back in ancient times."*

The four were silent a moment as they all realized the portent of the ancient words.

Jacob put a hand on his son's shoulder. "It is the Most High, then, who moves the hand of Caesar to fulfill his Word."

Joseph nodded, tears in his eyes. "May the Most High forgive me for ranting against the hand of the Lord."

Rachel reached out and embraced Mary. "You must go, daughter, Adonai will watch over you both. You carry his son. We will pray for your safe return...with my grandson."

EIGHTEEN

Joseph chose the thickest blanket for the back of their donkey. It was a young animal and strong. Joseph felt it would be able to make the journey and handle Mary's weight. She assured Joseph that if needed, she could walk short distances and give the animal a rest.

Anna and Heli were summoned and stood quietly, watching his preparations. Anna wrung her hands and wept. Heli's face was drawn and pale. Jacob had shared the Scripture with them and there was nothing they could do.

Heli sighed. "We cannot understand the ways of the Most High. Better to be obedient than fight against him."

They could only give the young couple their blessings and prayers.

"Send us word, if you can, daughter," Heli asked. "Just let us know you and Joseph and my grandchild are safe."

"We will send word if there is a way, Abba."

"Mary, you must be sure to have Joseph seek out the local midwife, as soon as you reach Bethlehem. I cannot be with you as I long to be, but you will need her help." She embraced Mary and whispered in her ear. "A firstborn can take more time."

Heli clasped Joseph on the shoulder and after embracing Mary, stepped back.

Rachel and Anna had both prepared food for their journey: dried meat, nuts, date cakes, some fruit, and a loaf of fresh bread.

The travelers would have to buy additional food and pay for lodging on their way.

Mary prayed the night before with Joseph, and they both acknowledged that Adonai knew their way and would guide and protect them as they traveled. Mary knew in her heart that nothing would interfere with the plan of the Most High to bring his son into the world.

After the tearful farewells from Rachel and Anna, and stoic words from Heli and Jacob, Joseph lifted Mary and sat her carefully on the back of the donkey. They turned their faces toward Bethlehem, and whatever lay ahead.

⁓

They reached the Roman road and Mary gave thanks for the ability of the builders. She had been jostled back and forth, up and down, on the rutted roads from Nazareth until she had to bite her lip to keep from crying out and causing Joseph even more concern.

As the hours passed by, she thought of her journey to Elizabeth's. Had it only been a few months ago? Timnah, pregnant at the time, had to ride for hours in the cart on a hard bench. Mary sighed. How could she have known she herself would make this journey again, and in her last month of pregnancy? There would be no mother and mother-in-law to see to her needs, but hopefully a midwife to oversee the birth. Then a thought struck her and she pursed her lips to keep from making a sound that would worry Joseph. What if there was no midwife? Who would help her? Would she birth this heavenly child by herself? Would Joseph have to help her? She blushed at that thought. What did a man know about birthing a child? She shuddered slightly as she fought down the fear that threatened to engulf her.

"Oh Adonai, please help me. I am afraid of what lies ahead. I know your ways are beyond understanding, but I submit to your will. Show us the way. Go before us."

Fighting the fear, she continued to pray silently as the donkey plodded slowly along, each step taking her steadily toward her destiny.

Even with the padded blanket, Mary felt she was riding on the hipbones of the donkey. She walked when she could, but as her steps got slower and slower, Joseph put her back on the donkey.

"Save your strength, beloved, we have a long way to go."

She pressed her lips together to not cry out when the road was rocky and found herself nodding as the animal plodded along. Joseph led the donkey by its bridle but glanced back at Mary from time to time.

"I'm all right, Joseph."

"I don't want you to fall asleep and slip off the donkey."

She smiled reassuringly at him and concentrated on staying awake.

They joined other travelers on the road heading for Jerusalem and other towns to register for the census and were able to camp one clear night in their midst. The women clicked their tongues over Mary and made sure she was comfortable. Many travelers shared what food they had. When she overheard the men commiserating with Joseph on having to make this trip with his wife in such a state, Mary smiled to herself. They were probably thanking the Most High that they did not have Joseph's dilemma. The next two nights they were forced to find lodging in an inn and wait out the sporadic rains.

The fourth day they were able to travel and Mary saw farmers already plowing their fields, taking advantage of the ground softened by the early rains. She thought of Nazareth. Abba would be plowing his field also. As she watched the plows turning over the earth, she realized she missed the flowers that grew through the land in the spring of the year. The prolific cornflower almost took possession of the fields of ripened grain. Then there was the scarlet anemone and the morning glory. Her favorite flower was the blue lupine, which she loved for its intense color. Sometimes the lupines filled whole fields near Nazareth. Now the fields were bare of flowers and only stalks remained of those that had bloomed so gloriously months before.

She looked up and for a time watched a hawk soaring on the wind over the fields. The hawk suddenly dived toward the field and rose again with a small creature in its talons. It had found its dinner.

That evening as they camped, Joseph tore a piece of bread and stared in the direction of the Holy City.

"I will not be able to celebrate Sukkot in Jerusalem as required; there is just not enough time. You will not be able to travel after the birth of the child, and I cannot leave you alone in a strange town, even if there is time to finish out the feast."

"Our timing is in the hands of the Most High, Joseph. He has ordained our way. Surely you are forgiven for missing Sukkot."

He smiled at her then, and reached out to tuck a strand of hair up into the cowl of her mantle. "I am the most fortunate of men, beloved, to have the wife of my heart, and this child. Sometimes I am overwhelmed by the task Adonai has set for me, to be a father to his son."

"He knew your heart, my Joseph, and chose you of all the men of Israel. He knew you would be willing and able to be the earthly father Yeshua will need."

They looked out from under their shelter at the travelers crowding the road, not only heading to Bethlehem and other towns to register their families for the census, but coming to Jerusalem for the required Feast of Tabernacles.

Joseph turned to Mary. "We have cousins in Jerusalem we stay with when we come for holy days. If we are early enough, they might have room."

At last the glistening walls of the city of Jerusalem loomed before them. As they joined the throng making their way up the road into the city, people were pressing them on all sides and many jostled them as they crossed the city to the home of Joseph's relatives. Mary prayed others had not come before them and the relatives would have room. She longed to sleep on a pallet in a house again.

Joseph's elderly cousins, Able and Huskim, did have an extra room and no other family members had come yet to claim it. They were gracious to share their small house with the young couple.

When they saw Mary's condition, Huskim clicked her tongue in disapproval. "How could the emperor expect you to travel at this time? Where will you stay in Bethlehem? You must stay with us until the child is born. What if you have to give birth by the side of the road? It is unthinkable."

Joseph shook his head. "We must go, dear Huskim. For reasons we cannot speak of at this time. Adonai will watch over us."

"But, Joseph, where will you stay?" This from Able.

"It will be all right. We will find a place."

Huskim still fretted. "But if you cannot get there in time?"

After Mary's repeated assurances that she still had some time until the birth, Huskim sighed and, shaking her head, said no more.

The next morning, Joseph prepared to continue on to Bethlehem. Huskim still felt they should remain until Mary delivered her child, but Joseph gently spoke to her concern and packed their things on the donkey once more. After thanking their hosts for their kind hospitality, Joseph and Mary left the city, passing through the throng of pilgrims entering Jerusalem for Sukkot, the Feast of Tabernacles.

As they neared Bethlehem, Mary noticed shepherds watching flocks on the hillsides. In another two months, they would be bringing the sheep into the walled enclosures near the town to protect them during the winter. Here and there she saw a lone figure huddled around a fire, gathering a bit of warmth while keeping a sharp eye on the sheep. She pulled her cloak closer around her shoulders and prayed for a warm place to stay in Bethlehem.

NINETEEN

*M*ary felt her body reaching the point of exhaustion when at last they entered the gates of Bethlehem. Could she go any farther? The baby, low in her body, was like a great stone in her abdomen and no position was comfortable.

Looking around, Mary saw crowds of people; women ushering children toward houses, young boys tending to livestock and joking with each other, soldiers lounging in groups, families with bundles staring unfamiliarly at the bustle and likely traveling for the census like Joseph and herself. Mary sent up a silent prayer once again for a room, and as a dull pain moved through her lower back, she knew it would need to be very soon.

A Roman magistrate sat at a table near the gate where a line of people waited and Joseph led the donkey to the end of the line. It seemed an eternity as they waited for their turn. When Joseph reached the head of the line, he gave his information to the magistrate.

"You have parents? Why did they not obey the order and come with you?"

"My father is elderly, sir. The trip would have been too difficult for him. My mother remained behind to care for him. I will register for all of us."

The official frowned and after a pause, marked Joseph's documents. He glanced at Mary and seeing her condition, shook his head.

"You'd best find a place before nightfall for your woman. It is not safe on the streets after dark. We have had some incidents. Go your way." He dismissed Joseph and motioned to the next man in line.

Joseph grasped the donkey's bridle and quickly led them away from the official. He turned toward the town and with a glance back at Mary, hesitated.

"Adonai, guide him," she breathed as she saw his indecision. Then another pain racked her body and in spite of her determination to remain silent and not worry Joseph, a low moan escaped her lips. Joseph was instantly by her side, looking anxiously up at her.

"Mary, are you all right? What can I do?"

She clutched her belly. "The pains have begun. Joseph, you must find us lodging, quickly."

Joseph ran to a nearby house and pounded on the door. A woman cracked the door open a few inches.

"A room. We need a room. My wife is with child."

The woman shook her head. "We have relatives here. No room." She shut the door.

With growing desperation, Joseph tugged on the bridle and turned to another house. Mary bent over the donkey clutching its mane as Joseph knocked on door after door with the same response. Many others had come for the census. There were no extra rooms available.

Glancing at Joseph before she doubled over with another pain, she saw concern on his face. What were they to do?

The last house they stopped at was larger than the rest. Mary prayed fervently in between the pains that gripped her. "Oh God Who Sees, it is my time and this is your child. Please, find us a place to stay."

A tall, heavy-set man opened the door, his voice gruff. "Yes?"

"My wife is ready to give birth. We need a room...and a midwife."

"Our extra room is taken. There is no place for you here."

A woman's voice was heard behind him. "Did he say he needs a midwife?" She came to the door. As tall as her husband and amply proportioned, the woman eyed Joseph a moment and then looked around him to Mary who was doubled over on the donkey. The woman's eyes grew large. "It is her time?"

Joseph nodded. "Please, can you help us?"

She turned to her husband. "Would the Most High be pleased with us to turn them away at this time?"

He shrugged and spread his hands. "There is no room."

"Our house is full, but the stable has been cleaned and prepared for winter and those who come for the census." She nodded to Joseph. "You are fortunate it has not been occupied as yet. Come with me."

Joseph grabbed the donkey's bridle and followed the woman. A path behind the house led to a cave carved out of the hillside.

"My son Tema spread fresh straw today and the manger is clean. I will move the animals to the side."

"We are grateful indeed for your kindness. I am Joseph and this is my wife, Mary."

She nodded her head at them. "I am Keturah." She looked up. "The sky is bright tonight. With that star who needs a lamp?"

As they entered the cave, Mary expected her nose to be assaulted by the odor of animals, but the cave was neat and clean. The few scrawny chickens squawked and resettled in their baskets of straw as a donkey contemplated them with large liquid eyes. Joseph led his donkey over next to their animal and tied it quickly. Keturah grabbed a blanket that hung from a supporting post and, with a snap of her wrist, spread it on a mound of fresh hay. Another groan escaped Mary's lips as Joseph quickly lifted her off the donkey and laid her on the blanket.

Mary gasped. "The midwife. I need the midwife, quickly."

Joseph turned to the woman but before he could speak, she shook her head and rolled back the sleeves of her tunic. "I have birthed six children. There is no time to find the midwife. I will help you."

She glanced at Mary and then turned back to Joseph. "Go to the house. My daughter is tending to our other guests. Just tell her I need these things: thread, a bucket of water, clean cloths, a bowl of salt, and a knife." She had him repeat the items as she named them and then with her hands, shooed him on his way. "I'll stay with your wife."

Another deep moan from Mary sent Joseph running.

Mary took shallow breaths at the urging of Keturah and glanced at the opening of the cave between pains, desperate for Joseph's return. He must hurry back, what if the child came now? It would only be Keturah and her. Silently she willed Joseph to hurry. *Most High, I am in your hands. My mother is not here, only this kind village woman. Help me. Help me, Lord.*

It seemed like hours. A tear slid down her cheek, and she gasped with relief as Joseph dashed into the cave carrying a bucket of water and the other items Keturah had requested.

Joseph stood glancing from one to the other, "What else can I do?"

"Take her other arm and help her stand," Keturah instructed him.

Joseph held one of Mary's arms and Keturah the other as they lifted her upright.

Mary felt the child moving and with each wave of pain, she pushed with all her might. She bit down hard on the clean rag Keturah had put in her mouth. Still the babe was not ready. They laid her down on the blanket again and waited. Soon her pains returned in earnest. They lifted her to her feet.

"Hold her up!" At the woman's sharp order, Joseph wrapped both arms around Mary as finally, the baby slid into Keturah's waiting hands. At his first cry, she smiled. "Ah, Adonai has blessed you with a son. What will you call him?"

Joseph glanced at Mary, relief and joy flooding his face as he murmured, "Yeshua. He will be named Yeshua."

Keturah nodded. "A good name. It is your family name?"

"No, it is a promised name."

The woman considered that a moment and then shrugged. "It is a good name." After cutting and tying the cord, Keturah used the bucket of water Joseph had brought from the house to wash the baby. Then she rubbed him with salt from the small pottery bowl. Joseph got the swaddling cloths Mary's mother had packed in their belongings, and Keturah wrapped the baby in them.

As she watched Keturah and waited to receive her baby, Mary thought her heart would burst with joy. Yes, a promised name. Yeshua was here, the child who would grow to govern her people.

As Mary rested, breathing heavily from her ordeal, Keturah handed the baby to Joseph. "Hold your son. Your wife has more work to do." She smiled at the small bundle. "A fine boy. That is a good omen for a first child." When Keturah had done what was needed to help Mary finish the birthing process, she took the baby from Joseph and placed him in Mary's arms.

The words of the angel came back to her as Mary gazed down at the face of her son.

"My little one," she whispered, "so much rests on your shoulders." She looked up at Joseph, his eyes glowing with love as he knelt down in the straw and ran a gentle finger down the baby's face. "He is so beautiful, beloved."

Mary looked into the face of her child, once again overcome by who he was. This small being, waving his fists, was the son of God. She clasped him to her, praising Adonai in her heart for this precious gift.

Keturah put a hand on Joseph's shoulder. "Your wife did well. She will recover her strength but you should keep watch. I must return to my duties and my guests. I will send food with my daughter. You will both need your strength after this night. I will be back in the morning to see to your wife."

She paused at the mouth of the cave and looked up at the sky. "Strange, I have never seen a star like that, so bright." She stood for a moment, watching it, and then hurried down the path to her home.

TWENTY

$\mathcal{J}$oseph put fresh straw in the nearby manger and, gently lifting Yeshua from Mary's arms, he placed the baby there. Then he settled on the straw near Mary. "Rest, beloved, I'll keep watch."

A young girl, Keturah's daughter, brought bread and some raisin cakes and wine. She peeked at the baby and, with a shy smile, hurried away again.

Mary was hungry and eagerly reached for the bread. They devoured the meal quickly and Mary lay back on the straw. She needed sleep to regain her strength.

Suddenly, the silence of the night was broken by the sound of excited voices. They stopped at the house and Joseph heard Keturah's voice lifted in protest. The commotion grew louder and louder. Joseph stood quickly and grabbed his staff. He gripped it with both hands, braced his shoulders, and walked to the doorway.

Keturah was arguing with a group of ragged shepherds, who were ignoring her and heading straight for the cave. Behind them followed a wide-eyed family, obviously the guests of the house. Keturah hurried to the front, waving her hands. "I told them they should not disturb you." She looked with distaste at these unwashed shepherds who had obviously come straight from tending sheep.

The small group approached more cautiously, stopping in front of Joseph. Noting his stance and the staff in his hand, they glanced anxiously at one another. One of the older men stepped forward. "I am Jonathan. Forgive our intrusion, but we were told to come." Keturah muttered something under her breath at this explanation, but the shepherd continued. "An angel bid us come."

At the earnest look on the man's face, Joseph lowered his staff. "An angel?"

Jonathan and the other shepherds nodded. One of them, his eyes alight with wonder, spoke. "The sky was full of them. Never have we heard such singing. Then one great being told us not to be afraid, that they were bringing tidings of great joy."

Jonathan glanced at Mary.

"He said that the Savior had been born, here in Bethlehem. We looked at each other wondering what to do. Then the angel told us we would find him in a stable, wrapped in swaddling clothes and lying in a manger. We left our flocks with one of the other shepherds and hurried into the town." He looked up at the night sky. "We weren't sure where we would find the stable, but there is a very bright star, lighting the sky overhead."

Joseph had been standing protectively in front of the manger. Mary smiled up at him. They knew about angels! Joseph nodded and slowly stepped aside. There was a collective gasp from the shepherds and they slipped to their knees, gazing at Yeshua with rapt faces. The family moved closer, the mother holding her two wide-eyed boys back by their shoulders. Her husband shrugged. "It is just a baby. I do not see what all this talk of angels is about."

Jonathan frowned. "We saw them. I am not given to visions and foolish talk. It is true as the angel told us. The Savior has been born."

The other shepherds nodded. "We saw them…multitudes of angels. And the child is here, just as the angel told us."

Jonathan turned to Joseph, his eyes moist with tears. "May Adonai be praised that I have lived to see this day."

Another shepherd raised his arms to the sky. "We will tell all we see of this great thing that the Most High has done for us."

Joseph shook his head and put a hand up to the small assembly. "My friends, I know you cannot help but tell what you have seen, but the child and his mother need rest. Surely it would not be a good thing to have the entire village making their way here."

"He is right," Jonathan murmured. "Can we not tell all who will listen of the visitation of the angels and that they told us the Savior, Messiah the Lord, has been born?"

The shepherds looked at one another and then at Jonathan, nodding their heads.

He turned to Mary. "We will protect you and this blessed child, my lady."

Mary had been holding her breath and now let it out slowly. She was sure her relief was visible. Joseph also sighed with relief as he smiled and faced the ragged group. "The Most High has chosen a most glorious way to announce his son. May you be forever blessed by that knowledge. The child's mother and I thank you."

One of the other shepherds stepped forward and pulled a soft fleece from under his cloak. "This is for the child. We have little to give him, but this will keep him warm."

Joseph took the fleece from him. "Thank you. We are grateful for your kindness."

"Let us return to our flocks," said Jonathan.

When they had gazed at Yeshua for the last time, the shepherds went on their way, exultant in the knowledge that they, simple shepherds, considered outcasts of society, had been given this precious gift.

Keturah waved her hands at her other guests, indicating they should return to the house.

"A strange tale," Mary heard the man murmur. "Who can believe the word of a shepherd? Whoever heard of such a thing? Angels indeed." His wife gave Mary a quick look of sympathy.

"Blessings on your child," she added, and hurried after her husband and sons.

"Who else will come, Mary?" Joseph scratched his head. "This has been a full night." Then he added wistfully, "I would have liked to have seen a sky full of angels."

"Oh Joseph, I believe we have had our share of angel visitations!"

Yeshua began to move and make small sounds. Joseph picked him up, and tenderly held him to his chest a moment, then handed him to Mary to nurse.

"Joseph, he is so beautiful."

The tiny hand curled around her finger and she looked into an incredible face. To her amazement, his eyes were open, strange for a newborn. As she stared down at her baby, the eyes that held hers were almost as bright and sparkling as the stars, and rather than childish innocence, they held wisdom. She looked into those depths and marveled at the enormity of the task she and Joseph had been given. She thought of the fine house he should have been born in; attendants around him, giving God glory and exclaiming praise at his birth. But his worshippers were a small group of simple shepherds who said angels appeared, a host of them in the sky, praising God. Adonai had sent a bunch of scruffy shepherds here to worship the newborn king!

Mary looked around her. The glorious place of birth for the son of God—a stable with a goat, donkeys, and chickens. The newborn king's attendant—a sympathetic village woman who had birthed enough children to know what to do. Mary wondered what she would have done without Keturah. Even poor Joseph was pressed to hold her up for the birthing. She shook her head slowly, smiling to herself. Men were never present for the birth of a child, it was not their custom. It was a woman's time, yet she sensed no embarrassment from Joseph, only concern. Mary longed for her mother, but Anna was many miles away in Nazareth. If her mother could see her now, she would wring her hands. A stable?

Joseph sat down near her and touched the soft cheek of his son. His look of awe changed to one of consternation. "We were given a holy task by the Most High, and I brought you to this." He looked around and shook his head. "We must trust that Adonai knew what he was doing. If I did not, I would be in despair."

She put her hand on his arm. "We got here safely, thanks to your care, Joseph. Our child is born, and we are not somewhere on the road. We can be thankful for that."

Joseph looked out toward the direction the shepherds had gone. "They said they would tell everyone they saw about Yeshua and what the angels said. Suppose more people come here to see him. I am only one. We need a safer place for Yeshua, but where do we go from here? I must wait until the eighth day and have the local rabbi circumcise him according to the law. He is our firstborn son—we must dedicate him at the Temple."

"Shall we return to Nazareth? Our parents will be anxious, but I don't know if I am ready to face all the shame and knowing looks at home. Our parents know our secret, but it will be hard to face the judgmental looks from women of the village again at the dedication."

Joseph stroked his beard and there was a long silence as she waited for him to decide what to do.

Finally, he tipped her chin with one finger. "I believe we must find a house to live in. We cannot remain here. We are vulnerable and we do not know whom the shepherd's story will bring. We will ask Keturah if she knows of a house we can rent. Then, when you have completed the days of your purification, we shall go to the Temple in Jerusalem and present him to the Lord. We have little money until I can find work. I can only buy turtledoves for the offering." He thought again. "If you wish, we can afterward return here to Bethlehem. Perhaps the local carpenter can use my skills."

Relief flooded through her. "That is a good plan, Joseph. I will pray we find a house as soon as possible." She glanced toward the opening of the cave. "At least in a house I would feel safer." And then she would not have to return to Nazareth...yet.

TWENTY-ONE

*T*he animals moved restlessly, seeming to understand something had happened in their cave home. Mary held Yeshua after she had nursed him and sang quietly to him in the moonlight. The stable became still as if her gentle lullaby soothed the animals also.

> *Laila, laila, haruach goveret,*
> Night, night, the wind grows strong,
> *Laila, laila, homa hatzameret,*
> Night, night, the trees rustle,
> *Laila, laila, kochav m'zamer,*
> Night, night a star is singing,
> *Numi, numi, kabi et haner.*
> Go to sleep, blow out the candle.

> *Laila, laila itsmi et enayich,*
> Night, night, close your eyes,
> *Laila, laila baderech elayich,*
> Night, night, on the way to you,
> *Laila, laila rachvu chamushim,*
> Night, night, they rode armed in full gear;
> *Numi, numi, sh'losha parashim.*
> Go to sleep, three knights.

> *Laila, laila haruach governet,*
> Night, night, the wind grows strong,

Laila, laila homa hatzameret,
 Night, night the trees rustle,
Laila, laila rak at m'chaka,
 Night, night, only you wait,
Numi, numi, haderech reka.
 Go to sleep, the road lies empty.

It had been a long night. Mary had risen silently at the first
fussing of her baby to feed him without waking Joseph. She looked
down on his face and saw the same weariness she felt. It had been a
long journey but had ended well. How blessed they were, and how
Adonai had watched over them and cared for their needs.

As the dawn broke through the clouds of the early morning,
the chickens awakened and began to scratch around the stable.
The nanny goat, with a full udder, let it be known she was ready for
milking. Keturah appeared with a wooden bucket and a bowl of
scraps for the chickens. With a smile and nod at Mary and Joseph,
she picked up a small stool, settled her bulk on it and began to
milk the nanny goat.

Joseph watched her work. She was quick. "Keturah, do you
by any chance know of a house in Bethlehem we could rent? We
cannot stay in your stable forever and my wife is not ready to travel
any distance yet.

Keturah thought a moment. "Ah, a perfect home for you. I
know of a family leaving for another town. The parents are ailing
and they must go to take care of them. They may be gone for some
time. I will direct you to their house. It is on the outskirts of the
village—not the most desirable location, but I am sure they will
be happy to have someone renting their house rather than leave it
vacant."

Joseph looked outside the stable. Keturah had come alone.
"Has there been any gossip in the village about the word of the
shepherds? We have seen no one else."

She sighed. "I don't know that anyone believes them. What does a shepherd know? They cannot be trusted. They have seen a vision to be sure to give them such boldness, but at the well this morning the gossip was that perhaps they were dreaming. A baby is a baby." She got up and picked up her pail, then came over and peered down at Yeshua. "He is a beautiful child. Perhaps such an unusual beginning means the Most High has a special task for him."

Joseph glanced at Mary and hastily interrupted Keturah's perusal. "Yes, of course. All parents want their child to be favored of God. Now about that house?"

Keturah nodded, took her milk to the house, and came back with two cups of milk and some fresh bread and cheese. "I will stay with your wife. Away with you now and see about the house."

Joseph hesitated, and Keturah shooed him off with waving motions of both hands. "They will be all right. The sooner you go, the sooner you can return. Now go!"

He left. Keturah settled on the hay next to Mary and took the sleeping baby from her.

"Rest now, I will watch the babe. You are tired from your birth. Rest now."

Mary nodded, her eyes already closing. She felt so weary. With a last anxious look at Keturah and her baby, she slept.

When Joseph returned a little over an hour later, he was jubilant.

"The family is anxious to leave and have agreed to rent the house to us!" He thanked Keturah for all she had done for them. "We will be on our way today. We owe you a great debt. What would we have done without you?" He reached for his small bag of coins in his belt.

Keturah shook her head. "How can I receive payment for bringing our Messiah into the world?" She spread her hands and shrugged. "Perhaps the Most High will look upon me with favor?"

She started to leave, but then turned back, "It was the hand of Adonai that sent you here. You could not have remained in the street."

When Keturah had gone, Joseph turned to Mary. "When I talked with the husband, he said we could stay until they come back. They will send word when they are returning to give us enough time to find other lodging. Also, when he asked me my trade, and I said that I was a carpenter, he mentioned the village carpenter was not well and could use some help. I went to see him and I will start work as soon as I settle you and the baby in the house."

"Oh Joseph, that is wonderful news." Mary smiled up at him, silently thanking Adonai for giving her Joseph, a man who would protect her and care for her no matter what they went through.

Joseph settled Mary on the donkey again, and after handing Yeshua up to her, led them down the narrow streets to a small house on the other side of the town.

Mary was surprised to see chickens scratching in the yard, and a goat tied under a makeshift shelter. It was obvious the family had left.

Joseph shrugged and grinned at her. "I agreed to care for their animals."

Mary was delighted. "We will have eggs and I can make cheese from the goat milk." Once again, Adonai had gone ahead of them and provided for their needs.

The furnishings were simple, but Mary knew Joseph could make anything else they needed. The dirt floor had been swept clean and there were some dishes and pots on a shelf. A clay stove on the rough table. She looked around with pleasure. For a time, at least, she would be mistress of her own house.

She laid the fleece on a pallet and carefully placed Yeshua on it, wrapped in a blanket. As she began to put their things away, she thought of the strange words of the shepherds: a sky full of angels, they said, praising the Most High. She considered all that had happened. How strange were the ways of her God. The King who would save her people, born in a stable. It was not as she had imagined. She sank onto a small stool to rest, and wondered. What else did Adonai have in store for them?

~

The visitors were moving on, gradually emptying Bethlehem of travelers. Heads of households had registered their families and were anxious to return to their own homes in other villages. Joseph spoke with the local rabbi and on the eighth day, Yeshua was circumcised. Joseph attended the local synagogue to worship with the men of Bethlehem. But until her days of purification were over and she was no longer considered unclean, Mary didn't accompany him.

Tekoa, the local carpenter, had fallen behind due to ill health and gladly welcomed Joseph's help. When the villagers saw the quality of Joseph's work, the shop had no lack of customers.

Mary took Yeshua in a sling of cloth to the marketplace when she shopped each day for their meals. Her mother had shared her secrets in using herbs in the dishes she prepared, and today Mary hummed as she kneaded the dough for their bread. When it was set to rise, she swept the courtyard and made sure the animals were fed. Yeshua lay in the new cradle Joseph had made for him, looking up at the sky and waving his hands. He was a good baby and seldom cried unless he was hungry.

Mary kept track of the days and when the additional days of purification after Yeshua's circumcision passed, she and Joseph journeyed to Jerusalem to present their firstborn son to the Lord.

Mary handed Yeshua over to Joseph and went to the *mikvah*, the ritual cleansing bath for women. She then entered the Court of Women and dropped five shekels into the cone-shaped container presided over by one of the priests. Finally, she rejoined Joseph and they wended their way through the crowds, stopping to purchase the two turtledoves. She looked at the innocent birds, cooing at each other. They were so beautiful in their white feathers, and Mary had a pang of regret for their short lives, yet knew they must do for their firstborn son according to the law.

They approached the presiding priest who expertly wrung the necks of the sacrificial birds and performed the ceremony for the dedication of a firstborn. They nodded their thanks and turned away to make room for the next couple.

Suddenly, an old man made his way toward them. He stopped in front of Mary and looked at the baby in her arms as tears made their way down his wrinkled cheeks into his beard. His face was lit with a wondrous smile. He reached out his arms and Mary, glancing at Joseph, reluctantly placed Yeshua in them. Was this a prophet? The old man looked down at Yeshua with awe and delight. Then he spoke clearly: "Lord, now you are letting your servant depart in peace, according to your word; for my eyes have seen your salvation which you have prepared before the face of all peoples, a light to bring revelation to the Gentiles and the glory of your people Israel."

Mary marveled at this strange revelation. The man blessed her and Joseph, and then turned to Mary. "Behold, this child is appointed; destined for the fall and rising of many in Israel, and for a sign that is spoken against, yes, a sword will pierce through your own soul so that the secret thoughts of many hearts may be revealed."

As he spoke these words of promise over Yeshua, Mary marveled. How did he know this? As if in answer to her unspoken questions, he said. "Adonai promised me through his Spirit that I should not see death until I beheld his Messiah." He turned his eyes to Mary, and holding the child in the crook of his left arm, put the other hand on Joseph's shoulder. "This child will be misunderstood and contradicted," and he turned to Mary. "You will feel the pain of a sword thrust through you...."

Mary shuddered when he mentioned the sword, and pondered in her heart what all this could mean. She bowed her head in submission, her heart pounding at the implication of his words, then stretched out her arms, anxious to receive her child back again. As they walked away, the old man stood watching them. Just as she and Joseph neared the entrance to the Temple, they were stopped again, this time by an old woman who also marveled over Yeshua and spoke words of prophecy. As the old prophetess lifted her voice, people stopped to listen and watched them with curiosity.

Joseph glanced at Mary and she sensed his anxiety matched her own. They did not wish to draw attention to themselves. Thanking the old woman for her words, Joseph took Mary's arm and hurried her out of the Temple. As they passed the Temple guards, the men were regarding them with more than curiosity, their hands on the hilt of their swords.

A sword. The old priest spoke of a sword. Mary clutched her baby closer to her. No sword would touch her child; she would guard him with her life.

TWENTY-TWO

As Mary took care of her home and child, it was easy for her to forget the words of the priest. Life was pleasant and Mary found a friend in Judith, a young neighbor who had a three-year-old daughter, Tabitha, and baby boy they named Ephraim. It was good to have someone her age to talk to.

Judith glanced at Yeshua. "He seems an unusual baby. He seldom cries." She shook her head at her own son, who had not stopped fussing since they arrived.

Mary knew to keep her thoughts to herself. She pondered the future of her son, yet knew she and Joseph must wait on the Most High for their direction.

The two women put the babies on a blanket while they talked and Judith charged Tabitha to help watch them. The little girl smiled and plunked herself down by the two babies, pleased with her responsibility. When Yeshua reached out a small hand and touched the face of Ephraim, the baby stopped fussing and smiled.

Judith watched, amazed. "That must be a sign. They will be good friends."

Mary just smiled. It was not the time to mention that they may not be staying in Bethlehem. It was pleasant, at least for now, to have Judith's company.

Later, when Judith had gone, Mary contemplated their evening meal of fried fava beans and dilled cucumbers with brine-cured olives and goat cheese. She would add the bread she had baked that morning.

Joseph seemed preoccupied since they had come back from Jerusalem, and Mary recalled seeing Joseph's face in an unguarded moment. He was her husband, but he had kept himself from her. He was to be father to God's son, and he didn't know what do.

She paused in her preparations and knelt on the ground. "Oh God Who Sees Me, show me what I should do. I am your hand-maiden. I want only your guidance and your will."

Then the words came to her in the afternoon breeze. *He longs for you. Be his wife in every sense of the word, for thus you fulfill the laws of marriage in the Torah. Be at peace, my daughter.*

Her heart rejoiced. She also longed to be the wife Joseph needed. She gathered up her son and, leaving him for a short time with Judith, went to the local *mikvah* to bathe herself. When she reached home, she nursed Yeshua and placed him in his cradle. Then she arrayed herself in her white tunic and brushed her long hair until it gleamed.

To her surprise, Joseph returned from the carpenter shop early. He went to the cradle and gazed down at their young son, sleeping peacefully. Then he looked at Mary and with a puzzled look on his face, started toward her, his eyes warm, taking in her appearance. Then he turned abruptly and began to wash his hands before their meal. Mary stood quietly waiting, her eyes shining with love.

He looked up from the washing bowl. "Mary? You look so beautiful. He started toward her again, then stopped. "Forgive me, beloved." He restrained himself and stood awkwardly, staring at her, his eyes filled with longing.

She went to him and cupped his face with her hands. "Is it not time, my Joseph? My days of purification are fulfilled and Ha'Shem has spoken to me. I am to be a true wife to you."

"Ha'Shem spoke to me in the shop. He said to go home to my wife. I wasn't sure what he meant." He gathered her in his arms and buried his face in her hair. "Beloved," he breathed.

The dinner grew cold on the table.

TWENTY-THREE

The months went by and Yeshua was nearly two. One evening Mary sat mending one of Joseph's garments by the light of an oil lamp and thinking about Nazareth. Was it possible to return home now? Would the gossip have died down? Surely her parents and Joseph's parents were anxious, not knowing what had happened to them.

Joseph worked on a carving of a small donkey for Yeshua to play with as they enjoyed a companionable silence. Yeshua had finally gone to sleep after a busy day watching lizards climbing the wall, a trail of ants across the courtyard, and a nest of birds in the mulberry tree. Earlier she'd found him studying a large beetle that sat quietly in the palm of his hand.

"No bugs," she admonished him gently, brushing the beetle off his hand onto the ground. The offending creature scurried off quickly and disappeared in a crack in the wall.

Yeshua watched it go. "Bug, Ima," he looked at her reproachfully, his lower lip protruding. Mary distracted him with part of a date cake and scooped him up for his dinner.

Now, glancing at her sleeping son, Mary's heart filled with gratitude. As each day passed, she hoped for a brother or sister to keep him company.

Her reverie was interrupted by a soft but firm knock on the door. She looked up. "Who could be coming after dark?"

Joseph rose and cautiously opened the door with Mary close behind him. To her amazement, three men stood outside. Their garments, while dusty and travel-worn, were of the finest material and from their regal bearing, Mary knew them to be men of great importance.

"May we enter?" one of them asked respectfully, and Joseph, his face still showing surprise, bowed and murmured, "Enter our humble home, my lords. Can we be of help to you?"

Mary stepped back quickly and bowed her head.

The tallest of the men spoke. "May I introduce myself and my friends? I am Balthazar." He indicated the second man. "This is Gaspar," and nodding to the third man, "This is Melchior."

Joseph looked from one to the other. "You are welcome, my lords, I am your humble servant." He raised his eyebrows. "May I know why we have the honor of your presence?"

"We are called Magi, astronomers and priests from the court of the kings of the Parthian Empire. We bear the gifts of interpreting dreams and celestial occurrences. We also serve the Most High God. For many years we have studied the heavens, seeking for signs of the great king whose birth was foretold many years ago by our forebear, Daniel. When the star appeared in the heavens, we knew the time had come at last."

Melchior spoke up. "We observed the new bright star that appeared in the heavens with great curiosity, and each of us came to the same conclusion; its portent told of the royal birth. When it appeared to be moving, we determined to follow the star, believing it would lead us to the king."

"And so it has," murmured the man named Gaspar.

Joseph glanced back at Mary and asked the question Mary longed to ask, "How did you find us?"

Gaspar spoke, "The star. To our amazement, it moved through the heavens. It led us to Jerusalem and then this village and this very house. It shines down on you at this very moment."

Mary shook her head in wonder. She had thought the light was from a very bright full moon! Then she recalled how the woman of the house had commented on the brightness of a star the night Yeshua was born. It had shone steadily as the months went by and she had wondered about it from time to time, but felt it was just a sign of the blessing of Adonai. She thought it strange that it did not move, for when she was little, her father told her how the stars have appointed places at certain times of the year.

The men then looked down on Yeshua who had awakened and was regarding them calmly. Mary picked him up and placed him on her lap. When he smiled at their visitors, they suddenly sank to their knees. Mary watched wide-eyed as they laid costly gifts on the earthen floor before her young son.

"Frankincense," intoned Melchior, "for the anointing of his priesthood."

"Gold," said Gaspar, "for his kingship."

"Myrrh," murmured Balthazar, "for a great prophet." He hesitated, then said, "and for his...death."

Mary raised her eyebrows, pondering his words. Myrrh was used in preparing the bodies of those who had died. She held Yeshua tighter. She didn't want to think of death at this moment.

Balthazar gave her a sad smile. "Death comes to all of us in God's time, dear lady."

Joseph looked stunned but found his voice and haltingly thanked them for their kindness. He looked from one to the other, then asked, "Does anyone else know of your journey here?"

Gaspar nodded. "We went to Jerusalem first and conferred with King Herod. He was greatly pleased at our news and asked us to find the child and tell him so he could come and worship also."

Mary's heart pounded. Herod knew? She glanced at Joseph and saw her fear reflected in his eyes. Herod was a bloody king, murdering even those of his own family to protect his kingdom if the rumors were to be believed. Would he not surely seek them out?

Mary knew they were to give hospitality to strangers, but as she looked around their small house, there was really no space to offer them for the night.

Mary served their guests fresh bread, goat cheese, and wine. When the men had partaken of their hospitality, Joseph took a deep breath and made the expected gesture. "You are welcome to spend the night, my lords. Our humble home is yours."

Melchior smiled broadly. "You indeed honor us with your welcome, my friend, but we must leave. We are anxious to return to our own country once again."

Gaspar added his voice. "We rejoice exceedingly that we have found the object of our long search."

Each in turn thanked Mary and Joseph for allowing them to see the young king and worship him.

Balthazar spoke softly. "We do not know what God has in store for you and this child, but we will pray he will fulfill all that he is to accomplish."

Three camels waited outside the house, their halters held by servants. Nearby, several armed guards watched the surroundings. At a command, the camels knelt for their three visitors to mount. Mary and Joseph stood in the doorway, Joseph holding the squirming little boy who was fascinated by the camels. Yeshua reached out a hand toward one of the great beasts as if to pet it. A servant shook his head. "Not a good camel," he said.

Mary looked quickly around for any lamps in nearby homes, indicating a neighbor was awake and had possibly seen their visitors. To her relief, the homes were dark.

"Will you be returning to Herod, my lords?" asked Joseph, his tone cautious.

Melchior stroked his beard. "Actually we will not. Our esteemed brother, Gaspar, had a strange dream last night. We were told to return to our country by another route."

He looked thoughtfully at Joseph. "I would be cautious, my friends. There is evil waiting for you, I feel it."

Realizing God's provision, Mary's heart was full. "Thank you for your wisdom, and the kindness of your gifts. We will remember you in our prayers that Adonai will give you safe travel as you return to your countries."

Melchior nodded, "The joy of our discovery will sustain us. We have found the object of our quest." Then, seeing Mary looking around, he spoke again.

"If you seek our caravans, we left them some distance from the town, dear lady. We did not wish to disturb the populace." He smiled at her and then the camels rocked forward, rising with their passengers and, with the guards following at a quick pace, glided silently into the darkness.

When Yeshua was asleep again, Joseph encircled Mary in the crook of his arm. "I don't like knowing those men went to Herod. How will he take the news our visitors gave him of a newborn king?"

"Joseph, I'm afraid. What are we to do?"

"I don't know. Let us rest, beloved, and face that decision in the morning."

Mary fell into a troubled sleep only to be awakened in the middle of the night by Joseph gently shaking her shoulder. "Mary, get up quickly and gather our things."

"What is it?" She sat up, fully awake now.

"Adonai has sent his angel again, in a dream. Herod seeks the child to destroy him. We are to flee to Egypt, at once."

"Egypt? We are to leave now? Joseph, that route is dangerous, and we would be traveling alone."

"We have no choice. Adonai will go before us. The angel told me that even now the soldiers are on their way."

Jerusalem was only a few miles from Bethlehem! Her heart pounding in her chest, Mary dressed quickly. She would need the *glimah*, her traveling-cloak, and pulled it from the peg on the wall. Wrapping her head in her mantle, she prayed silently as she swiftly gathered a clay jar of honey, some date cakes and flour. Then she filled two leather bags with water. She took one of the wineskins, then looked around for anything else she could safely take, putting them into her bag. She looked at her sandals, the soles nearly worn. She had intended to have Joseph purchase a new pair for her in the village, but there was no time. She tied them on and turned to the cradle. Running her hand over the smooth wood of the cradle Joseph had made for Yeshua, she felt a pang of regret that they would have to leave it behind. Joseph had worked many hours on it. She carefully lifted her sleeping son, wrapping him in a sling of cloth, and hurried to join Joseph who had finished loading the donkey with his hand tools and a few bare essentials. He placed the bag Mary brought in a side basket on the donkey.

To make good time, they would have to travel as lightly as possible. The containers of frankincense and myrrh were stored in the other basket with some clothing. Joseph tucked the container of gold down in the bottom of one of the baskets, under the clothing, then with a glance at Mary, tucked a smaller bag with just a few gold coins into his sash.

"The gifts from our royal visitors will sustain us in Egypt," he murmured.

Mary's heart lifted. Adonai would go ahead of them to provide for their needs. She turned toward the neighboring houses. "I wish I could have said goodbye to Judith. No one will know why we left so suddenly."

There was no time to notify their landlord or any of their neighbors. Mary prayed for the safety of Judith and her children.

Hopefully, the soldiers were looking only for Yeshua, and if they didn't find him, they would seek elsewhere.

"I don't know if I should leave money for the family that rented the house to us. We don't know when they will return. If the soldiers enter the house first, they will surely take it."

He looked around quickly and then with a shrug, placed the amount owed in the cold cooking pot. Perhaps the soldiers, looking for people, would glance in and go on their way. It was all he could do.

Mary looked at the chickens and the goat. "What will happen to the animals?"

Joseph glanced at them and shrugged. "I've fed them the best I could. When the neighbors realize we are gone, hopefully they will care for the animals. We have no choice, Mary. We must travel with haste."

Joseph reached for a small bench nearby. He put it by the donkey and helped Mary get settled as she held Yeshua tightly against her. With a firm hand on the bridle, Joseph led the donkey through a field and then the hills dotted with fruit trees until they entered a rocky pathway that wound into the hills above Bethlehem. They would leave no trail. Even the donkey seemed to sense the urgency of their journey and did not balk but trotted swiftly along. The starlight was bright enough to guide their way on the path.

As they left Bethlehem, Mary felt her apprehension ease. In a few hours, the sun began to spread its orange and gold fingers across the land. They stopped to let the donkey rest. When Yeshua awoke and stirred, Mary realized he must be hungry but thankfully, he did not cry. With a cautious glance in the direction from which they'd come, Joseph lifted her down. Mary sank onto a flat rock nearby and held Yeshua close as he nursed. Looking down at this beautiful child Ha'Shem had given them, she was glad he was not yet weaned. It was another blessing, for there was no goat to provide his breakfast. He was still sleepy, and soon slept again in Mary's arms.

As they prepared to continue their journey, Mary raised her eyes and looked in the direction of the town they'd called home for almost two years. Suddenly she frowned and strained her ears to listen carefully. Did she hear something? In spite of the distance, sounds were amplified in the clear morning air. Was that screaming? She reached out for Joseph, her heart pounding like a drum in her chest.

"Joseph!"

"I hear it." He gripped her hand, his mouth tight. And she knew. Herod's soldiers had arrived in Bethlehem.

TWENTY-FOUR

*F*ear made Mary catch her breath. Joseph quickly lifted Mary back on the donkey, and, as she held her sleeping son close, Joseph struck out on a faster pace. They must reach the border of Egypt before the soldiers came to look for them. They traveled steadily for hours, stopping only to take care of Yeshua and eat from their meager provisions.

Coming out of the hills, they reached the town of Modein and they were able to add some fresh bread and fruit to their provisions. A small inn allowed them a night's sleep out of the cold. The next day after a hasty meal, they traveled on to the coastal plain of Philistia and reached the town of Ashkelon. The Roman presence was everywhere, and Mary was relieved to pass through the town quickly to the coast of Gaza. The land was barren and they drank their water sparingly as they crossed the sunbaked desert wastes. For a time, Joseph held Yeshua who was restless as most little boys are at being contained. They let him walk as much as possible to exercise his small legs. Mary walked beside Joseph and led the donkey. Mary prayed as they traveled, for the provision of Ha'Shem to watch over them, and she felt the warmth of his presence over her. They did not run into bandits or other travelers, which was unusual, and they rejoiced. Surely the Most High had sent his angels to see them safely to Egypt.

Traveling along the Roman road that skirted the coast of the great sea, Mary took deep breaths of the salty air and was relieved to see Yeshua distracted by the birds that called to one another as they flew in great numbers above the sea. Near the end of the third day, they crossed the Wadi-El-Arish, called the River of Egypt. Misnamed, she thought, as it was more a trickling stream, easily forded.

Traveling along the border of Egypt, Mary breathed a sigh of relief as they entered the large city of Pelusium. It was a seaport and she could see it was an important city. They passed marshes and swamps on their way. Pelusium had been named for the mud of the swamps. In the marshes, they passed clumps of papyrus, and also the Egyptian bean, which Mary had seen in the marketplaces in Egypt. The Egyptians used it as a kind of drinking cup.

They passed a caravansary, teeming with herds of camels. Mary frowned as they passed by. "So many animals, Joseph. What do they do with them all?"

"It is my understanding that they hire them out to travelers crossing the desert to Jerusalem."

Jerusalem. Just the mention of the name sent chills down Mary's back. With Herod as king, she felt sorry for the Jews who lived in that city, even though it held their beautiful Temple. Now Mary and Joseph were out of Herod's territory of influence, but Egypt was still ruled by Rome, for a man named Gaius Turranius served as the Roman prefect over Egypt.

They crossed the narrow isthmus of al-Quantara, the bridge that separated the Lake of Menzaleh from Lake Balah, and found themselves at last in the Land of Goshen.

They came to the town of Bilbais, and weary of traveling, Joseph found them lodging in a small caravansary to rest a few days. Yeshua had been a good traveler, but he was a toddler and they could only contain him on the donkey for short periods of time. When he fell asleep, they traveled as far as they could until he awakened and was hungry.

With the donkey properly stabled for a time, Mary and Joseph wandered through the marketplace with Yeshua, who was fascinated by everything he saw. Mary felt as though she was seeing the world through new eyes. Yeshua wanted to taste and touch everything.

Joseph bought Mary a new pair of sandals at last, and she was able to throw the old ones away. They wouldn't have lasted much longer.

Mary smelled the saffron and the cinnamon in the air. Plucked chickens hung from a wire and another booth had chunks of lamb and goat's meat for sale. While she thought longingly of the dishes she could prepare, she had no place to cook. They had to eat only what they could carry in their hands. One stall was selling a fava bean and goat's meat stew in cups made of the Egyptian bean. Joseph quickly bought two of them. Mary dipped some fresh bread in the stew and blew on it before handing it to Yeshua. She smiled as he devoured the morsel and she let him eat what he wanted. He had developed all of his teeth, and she contemplated weaning him when they got settled somewhere.

When at last they traveled again, they passed through a small village of Matariyah and several more small towns and finally reached the great city of Ramses on the edge of the Nile Delta. Mary and Joseph marveled at the pyramids built by their ancestors when they were slaves in Egypt.

They skirted the deserted pagan city of Beth Shemesh, and, after many days, they came to the small village of Matariyah and were welcomed by a few Jewish families who had settled there after escaping the terrors of Herod's reign. One family shared their humble home with them and provided a meal in the morning.

The family urged them to stay, but Joseph, wishing to press farther into Egypt for safety, thanked them and led his family along the road. When they had traveled a while, they came to another village. People smiled and nodded to them as they passed along the street. Many of the men wore the *kippah* on the back of their heads.

"This looks like a friendly town, Mary. There are many Jewish families here. Perhaps it is a good place to settle. I do not wish to travel for much longer."

"I feel also that this is good." Mary sensed the warmth of Adonai's presence steal over her and felt he was confirming their choice. She and Joseph thanked the Most High God for leading them to a safe place.

Joseph approached one of the men and inquired about a dwelling. The man nodded and pointed to a crude building, used as a synagogue, where they would find one of the town elders named Japheth.

He listened to their request and studied them through narrow eyes. Finally he shrugged. "There is a house. The family left some time ago. I was given charge of the house, but no one has come to rent it. I will show it to you."

He led them down a narrow side street to a small stone house not much bigger than the one in Bethlehem. Weariness had settled on Mary like an unwelcome cloak. At least it would be a place to call home until they had further directions from Ha'Shem.

In the corner of the yard was a clay oven for baking bread and nearby a well-worn millstone for grinding grain. They hesitantly peeked inside and Mary sighed. It was dusty and there were no dishes or a clay stove. She approached a large clay jar and lifted the lid. It held some water that looked usable. There was a shelf above a crude table, but it was empty. She wasn't discouraged. Joseph would make what they needed, or buy it in the marketplace. She smiled at him.

"It will be fine, Joseph."

He carefully retrieved a gold coin, taking care the elder saw it was only a small bag, and paid Japheth for their rent.

"Thank you for your kindness. We will take good care of the house."

Japheth stroked his beard and squinted at them. "How long will you be staying?"

Joseph shrugged. "We are waiting on word from a…relative. We are not sure."

"People come and go here. Always they are just passing through. But that is life. You will let me know when you must leave? The family that was here left suddenly and did not pay the last month's rent." He squinted at Joseph again.

"We will let you know when we have to leave."

Mary listened to the exchange. What could Joseph tell the man? They could certainly not say they were waiting on the Most High to tell them when to leave Egypt. She looked around the yard. There would be work to do to make it presentable, but it was a house.

This time there were no other animals so when the man had gone, Joseph unloaded the donkey and led him into the town to get some hay.

Mary made sure the gate to the yard was closed so Yeshua could not wander away. She found a weathered broom in the house and began to sweep. As she worked, she sang one of the hymns from the Psalms, praising Ha'Shem for his care and provision for them. When the house was in order, she looked around. Joseph would be pleased. She waited eagerly for him to return. There were other things she needed.

The gate creaked open and Mary looked up anxiously as Joseph hurried to her side. He was beaming.

"A family is leaving and were selling some things in the marketplace. I bought what I thought we could use. They have a cart and are bringing them here."

Mary raised her eyebrows. "What did you buy?"

He glanced over to see where Yeshua was and seeing the child occupied with a feather that had floated down into the yard, turned back to Mary.

"A clay stove, some dishes, two more blankets, some straw, a cooking pot, and two feather pillows."

She reached up and put a hand on his cheek. "How resourceful you are, my Joseph. Just the things we need."

A voice shouted out "Whoa" and the cart was there at the gate. Joseph helped the man unload and Mary carried the dishes into the house: three wooden platters, three clay cups, and the cooking pot. Joseph carried the hay to the corner of the yard where the donkey stood in a small lean-to. He got the stove and placed it on the ground by the house. The weather was still pleasant and Mary was happy to be able to cook outdoors as long as possible.

When the man had gone, Mary looked at her cooking area. She could make do, but there was nothing to cook. They had a couple of date cakes, and a little bread that was getting stale. The provisions Joseph had purchased at the last town were gone. Mary felt like she had not baked bread for too long. She was anxious to begin in her own cooking area.

There was a knock at the gate and Joseph opened it to admit a young woman carrying a covered basket.

She looked at Mary and spoke shyly. "I am Reba. We live in the next house and saw you arrive with the baby. My mother thought you might not have supplies for your supper and sent this." She uncovered the basket. There was a pot of stew with lentils, barley, and mustard greens, a bowl of dates, figs, and flat bread, along with some dried fish.

Mary silently thanked Ha'Shem, then said out loud, "We thank you, Reba, and the kindness of your family. I did not as yet have provisions for our meal. Please thank your mother for us."

The girl gave them a brief smile and a nod and hurried away.

"Oh Joseph, how wonderfully Adonai has cared for us."

They washed their hands in the jar of water in the kitchen and bowed their heads as Joseph intoned the blessing, thanking the Most High for his care and for the kindness of their new neighbors.

When they had eaten, Mary carefully stored what was left over. Then she nursed Yeshua one last time and settled him down on the pallet Joseph had made for him. Joseph checked the donkey and made sure he was secure for the night. Had the animal decided to challenge the gate, it would have crumpled easily.

When they were sure Yeshua was asleep, Joseph flung their blankets down on their pallet and with Mary's head resting on his arm, they fell into an exhausted sleep.

Mary awakened in the dawn with a sense of foreboding. She glanced over at their son's pallet and shook Joseph awake.

"Yeshua is gone!"

Joseph leaped up and they hurried out into the small courtyard. Yeshua was sitting in the dirt, his brow furrowed as he gazed down at a lizard he held in the palm of his hand. He heard Mary's gasp and turned to smile at her.

"See, Ima. See, Abba."

Mary released the breath she'd been holding and Joseph lifted Yeshua up, still holding the lizard.

"Who gave you the lizard?"

"A man, with wings. Like bird."

Mary frowned. A man like a bird that could fly? She pondered a moment. Could it have been an angel? Were there angels she could not see, watching over Yeshua? It was a comforting thought.

Joseph however, was more practical. "I need to put a latch on the door. We cannot have our son wandering outside when we are asleep."

They ate the last of the bread and fruit for their breakfast and Mary prepared to go with Joseph to the marketplace.

Wanting to keep the gold they carried a secret as long as possible, Joseph sold the frankincense in the marketplace and Mary bought olive oil, barley, wheat flour, coarse horse beans, lentils, cucumbers, more dates and figs, and a small clay jar of honey. Moving from stall to stall, she found leeks, garlic, and a block of goat cheese and purchased a small chunk of goat's meat. At the spice vendor, Mary replenished the spices she'd had to leave behind in Bethlehem.

One farmer was selling chickens in basket cages and Joseph bought two of them. There was a young female goat available that had borne and lost her kid. She was ready for milking and Joseph bought her from the farmer. Yeshua was not weaned as yet, but they could use the milk.

At the local well, Mary became acquainted with two of her neighbors: Dorcas, who was the mother of the young girl who had brought the basket of food, and Salome, an older woman who lived with her grown children.

"Dorcas, I thank you for your kindness in providing our evening meal last night. It was much needed."

The woman smiled, showing a missing tooth. "It is good to have a young family nearby. How old is your son?"

"Yeshua is almost two."

"Where did you come from?"

Mary hesitated. What did it matter? "We came from Bethlehem, but my parents live in Nazareth."

Dorcas' eyes grew wide. "You are from Bethlehem? How fortunate you are to have left that place."

"Fortunate? Why?" Her heart filled with apprehension. She knew the soldiers had come to search for Yeshua, but no more after their hasty retreat.

Salome glanced at Dorcas and shook her head. "Then you have not heard?"

Mary frowned. "What is the news from Bethlehem?"

Dorcas put a hand on her arm. "Herod's soldiers came. They killed all the male children from newborn to two years old."

Fear struck Mary's midsection and her chest tightened as she suddenly sank down on the edge of the well. "He killed...all of them?"

Salome and Dorcas nodded. "All."

Tears pooled in Mary's eyes. "I had a friend there. She had a daughter about three and a little boy...." She could not continue. Judith's son, Ephraim, would be among the dead.

TWENTY-FIVE

*T*hey had been in Egypt six months, and life was peaceful. Mary went about her household duties, and Joseph kept busy repairing things around the house and doing small carpentry jobs for the neighbors. There was a synagogue, and Joseph met with other men in the village for prayer. They could always count on a *minyan*, at least ten Jewish elders.

Always on Mary's mind was the question of when they were going to be able to return to Judea. At night, they prayed fervently for word from Ha'Shem that would allow them to return to their home in Nazareth. Mary grieved that her parents had not yet seen their first grandchild.

Then, at last, just as the rooster next door heralded the coming dawn, Joseph gently shook Mary. "Wake up, beloved, it is time."

"Time? Joseph, it is not yet even light."

She could hear the smile and excitement in his voice. "The angel has come to me again. Herod is dead and we can return to Judea."

"It is safe to return? Where shall we go?"

He paused. "The Most High will show us where to go." The sun was rising and Mary looked up at the dear face of her husband. His brows were furrowed as he asked, "Are you ready to return to Nazareth?"

She nodded. "I have missed my parents and they will be anxious to see their grandson. They have probably wondered many times what happened to us." She put a hand on his arm, smiling now. "Besides, I do not relish his brother or sister being born in another stable."

"You are with child?" Joseph gathered her in a fierce embrace. "I have hoped for a long time."

"Joseph! It is a time to be careful."

Joseph released her and touched her cheek. "Let us prepare at once." Then he stopped as a thought crossed his mind. "How soon…?"

She laughed then. "It is early. We have many months to go."

Joseph drew her to himself, this time gently, and she could feel his heart beating strongly against hers.

She lingered in his arms, but a small voice interrupted the moment. "Ima? I am hungry."

When Joseph had gone outside to gather his tools and see to the animals, Mary's heart leaped within her. Home. They were going home.

She nursed her son and then broke off a chunk of bread and spread a little honey on it to keep Yeshua occupied. She quickly milked the goat and poured fresh milk for her and Joseph. With a lighter heart than the night they left Bethlehem, Mary prepared to pack once again. This time they would travel farther, but not in haste. They debated on a cart, but Joseph decided that with the rough roads ahead, it was better to purchase another donkey to carry extra goods. Having been alerted early by the angel, Joseph was fortunate to find the one suitable donkey in the marketplace. Soon other Jewish families heard the news of Herod's death and were making plans to leave Egypt to return to homes and families in Palestine and Judea.

There was almost a festive air in the town as families wished each other a safe journey. Mary and Joseph would travel with three other families up the coast of Gaza. Two families were traveling to Caesarea, and one family to Megiddo in the huge Jezreel Valley.

Mary was delighted when she heard where the family was headed. Nazareth was only about fifteen miles from Megiddo, across vast fertile plains full of grain.

When all was ready, in the early dawn, they joined the other three families in the center of the village and with the braying of donkeys, the squawk of chickens, and the bleating of goats, they began their journey.

After passing through the small towns Mary and Joseph had encountered on their way from Nazareth to Egypt, their group reached Gaza and camped. Mary was thankful that one of the families had a young son about the age of Yeshua because the two boys entertained each other.

In ensuing days, they camped outside Ashkelon, and another night lodged in a caravansary in Joppa. Entering the Plain of Sharon, they traveled through heavy forests and marshes. When they reached Caesarea, Mary and Joseph and the other travelers said goodbye to the two families leaving their group and wished them well. The women hugged each other and vowed to meet again "next year in Jerusalem," when they would come for Passover.

Mary, Joseph, and the remaining family left the Plain of Sharon and the land became drier as they ascended into rounded limestone hills. Isolated fertile areas were filled with gardens, vineyards, and olive groves. Fortunately there were scrubby grasses in the higher elevations for the donkeys to graze on.

The goat, tied by a rope to the second donkey, slowed their progress, but the other family had animals they were bringing with them so the group could only travel as fast as the goats and sheep could walk. Joseph and Mary's chickens rode in baskets on the second donkey.

Leaving Caesarea, the group traveled up through Mount Carmel and into the Jezreel Valley to Megiddo. The women bade each other tearful farewells and, finally, Mary and Joseph continued on through the Jezreel Valley to the hill country of Nazareth.

TWENTY-SIX

As they traveled through the Jezreel Valley, Mary felt a sense of joyous anticipation at the thought of seeing her parents again after so long. She saw the same look on Joseph's face as he urged the animals along the road.

At last they neared Nazareth, nestled in a sheltered basin some 1,300 feet above sea level, and Joseph stopped to rest the donkeys and point out some sights to his young son. Mary was amazed that in spite of his young age, Yeshua listened attentively to his father.

"See those limestone ridges? They surround Nazareth and form the southernmost border of Lower Galilee. That is Mount Carmel in the distance. And there, to the east, is Mount Tabor." Joseph pointed in the direction of the north where they could make out snow-covered peaks. "That is Mount Hermon." Yeshua nodded sagely.

Mary looked to the south, where she could see the fertile Plain of Esdraelon stretched out before them. Her father told her it had been the battleground of conquerors, but it had formed a crossroad for trade and travel as long as people in the village could remember.

Joseph urged the weary donkeys on and Mary could hardly contain her excitement. She had talked to Yeshua about his grandparents, and what Nazareth was like. He listened, but with the attention span of a young child, was easily distracted. Now, when she told him they were almost home and he would meet his *sabta* and *saba*, he seemed to catch her excitement and clapped his hands.

Joseph led the animals through the winding streets and neighbors that recognized them came out of their homes.

"Joseph, is that really you?"

"We thought you were dead."

"Welcome home."

"A son! The Most High has blessed you!"

Mary saw only smiles and the natural surprise of seeing them again.

Word spread rapidly in the small village, and only moments after Joseph brought the donkeys to a halt in front of his parent's home, Anna came running. She was puffing from the effort and tears of joy ran down her cheeks.

"My daughter, you are safe and have returned at last. With Joseph and…." She looked at Yeshua and beamed.

"My son, this is your *sabta*."

Yeshua smiled at Anna and she held out her arms to gather her small grandson to her heart.

Rachel and Jacob opened the gate to their courtyard and Jacob, with tears in his eyes, clapped his son on the back. "May the Most High be praised for your safe return. We have sorely missed you." He frowned. "After you registered, and the child was born, why did you not return to us?"

Rachel waved a hand. "Husband, they have just now arrived. They are tired and probably hungry. There will be time to hear all they have to say."

Heli had been in the fields and now hurried up to them, embracing his daughter and Joseph. He marveled at Yeshua who was now in the arms of Rachel as both grandmothers exclaimed over him.

"He seems a calm child, Mary," Anna noted. "Does he cry much?"

"Mostly when he was a baby. He seldom cries now."

She looked at Joseph helplessly as both grandmothers vied for attention from Yeshua. "Ima, Mother Rachel. Yeshua needs rest. It has been a tiring journey. Besides, there will soon be another grandchild for you to fuss over."

This brought more exclamations of joy from both sets of grandparents and Rachel reluctantly relinquished Yeshua to Mary who put him down on a pallet where, with the ease of young children, he promptly fell asleep.

Jacob tethered the donkeys and tied the goat nearby, giving them some hay. Joseph untied the chicken's cages and let them out in the yard. The birds, loudly ecstatic with their freedom, ran back and forth in the yard fluffing their feathers. Anna and Rachel unloaded the food and clothing and brought them into the house. Mary put her things in the room Joseph had built for them and looked around. It was clean and inviting, as if it had been waiting for them to return. In the corner of the room was the cradle Joseph had made for Yeshua. At least it would be used again in a few months.

With Yeshua napping, Joseph and Mary settled on a rug with diluted wine and a bowl of fruit. Heli, speaking for all of them, asked the question on their hearts.

"So what happened in Bethlehem? We heard news of...."

Anna interrupted. "Were you able to find a midwife? A room or house somewhere for the child to be born in?"

Mary glanced at Joseph for a moment, and he nodded for her to go ahead.

"The rooms were all taken, Ima. The city was so crowded with travelers. The last house already had guests and there was no room there."

The two grandmothers tsked at each other and shook their heads.

"So where was Yeshua born?" Rachel ventured.

Joseph spoke up at last, trying to hide a smile. "In their stable. The woman of the house took pity on Mary and helped us." Ignoring the startled looks on the faces of their parents, he continued. "We had a fine audience of donkeys, goats, and chickens. Fortunately the hay was clean."

Mary saw the look of horror on her mother's face. "Was there not a midwife in Bethlehem?"

"No, Ima. There was no time. The woman had birthed several children, and between her and Joseph, I managed. Fortunately the labor was not as long as I feared."

"A stable?" Rachel croaked, "My grandson was born in a stable? Joseph had to help with the birth?"

Jacob and Heli exchanged looks.

Joseph shrugged. "There was no one else to help."

Heli looked around at the group. "I believe Joseph and Mary have much to tell us. There have been rumors of terrible things wrought by Herod's soldiers. We feared for your lives. When we didn't hear for so long, we thought you were dead."

"We would have been, Abba, or at least Yeshua would have been, if Joseph had not been warned in a dream to leave Bethlehem in the middle of the night."

Joseph took Mary's hand. "It is probably best to start at the beginning." Joseph shared more about the unusual birth of Yeshua, assuring their parents that a rabbi in Bethlehem had properly circumcised Yeshua, and that they had dedicated him in the Temple. Mary shared the words of the prophecy over Yeshua by the priest and the old woman.

Both fathers stroked their beards and nodded, pleased. Joseph had followed the law, and the prophecy only verified who Yeshua was.

"My son, how did you live? You had only enough money to go to Bethlehem and return home."

Joseph turned to his father. "This has been a time of miracles, in so many ways." He then told them about the night the three Magi, great men and astrologers, had appeared at the door of their house, and the gifts they had presented to Yeshua.

"They came all that way to worship a newborn king according to a great star they followed. Then they told us they had stopped in Jerusalem and spoken to Herod about their quest for the newborn king. He asked them to return and tell him where they had found the child."

Rachel gasped. "Herod? Worship a newborn king?"

Mary put a hand on her mother-in-law's arm. "You surely remember the events before his birth. We all knew who Yeshua was to be. Joseph and I feared for his life, yet Ha'Shem took care of us. The Magi told us they'd been warned in a dream not to return to Herod. They were going to return to their country by another route."

"We wondered what we should do," Joseph added, "and that night an angel warned me in a dream to leave immediately and flee Bethlehem."

Heli stroked his beard. "The Most High protected his son."

Joseph nodded. "We left in the middle of the night and were far away from the town when we heard the cries from Bethlehem. We didn't know what had happened until we were in Egypt. The soldiers came and...." His eyes watered and he could not continue.

Heli shook his head. "Yes, word finally came to us of what happened in Bethlehem and we feared for you all."

"Oh Abba, those poor mothers. Herod killed every male child in Bethlehem from birth to two years old." Mary shuddered.

"You have been in Egypt all this time?"

Joseph nodded. "Yes, Abba. The angel of the Lord came once again and told us Herod had died and it was safe to come home." Then he told how the gifts of the wise men had sustained them along with his carpentry work.

"Then let us rejoice and celebrate, for my son and his wife have returned to us with a grandchild and good news of Adonai's blessing of another child. Let us leave the past events behind us."

Neighbors, who had begun to gather outside the courtyard in curiosity, were welcomed in, and the women hurried back to their homes briefly to gather food to share.

Mary found herself smiling at the memory of her anxiety, rejoicing that there were no more remarks about the birth of Yeshua. Somehow, knowing the couple had been through an ordeal, hearts had been softened. The neighbors were only told part of the story. There was no need to mention the stable, the shepherds, the angels, or the visit from the astrologers from Chaldea. It was enough to tell that they had been able to flee the bloody deed of Herod.

TWENTY-SEVEN

*J*ust before the birth of their second child, Yeshua was finally weaned. The neighbors gathered and with a small feast, the auspicious day was celebrated. Joseph recited Psalm 104 from memory:

"Bless ADONAI, *my soul!* ADONAI, *my God, you are very great; you are clothed with glory and majesty, wrapped in light as with a robe. You spread out the heavens like a curtain, you laid the beams of your palace on the water. You make the clouds your chariot, you ride on the wings of the wind. You make winds your messengers, fiery flames your servants."*

To Mary's delight, their relatives Elizabeth and Zechariah came with their small son, John, who was a quiet and serious child. They had been to the wedding of a nephew of Zechariah's in Sepphoris and, hearing of the celebration, eagerly joined Mary and Joseph in the celebration.

"The child grows well," Elizabeth commented, observing Yeshua. The two young children seemed at ease with each other. She gazed meaningfully at Mary, and the two women smiled at their shared secrets. Two unusual sons, chosen for a destiny their mothers could not begin to know.

Seeing Elizabeth to be in her later years, the neighbor women, as well as Rachel and Hannah, oohed and aahed over John, counting Elizabeth to be truly blessed that Adonai had looked on her barrenness and granted her a son.

After being blessed by the local rabbi, Yeshua clapped his hands and swayed to the music of the flute. He smiled at everyone and seemed to know this was a special day. Mary was sorry to see Elizabeth and Zechariah leave but knew they had a long journey ahead of them back to Juttah. She thought of the moment Elizabeth had opened her door years before and the wonder of the revelation of Elizabeth. What role would John play in Adonai's plan for him, and for that matter, what was the reason for the birth of Yeshua? She sighed and shook her head. She and Joseph could only wait. Surely Adonai would reveal his plan in good time.

～

Mary's second son, James, was born at the beginning of the grape harvest. Yeshua was delighted to have a sibling and became his protector. Jacob's carpentry shop was doing well, and, with the profits, Father Jacob and Joseph had added to their humble home. A proper gate had been made by Joseph and fitted in place of the old one. Various pots with overflowing herbs graced their small courtyard. Nearly a dozen chickens roamed about and there was a pen for their five sheep which the local shepherd took to the hills each day along with a few sheep of other families to graze until evening. Joseph built a stone cistern by the side of the house with clay pipes to direct the rainwater. Along with water from the local well, their needs were amply met.

It was harder now with two active boys. Yeshua seemed to be endowed with insatiable curiosity. Everything interested him, from the ants moving in a single line along the wall to the birds that sang in the sycamore tree in the corner of the yard.

By the time Yeshua was six, a daughter, Miriam, and a third son, Joseph, named after his father, were added to the family. They called him Joses.

One day Yeshua ran to get Mary, and tugging on her hand, led her to a corner of the yard where a baby bird sat on the ground eyeing them fearfully. Mary looked up in the tree.

"My son, the baby bird has fallen out of his nest. See it up there on the branch?"

"We can put the baby bird back, Ima."

She frowned. "I don't know. We might frighten away the mother bird." She looked up in the tree again and saw the mother bird watching them. Yeshua got a small stool by the goat pen and put it at the base of the tree. Seeing what he had in mind, Mary shook her head. "My son, I think you are too little. You might fall out of the tree."

Yeshua gently picked up the baby bird in one hand and before she could stop him, clambered up the tree, stepping from branch to branch. To Mary's surprise, the mother bird did not make a sound, but watched as Yeshua carefully placed his small charge in the nest with her two other baby birds. He scrambled quickly down and Mary stood in amazement. She did not scold him, for he had not disobeyed her, but shook her head at what she had just observed. Her son definitely had a way with small creatures.

Yeshua smiled again, pleased with himself. "He is safe now. Mama bird will take care of him."

When she related the incident to Joseph that evening, he chuckled. "I do not think that is the last of the strange things we will observe as our special charge grows up, beloved."

In the darkness Joseph could not see her face, nor the one tear that made its way down her cheek. What was the destiny of this child they were raising? Well-liked by the other children in the village, adored by his younger brothers and sister. Who was he to be? What plans did the Most High have for his son? Long after Joseph was asleep, she let the thoughts tumble about in her mind.

With four children, Mary seemed to have little time to herself. Yet she was aware of Ha'Shem throughout her day and spoke to him in her heart. Sometimes, with Rachel's permission, Mary would walk by herself in the hills of Nazareth and feel the presence of the Most High with her. She did not see any more angels, but sometimes felt the soft breeze brush her cheek like a caress.

Yeshua was attending Hebrew school, which all Jewish boys attended from the age of six until they were twelve. In time, a fourth brother, Simon, was born and a second daughter, Jerusha, joined their family.

Mary hurried Yeshua and James through their breakfast and waved her older sons toward Joseph who had already finished and waited by the gate.

"My sons, you must hasten. You do not want to be late for school. Your father is waiting."

Yeshua gave her one of his brilliant smiles. "We are ready, Ima." And he turned to James who rose and hurried with Yeshua to join their father. Mary had listened as Yeshua shared with James and young Joses the night before and how eager Joses was to join his older brothers and the other boys of the village to study the Torah with the local rabbi. James seemed to drink in his older brother's words and listened eagerly to the stories Mary told from the Scriptures. James had memorized other parts of the Torah, and Mary, observing his joy of study, wondered if one day James would become a rabbi himself.

Each day Joseph walked Yeshua and James to the *beit hasefer*, "house of the book" where they would engage in a deeper study of the Torah with the rabbi.

One day Joseph came home with the two older boys and as he watched Yeshua begin his task of feeding the animals, a thoughtful expression spread over his face.

Mary, standing in the doorway of their house, noticed his absorption and finally asked, "Is something wrong at the school?"

Joseph hesitated and shook his head slightly. "No, it's just the words of the rabbi. He came to me and commented that we must have taught our sons well. Especially Yeshua. It seems that no sooner does the rabbi introduce a portion of the Torah, but Yeshua has memorized it. He was puzzled at the knowledge of one so young."

She raised one eyebrow. "What did you say to the rabbi?"

"I merely said that Yeshua has a good mind, and seems to remember things quickly."

Mary caught her breath. "I have taught him the stories of our people and you have taught him portions of the Torah as we are commanded to do."

"Mary, we must never forget who he is. Would not the son of God know the Torah?" He flung one hand in the air. "I pray he will not give the rabbi cause to be concerned…at least not at this age." He went to wash his hands for the evening meal.

She was silent then. She had not thought for a while of the burden the Most High had placed on Joseph. He was a good father, but was acting as father to one who had a heavenly Father. They both wondered at God's purposes for Yeshua's miraculous birth and all that had attended that occasion. She looked up. *Oh God Who Sees, will he manifest who he is so soon?* She cried out in silent prayer to the One she had trusted all her life, and was immediately comforted.

It is not his time yet.

She put her hand on her heart and breathed her thanks, yet as she went about serving her family, she pondered the rabbi's words.

⌒

While Mary rocked Joses, Simon was learning the *Shema,* from the book of Deuteronomy, as had Yeshua and James. "*And you are to love* ADONAI *your God with all your heart, all your being and all your resources….*"

Mary told her children the stories of their ancestors that had been passed down to her from her mother, and as he had done with Yeshua and James, Joseph oversaw their studies at home to make sure they were prepared for the next day at school.

The year Yeshua turned eleven, a fifth son, Jude, was added to the family and Mary sensed that this child would be different. Demanding from the day he was born and sleeping fitfully for scarcely two hours at a time, Mary felt her strength wane. Each day she prayed for wisdom and strength for this child who required so much attention.

Joseph added another room on the house for their growing family. Mary watched him work. "At least we have two daughters to train in household duties," she said up to him. Though the girls were young, they were eager to help their grandmother, Rachel, and Mary. Jerusha liked the chickens and it was her task to feed them and bring Mary the eggs. Miriam liked to help with the cooking and carefully watched her mother and grandmother to see what herbs they used in the various dishes they prepared. She watered those plants used for cooking and, from a young age, knew their names and their uses.

Joseph nodded, looking down at her from the ladder. "Yeshua is gifted in the carpentry shop and Simon shows a strong interest. James only helps when he must. He'd rather be in a corner somewhere reading a scroll and studying the Torah."

"Well, my husband, it is too early to tell what Joseph and Jude will be interested in."

Joseph came down the ladder and watched as Jude waved his fists from a pallet in the shade where Mary had placed him. "Jude is a handful, beloved. I pray his temperament will soften as he gets older."

Mary observed her youngest son. Yeshua seemed to be the only one who could calm his smallest brother down when he had a temper tantrum. She sighed. Yeshua was a calming influence on all of them. Did they sense he was different? He was gentle and kind with all of his brothers and sisters, yet firm when he needed to be and the children seemed to delight in doing his bidding.

She glanced over at Mother Rachel. A strong presence in the family, yet in the last year she had given much of the household chores and cooking over to Mary. Rachel's eyesight was failing and Mary became more aware of it as she saw Rachel squinting at the hand-dyed yarns when she was weaving. Soon she gave up weaving all together and Mary made most of the woven fabric for their clothing.

All in all, as Mary thought of her family, she felt her heart would burst with happiness. A family that had many children was considered by the village as favored by the Most High. One of the Psalms came to her mind: "*Children too are a gift from ADONAI; the fruit of the womb is a reward. The children born when one is young are like arrows in the hand of a warrior. How blessed is the man who has filled his quiver with them.*"

~

Simon started school and was also a diligent student. When Joseph had to spend extra hours in the carpenter shop, Yeshua patiently helped his brothers with the Scriptures. Mary smiled to herself. How his younger brothers and sisters adored him.

One day Jude sat in the corner of the yard, large tears running down his chubby cheeks. "What happened?" Yeshua asked him.

"I hurt my toe." With his older brother's attention, he began to sob louder. Yeshua took him on his lap and rubbed the sore toe. "It will be all right. There is no blood that I can see. It will soon stop hurting you."

Jude laid his head on Yeshua's shoulder and, comforted, soon dried his tears. Mary watched from across the yard. "How gentle he is with his brothers and sisters," Mary commented to Rachel, who had also paused to view the scene.

Rachel nodded. "He is an exceptional boy" was all she said, but she continued to observe, her brows knit in thought.

Seeing how Ha'Shem had blessed the family of Mary and Joseph, all traces of the questionable birth of Yeshua seemed to fade in the background. There had been no comments by the women of the village for some time and Mary enjoyed going to the well with Miriam and Jerusha, catching up on the latest gossip.

Mary watched her father-in-law, who had been an elder in the town, become increasingly feeble. He found it more difficult to get around and now used a staff for balance.

She commented on it to Joseph one evening when the rest of the family slept. "He spends less and less time in the carpentry shop. Your mother and I have to rub his legs to get the circulation going so he can rise and walk."

Joseph sighed. "He has seldom been able to take his place at the council of elders. Some of the town elders came by the shop. They were asking questions, and I felt they were thinking of asking me to take my father's place."

"Oh, Joseph, that would be hard for your father." Then another thought came. "Do they think he will not be able to participate anymore?"

He was silent a long moment and then Mary heard the sadness in his voice. "I do not feel he will be with us much longer. His cough is worse and he seems to have trouble breathing sometimes. I would not tell him what the elders suggested. It would mean they count him as dead already."

"Do you think he will be able to make Passover in Jerusalem this year? The month of Adar is nearly gone and the flax harvest is over. It is only a few weeks away."

"I pray he will be able to go, even if he has to ride the donkey. Yeshua is twelve and will now travel with me and the men of the village. He can walk by his grandfather and help keep an eye on him."

"If he goes then your mother will also go. My father and mother are going. She will help Mother Rachel and me with the children. Abba will travel near Jacob also."

Joseph frowned. "Are you able to make the trip to Jerusalem?" Their fifth son, Jude, was almost two—still a restless child, and temperamental. He of all her children seemed the most trying. Mary felt her weariness.

However, she smiled up at Joseph, her love for him filling her heart. "With Mother Rachel and my own mother to help, we can manage. Miriam already helps with her younger brothers and sisters. I love Jerusalem at Passover time. I would like to go."

"I know you will miss having Yeshua's help also, but he is anxious to travel with me and the other men this year. Now that he is twelve he is a son of the Torah." Joseph stroked his beard. "Did you ever imagine we would be blessed with seven children?"

Mary laughed then. When he turned away to see to their donkey, she sighed and instinctively put a hand on her abdomen. She would wait until after Passover to tell Joseph that she was to bear another child. It was a mixed blessing, for she loved all her children, but hoped Ha'Shem would forgive her for hoping her childbearing years were at an end. Caring for them absorbed her whole attention. Joseph did well in the carpentry shop, but with less help from his father due to his health, she knew Joseph depended on their oldest son more and more. At least Yeshua was proving to be very capable and skilled with wood, even though at twelve he was only an apprentice.

At a cry from Simon, Mary turned to see Jude pushing his brother. She sighed. If he was doing these things at two, what did the future hold for this child? She strode across the courtyard and took Jude firmly by his arm.

"Sit down here in the corner and stay there! My son, the Most High is not pleased when you treat your brother in such a way and neither am I."

Jude's lower lip protruded and while he obeyed, he did not answer her. He looked up at her face and rebellion spilled out of his eyes.

TWENTY-EIGHT

*Y*eshua was already tall, and seemed older than his years as he worked with Joseph and his grandfather in the carpentry shop learning their family trade.

With six younger children to oversee, Mary had an active household. Many times her mother, Anna, came to help. Mary would sit at the loom pushing the shuttle back and forth, or be making cheese or bread with Grandmother Rachel, while Grandmother Anna entertained the youngest children with stories.

Sometimes, when Rachel needed a rest, Mary would walk the children to her parent's home, knowing her father and mother were always glad to see them and would entertain their grandchildren, giving Mary a few moments to herself to walk the fields nearby and spend time in prayer with Ha'Shem.

The month of Nisan arrived and as the flax harvest ended, the barley was ripening in the fields. Families from the village made preparations to travel to Jerusalem for Passover, to fulfill the commandment of the Lord, knowing that as soon as they returned the barley harvest would begin.

Joseph was pleased they had an extremely acceptable lamb from their small flock to take as the sacrifice, a beautiful creature and without blemish, as required. James was given the responsibility of tending to the lamb for the family and he was diligent to make sure no harm came to it.

The sun shone brightly the morning the families gathered to journey to the Holy City, Jerusalem, the City of Peace, to celebrate Passover.

With light hearts, the pilgrimage began. Mothers herded young children, while behind them, the older boys walked proudly with their fathers and the other men, pleased they were no longer relegated to the head of the procession where the women and children walked. James, nine years old, was still required to travel with Mary and the younger children. He longed to go with the men and he let his mother know it many times before they left.

It was a five-day journey to Jerusalem and Mary knew Joseph, Yeshua, and her father would keep a close eye on her father-in-law, Jacob, who, while showing determination, drooped on the donkey. Joseph told Mary he would walk on one side of the donkey with Yeshua on the other side for fear Jacob would slip off. Mary's father, Heli, also stayed close by.

The roads had dried enough from the spring rains that they could travel without running into mud. They took a narrow road out of Nazareth and circled to the south of the Sea of Galilee, finally reaching a larger road that went downhill along the Jordan River. They followed the river, which started out as a narrow stream, but as tributaries merged into it, began to widen. As the river grew, so did the stream of pilgrims, merging with them until the road was clogged with travelers.

The journey took the pilgrims almost to the Dead Sea and at night mothers told the young children the story of Sodom and Gomorrah. Turning west, they followed the road up into the Judean hills. The air, heavy around the Dead Sea, became fresher and lighter in the high country but traveling was slower due to the steepness of the road.

At night Mary, Anna, and Rachel prepared food for their family and the men joined them for the meal. Miriam watched over Jerusha and Jude who stuffed a piece of bread in his mouth that had been dipped in a puree of dried garbanzo beans mashed with garlic, vinegar, cumin seeds, and olive oil. Jude was always hungry. Rachel sliced cucumbers, and Anna cut up date cakes and two loaves of bread along with the dried apricots she had brought. They parceled the food out carefully to last them until they got to Jerusalem.

Jerusalem was high above sea level and its temperate climate differed from the area around it. At the top of Mt. Olivet, Mary and the other pilgrims could look down on the plains of Jericho and the dull grey of the Dead Sea that they had bypassed. As they traveled, some of the pilgrims sang Psalm 122 from the songs of Ascent:

"I was glad when they said to me, 'The house of ADONAI! *Let's go!' Our feet were already standing at your gates, Yerushalayim [Jerusalem]! Yerushalayim, built as a city fostering friendship and unity. The tribes have gone up there, the tribes of* ADONAI, *as a witness to Isra'el, to give thanks to the name of* ADONAI. *For there the thrones of justice were set up, the thrones of the house of David. Pray for shalom in Yerushalayim; may those who love you prosper. May shalom be within your ramparts, prosperity within your palaces. For the sake of my family and friends, I say, 'Shalom be within you!' For the sake of the house of* ADONAI *our God, I will seek your well-being."*

"Pray for the peace of Jerusalem, Jerusalem shall live in peace."

As they sang the others joined in, making a joyful chorus as they walked. The songs lifted Mary's heart and she smiled to herself, as the presence of Ha'Shem seemed to enfold her.

The view of the City of Peace itself was magnificent. The group paused and Mary watched Joseph put his arms around Yeshua and as James hurried up to join them, Joseph quoted from the forty-eighth Psalm: *"Great is* ADONAI *and greatly to be praised, in the city of our God, his holy mountain, beautiful in its elevation, the joy of all the earth, Mount Tziyon, in the far north, the city of the great king...."*

Yeshua gazed at the sight before him. "Is it not the most beautiful city, Abba?" With the valleys surrounding it, the city was like a fortress, the sun glinting off the white walls of the Temple in its midst.

"That it is, my son. And this year you will come into the Temple when your grandfathers and I present the sacrifice."

As Mary watched, Yeshua turned to look at the lamb that had been bound to one of the donkeys. They could not take a chance on letting it loose to come to harm before they reached the Temple. She could not decipher the expression on the face of her oldest son, and wondered what he was thinking, but did not question him. She turned back to the younger children as the group moved along on the road.

The various families began to separate as each turned toward the home of relatives where they would stay for the duration of the Passover. Mary's parents would go to the home of a cousin. The family was too large to stay together with one household.

Heli smiled at his daughter. "We will meet again at the end of Passover. May Ha'Shem bless you and your family at this holy time." Mary sensed a feeling of loss as she watched her parents walk away.

Getting through the crowds was difficult, but Joseph made a way through the throng toward the street where his Uncle Beniah lived. Mary and Rachel followed close behind, making sure the older children held the hands of the younger children and did not get lost in the vast sea of pilgrims. Yeshua carried Jude and James carried Jerusha.

As they opened the gate and touched the *mezuzah*, Beniah appeared with a big smile on his face.

"Welcome, welcome. It is good to see family." His eyebrows raised as he noted the number of children entering his small court-yard. "There is room. There is room. We will be a little crowded, but all will be well."

Since Beniah, Joseph, and Jacob would sleep on pallets outside in the courtyard, Mary was glad the weather held. She, Rachel,

Jerusha, Miriam, and little Jude slept close together in the house while Yeshua, James, young Joses, and Simon were relegated to the rooftop. At least it had a proper parapet around the roof, and she need not fear one of them falling off.

There was barely enough room in Beniah's house and courtyard for all of them, but being a widower with no wife to cook, he was glad to have someone preparing delicious meals. A jovial man, he gladly helped by taking the little ones on his knee and telling them stories.

Mary glanced at Rachel who was obviously weary from the journey yet seemed determined to do her part. She diligently watched over Jacob and the smaller children while Mary and Miriam set about preparing the Passover meal. Mary sang to herself as she roasted the eggs in the small oven. The *beitzah*, or roasted eggs, represented life and perpetuation of existence. Miriam chopped the parsley, and Mary sent Jerusha to put water in a bowl and carefully add salt. The family would dip the parsley in the water to represent the tears shed in Egypt and the salt of the Red Sea they had passed through. Jerusha was given the walnuts to carefully add to the saffron millet as it cooked, and her face was a picture of concentration as she dropped the pieces in one by one.

Mary began preparing the salad of bitter lettuce and horseradish, to represent the bitterness of slavery in Egypt. Rachel chopped dried fruit along with nuts and apples and mixed them with red wine for the *charoset*, the compote that represented the mortar of the walls of the buildings built by slaves.

James, Joses, and Simon were charged with the responsibility of keeping an eye on Jude. *It may take all three of them*, she thought to herself as she watched Miriam pat the dough into flat bread to bake on the griddle. As Mary worked, she explained the foods of Passover to the younger children who began to gather around with eager faces, anticipating the feast ahead.

"When our ancestors left Egypt, there was no time to wait for the bread to rise, so we do not use yeast with the Passover bread."

When all was ready, the family rested and waited for Yeshua, Joseph, and Beniah to bring the sacrificed lamb.

The children eyed the food hungrily.

"Ima, when will Papa bring the lamb?"

"Ima, I am hungry. May I have a taste?"

"Children, you must learn patience," Mary admonished them, but as the smell of roasted lamb wafted in the air from other fires in the city, Mary realized she was as hungry as the children. She put Jerusha to work carefully laying the platters on the table. The younger boys occupied themselves with observing a stream of ants along the wall while Miriam went with James to look in hidden nooks in the courtyard for eggs. Jude wanted to play with a chicken that pecked at him, and Rachel shooed the chicken away then dealt with his tears of frustration. Mary watched and shook her head. She thanked Ha'Shem that most of the children were of a more docile temperament.

Mary was happy Yeshua had gone with his father and the other men, but when the children became restless, she wished she had the help of her oldest son, knowing he had a way with his brothers and sisters.

Suddenly there was the sound of voices and the gate opened to admit Joseph and Beniah, carrying the lamb on a pole with Yeshua following close behind. The fire pit was ready and the men quickly removed the intestines to wrap around the lamb's head as the crowned sacrifice.

The lamb's front legs were spread out to each side and tied to a horizontal skewer so everything in the chest cavity would cook thoroughly. The rear legs were tied together to a vertical skewer.

They waited a long time for the roasted sacrificial lamb. The women opened the wine they'd brought and Beniah provided two more bottles. As part of the Passover ceremony, the adults, to represent the four-fold promise of redemption, would consume four glasses of wine. And as was traditional, a special glass was poured and left for Elijah the prophet.

Jacob napped off and on but when he was awake, Mary noted the sadness in the eyes of her father-in-law as he looked longingly toward the Temple. It was the first time he did not have the strength to participate in the Passover ceremonies and present a lamb for sacrifice.

She went to him and putting a gentle hand on his arm, smiled. "You will get stronger soon, Father Jacob."

He patted her hand, but slowly shook his head, and dozed off again. Mary remembered what Joseph had said, that his father would not be with them the following year. She turned away with a heavy heart, recognizing the truth of her husband's words.

"Ima!" Jerusha's cry caught Mary' attention. "Joses teases me!"

Joses, grinning with boyish glee, dangled a lizard in front of her face.

"Joses, tell your sister you are sorry. She is too little for your pranks. Go to the woodpile and bring some more twigs for the oven."

The boy's shoulders drooped. "I am sorry, Jerusha." He reluctantly let the lizard go and went to the woodpile to do as he was told. James sat in a corner of the yard with a small scroll he'd brought with him and became absorbed in studying it. He told Mary he wanted the Rabbi to be pleased with the verses he'd memorized when they returned to Nazareth.

Simon liked to eat and hungrily eyed the *charoset*. Mary glanced his way and shook her head. He sighed and went to pet their donkey.

From the Temple, the air was filled with the choirs singing the *Hallel*, praises to the Most High God. The smell of roasted lamb grew stronger as it wafted from the number of ovens in the city. It took both women to keep the children occupied while they waited for the lamb. Fortunately for Mary's peace of mind, Jude had fallen asleep for the time being in the lap of his grandmother, Rachel.

The family gathered around the low table and Beniah, as the host and the oldest, spoke the *kiddush*, the sanctification blessing over the wine in honor of the holiday. The first cup of wine was drunk and the second cup was poured. The parsley was dipped in the salt water and eaten. As the family shook off the salt water, Mary thought the droplets looked like tears.

Joseph chuckled as he related how they were able to use their own lamb for Passover.

"The old priest tried as hard as he could to find fault with it."

Yeshua spoke up, his eyes twinkling. "We would have had to buy a lamb from the Temple flock. When he was unable to find anything wrong with the lamb, he just mumbled to himself and finally waved us on toward the sacrifice area."

Three pieces of unleavened bread were placed in the unity *echad* cloth. The middle *matzah* was removed, broken in half, wrapped in a white linen cloth and hidden by Rachel for the children to find later in the ceremony. At least it kept the older children in anticipation until they were sent to find it. Jacob told the story of the Exodus from Egypt and the first Passover. Joses was allowed to ask the four questions, the first being, "Why is this night different from all others?"

Mary had always been fascinated by the four questions, and had come to learn they were designed to meet the needs of four different types of people: the wise one, who wants to know all the details; the wicked one, who excludes himself and learns the folly of doing so; the simple one, who needs to know the basics; and the one who is unable to ask, who doesn't even know enough to know what he needs to know.

Mary sensed a feeling of kinship with other families of their faith, knowing that all over the city, children were asking the four questions as families proceeded with the centuries-old ceremonies celebrating Passover.

The lamb was tender and the children hungrily ate as much as they could hold. At the end of the meal, before the third cup of wine was poured, the children were sent to find the hidden broken *matzah*. Simon was the fortunate child and Joseph gave him a half a shekel as a reward. Everyone broke off a piece of the *matzah*, and it was consumed along with the third cup of wine, the cup of redemption.

Beniah poured the fourth cup of wine for the prophet Elijah, who would one day come on Passover to announce the arrival of the Messiah. Mary noticed that Yeshua was looking in the direction of the Temple. He had a faraway look on his face. Joseph noticed also, but when he saw Mary looking at Yeshua, he looked away with a small shake of his head. The words of the angel suddenly came to her mind, "*...the Lord God shall give him the throne of David....*"

What was the destiny of this miraculous son of hers? When would he step up and seize the throne of David? She comforted herself that he was only twelve and still young, yet the questions churned in her head. *What plans did the Most High have for Yeshua, and when would they come to fruition?*

Her attention was caught as the children vied to be the one to open the door for Elijah according to the custom. The door of every home is opened for a while, supposedly for Elijah to enter. Simon was chosen, and rose quickly to perform his task. Mary continued to watch Yeshua. No, Elijah had not appeared in the doorway to announce the coming Messiah, but there was a faraway look on the face of her oldest son. More and more she thought of the words of the angel, many years before. The truth crept into her heart and she involuntarily caught her breath. The one destined to be the Messiah was already in their midst.

TWENTY-NINE

*T*he small courtyard resounded with noise of preparation as the days of the Passover ended and the family prepared to return to Nazareth. The children were everywhere and Mary and Rachel had their hands full rounding them up. The donkeys were loaded and the food packed, along with bedrolls. Joseph carried Jude on his back in a sling. Little Jerusha would have to walk with their other children as long as she could, but Mary knew her chubby legs would not take her far. James offered to carry her piggyback when she got too tired, for Yeshua would again travel with his father and the men of Nazareth.

The first day was a long one, as the men wanted to get their families home as soon as possible. The barley was ripe for harvest. It was a relief to Mary when the leader signaled they were stopping for the night. As she prepared the evening meal with Rachel and Anna, she looked forward to the men and Yeshua joining them after a long day of separation. She especially looked for Yeshua. She could use his calming influence on his younger brothers and sisters.

As Joseph and Heli approached, helping Jacob who was wiping his brow, Mary looked up from her preparations for the evening meal. "Where is Yeshua?"

Joseph frowned. "I thought it strange he would want to travel with the younger children. Isn't he with you?"

A feeling of unrest fluttered in her heart. "No, he isn't. Joseph, search the other families. He may have been walking with some of the boys of the village."

Unable to stop the rising panic, Mary waited anxiously for Joseph's return. When he came, he was almost running.

"Yeshua is not anywhere among our people."

Rachel stepped forward. "Could he have strayed and gotten lost in Jerusalem before we left the city?"

Soon word passed through the group that one of the children was missing. After discussion, it was agreed that Mary and Joseph had to return to Jerusalem to search for Yeshua. Heli, Anna, and Rachel would proceed on with the other children. Jacob needed to return to the comfort of his home. The journey had been hard on him.

Mary breathed a prayer, *Oh God Who Sees, you know where your son is. I know you will keep him safe until we find him.*

It was no small thing to travel alone on the road to Jerusalem, but there were so many pilgrims returning to their towns that Mary felt they were safe. She and Joseph walked as quickly as they could manage, but it took them another day to return to the city. Some of the people they passed gave them odd looks, as if wondering why two people were hurrying toward the city when Passover had ended and most travelers were going home.

Joseph checked with the relatives Mary's parents had stayed with, but no one had seen Yeshua. Beniah also shrugged and spread his hands. "I have not seen him since you all left, but you are welcome to stay with me while you search."

Mary looked toward the street. "He may be twelve, but he is only a boy. Where could he be?"

Joseph put a hand on her arm. "He will find shelter. He has a good head on his shoulders."

"But Joseph, it is not like him to just wander off."

After a night of restless sleep, they were up early, searching the city all the second day and yet there was no sign of him. Joseph held Mary in the darkness on the roof as she wept in anguish. "Could something have happened to him?"

"Tomorrow we will go to the Temple and make a sacrifice. Perhaps one of the priests knows where we might find him."

That night Mary had a dream. Yeshua was smiling at her, and a voice whispered, *He will be found, beloved woman.*

The Temple was dedicated as a house of prayer, and so with high hopes of praying for the return of their son, Mary and Joseph hurried into the Court of the Gentiles where the learned men gathered to discuss religious matters among themselves and with all who came with questions.

A group of elders were indeed gathered. But in their midst, listening and then talking earnestly, was Yeshua!

Mary hurried up to him and he turned to her, not with chagrin at being found, but with a welcoming smile.

She felt her days-old anxiety coloring her words. "Son, why have you dealt with us in this way? We have been anxiously looking for you, fearing you were hurt or lost."

"How is it that you sought me, Ima? Did you not know I must be about my Father's business?"

His father's business? His *heavenly* Father. She sighed and turned to Joseph, but his face reflected bewilderment. "We must return home, my son. You still have responsibilities there," Joseph commanded.

The older men who had been talking with Yeshua looked at Mary and Joseph earnestly. "He is wise for one so young. How well he knows the Torah."

Another spoke up. "He has stayed with us in the Temple. We did not know where his parents were."

Joseph thanked them for their care and, turning to Yeshua, raised his eyebrows in question. Yeshua rose and, nodding to the men he'd been with, walked with Mary and Joseph out of the Temple grounds.

The company had gone on to Nazareth and, while Joseph didn't relish traveling alone, there was not enough time to catch up to them. At least there were enough families on the road returning to their own villages and towns that they were able to join a group to spend the night.

That evening, after their meal, Joseph went to speak with some of the other men. Mary walked with Yeshua in the nearby field. They looked up at the stars filling the heavens and Mary stood with her hands on his shoulders.

"How long have you known?" she asked quietly.

Yeshua turned his face up to her and said without guile, "I have known ever since I can remember, Ima. His presence is always with me."

"That is as it should be, my son. You have a destiny. I was told that before you were born. When you will fulfill it, only Ha'Shem knows."

He smiled at her then, and looking off into the distance, his eyes seemed to focus on something she could not see. "It will not be soon, Ima, but one day the Father will call and I must answer."

She could not speak, but nodded. A night bird called to his mate and they listened a moment, then quietly returned to the camp.

⌒

When they reached Nazareth, Rachel, Anna, and Heli came forward and the other children surrounded their parents. Jacob leaned on his staff. "Our thanks to the Most High. You have found him! Where was he?"

Joseph shrugged and shook his head slightly. "In the Temple conversing with the elders and learned doctors."

"Conversing with…." Jacob peered at his grandson, but said nothing more.

"I will explain later," Joseph murmured to his parents as neighbors and friends gathered round them to celebrate finding their lost son.

Mary comforted her youngest children who wept with relief that they had not lost their parents too.

THIRTY

Joseph said no more to Yeshua about his sojourn in Jerusalem. Yeshua was his usual pleasant self, helping with the younger children and working hard in the carpentry shop with Joseph and his grandfather.

Life seemed to go on as usual in Nazareth, but the words Yeshua had spoken to them in the Temple stayed in Mary's mind. As she went about her tasks with Rachel, she wondered. What did he mean about his Father's business? What was his Father's business? Sometimes at night, she replayed the angel's visit thirteen years before, and pondered the events of his birth in Bethlehem. Were they raising a king? Someone who would at last lift the yoke of the Roman Empire from the necks of her people? The words "a king...a king" reverberated in her mind.

Just after the first rains, at the beginning of the olive harvest, Mary gave birth to Rebecca. If children were like arrows in a hunter's quiver as the Scriptures claimed, she and Joseph had a full quiver! Yet she saw that feeding and clothing eight children was a task ever on Joseph's mind; though she and Rachel were creative with meals, it took a lot of carpentry work to put food on the table.

Joses started Hebrew school and Yeshua helped him, James, and Simon recite their lessons. Yeshua was endlessly patient at explaining things in the Scriptures they didn't understand. Mary caught her husband listening from time to time, a puzzled look on his face. In the night hours, when he and Mary talked in low tones,

Joseph, too, wondered where the Most High was leading this miraculous son of theirs.

When he was caught up on his lessons, James dutifully helped in the carpentry shop, but his heart was not in it. He wanted to read the Scriptures and seemed more on the studious side. Mary considered again that perhaps he might become a rabbi one day. Joses, on the other hand, seemed to have inherited a love of wood from his father. He was anxious to begin working in the carpentry shop and was allowed to come and help with small chores. Simon, who turned out to be a good and well-intentioned boy, now helped in the shop.

Joseph told Mary that Yeshua was skillful, and his work was beyond complaint, but Mary, considering his words in the field, knew Yeshua would not be working as a carpenter forever, but was waiting for something. What was it?

Jacob spent less and less time in the shop and more time sitting in the sun in the courtyard. His hearing was deteriorating and the family had to speak up when they talked to him. Then, one day in the month of Shevat, when the almond trees were in bloom, Rachel woke early, and turning to her husband, found he had left them sometime during the night. Her cries of grief woke Mary and Joseph and the children.

Joseph tore his garment over his heart and, weeping, knelt by the body of his father. In a broken voice he recited the blessing over the dead, acknowledging Adonai as the true Judge, and in acceptance, giving his father to his God.

Rachel threw her apron over her head as her shoulders shook with her grief. They had been married for over thirty years. Neighbors brought linen cloth and when Rachel saw them, she drew herself up and moved forward, struggling to begin the *aninut*, the preparation time of the deceased. The long strips of linen were wrapped around the body and spices were tucked into the folds. Then the *tallit*, his prayer shawl, was wrapped around his head to cover his face. As was the custom, Jacob was carried that same day to a burial cave outside Nazareth and placed with the bones of his father and mother.

Joseph's shoulders sagged with the weight of his loss. Hearing the others weeping, Jude and Rebecca began to cry. Yeshua, too, knelt by his father and with an arm around his father's shoulders, wept for his grandfather.

The women of the neighborhood joined Mary and Rachel as they walked to the burial cave, casting handfuls of dust and weeping to show their sorrow. Anna remained behind to help comfort the younger children.

Rachel sat outside the cave with the women of the village who came to grieve with her. Mary had followed the body of her father-in-law and wept for him at the cave, but knowing her mother was caring for the younger children alone, and she had a baby daughter to nurse, looked back toward her home. Rachel saw and, in spite of her tears, understood and, with a nod of her head, gave Mary leave to return.

Joseph closed the carpenter shop for a week as the family sat *shivah*, on low stools. Their clothes were unchanged and their feet bare to show their mourning. The family cooked no meals during this time and neighbors brought in food, quietly leaving it on a table in the courtyard. Anna brought eggs, a symbol of life, and fresh bread. It was called the *Se'udat hara'ah*, the meal of condolences. Joseph recited the mourner's *Kaddish* each day as required by a son for his father. A *minyan* of ten elders joined him in the prayers for the dead, affirming the worth of his dead father, and Yeshua was allowed to join them. Joseph would say the *Kaddish* each day of the eleven months of the *avelut*, the mourning period prescribed for a parent. Anna came to console Mary and help with the household duties until Rachel was ready.

Rebecca, the baby of the family, was barely four years old when tragedy struck the family again. Joseph was working on a table in the carpentry shop when he clutched his chest and fell, striking his head on a corner of the workbench. Yeshua, at sixteen, had grown tall and his arms were strong from working with the tools of the shop. He, James, and Simon were able to carry their father home while the local midwife and healer was sent for.

Joseph was laid on their bed and Mary bandaged Joseph's head with clean linen cloths. She and Rachel knelt by his side and beseeched Adonai to strengthen him and heal his wound. Yeshua shooed the other children outside and admonished the older ones to look after the younger. Neighbors came and the women helped calm the weeping children.

The midwife made a poultice for Joseph's head and while Mary and Rachel kept a steady vigil for two days, Joseph never opened his eyes or spoke. Yeshua told them how his father clutched his chest before he fell and the midwife shook her head solemnly.

"Then it was not just the fall, my lady. I fear that it was his heart. There is nothing more I can do for him."

Once again the family was torn by grief, as on the third day, Joseph breathed his last. Yeshua as the oldest son said the prayer for the dead, as he was required once again to sit the seven days of *shivah*.

Glorified and sanctified be God's great name throughout the world. Which he created according to his will. May he establish his kingdom in your lifetime and during your days,

And within the life of the entire house of Israel, speedily and soon, and say, Amen.

May his great name be blessed forever and to all eternity.

Blessed and praised, glorified and exalted, extolled and honored, adored and lauded be the name of the Holy One, blessed be he, beyond all blessings and hymns, praises and consolations that are ever spoken in the world; and say, Amen.

May there be abundant peace from heaven, and life, for us and for all Israel; and say, Amen.

He who creates peace from heaven, and life, for us and for all Israel; and say, Amen.

Mary's heart was broken at the loss of her dear husband, and the father of their children. What would she do with eight children to care for? She had depended so on Joseph, on his strength, and on his comfort. Her cries were added to those of Rachel, who had buried her husband and now grieved for her son.

Yeshua became head of the household. It would take hard work and long hours in the carpenter shop for Yeshua, James, and Simon to take care of the family. Mary also welcomed her father Heli's steady presence. She was greatly encouraged to learn that because of Joseph's good reputation in woodworking, the carpentry shop had all the work they could manage. Some days she suspected that neighbors brought work to the shop to help the struggling family.

THIRTY-ONE

*M*ary watched Rebecca carefully set the platters on the low table. It was hard to believe her youngest was already eleven. She was a helpful girl and Mary was grateful that with Jerusha and Miriam married and in homes of their own, she still had one daughter at home. Mary cut some date cakes in half as she contemplated her youngest daughter. While Rebecca was capable in her household duties, and eager to learn all she could in using herbs in cooking, she was a plain child and as they had discovered in her early years, slow in her mind. Would Yeshua be able to secure a marriage for her when she became eligible?

The loss of both her parents the previous year gave her a sense of mortality. The respectful term "Mother Mary" took on a whole new meaning as she watched the younger women tend to the household tasks. Rising from her pallet in the morning, she was wont to rub her arms and wrists and move her legs to loosen the stiffness from the dampness.

When she was able, Mary climbed up to the roof where she could be alone and seek the comfort of Ha'Shem. Other times she walked the hills of Nazareth in the cool of the afternoon. As she prayed, she felt a gentle breeze brush her cheek and sensed his presence strengthening her. She gathered herself together for her family's sake, but leaned more and more on Yeshua for his counsel and wisdom.

The tenants that had lived in Mary's former home from the time her parents died, left for another village, and Simon moved himself and his young wife, Bithia, into it. There was now only Yeshua, Mary, Joses, Rebecca, and Jude. She looked around for Rebecca and then remembered she had gone to the well for their household water. There was a sound from the corner of the courtyard and Mary's gaze turned to observe her youngest son, Jude, sitting with a scroll in his hand, and a scowl on his face. She sighed. Jude nearly drove her to distraction getting into mischief. He wasn't sitting in the corner because he was studious like James. His quick temper started arguments with everyone in the family. This Yeshua would not tolerate, and more times than she could remember, Jude found himself in the courtyard with a scroll and verses from the Torah to memorize.

Another thought gave her peace. James and his wife, Hodiah, were expecting their first child. Miriam, married to the rabbi's son, Aaron, had quickly produced two sons, Amasa and Reuel. Mary smiled to herself. She would welcome another little one to hold. Jerusha had been married a year to Nahor, a farmer, but there was no sign of a child as yet; Mary felt her daughter's anguish and beseeched Ha'Shem for her.

Since Hodiah's father was a stonemason, he had contributed stone and helped James build a house next door.

Joses would marry soon. She had seen his face one day as he talked to Sarah, a young girl in the village. Last night he had spoken earnestly to Yeshua in the corner of the courtyard and from the smile on her oldest son's face, she anticipated the two of them would soon call on Sarah's father.

Yeshua appeared well-liked by most everyone in their village. More than one young maiden looked upon him as a possible husband and many were puzzled that he didn't seek a wife. A young man in their community was usually betrothed by now. Yeshua was twenty-five. Some speculated that he had taken an oath of some kind. It was hard for Mary to turn aside from the raised eyebrows and thinly veiled questions:

"Mary, how is it that your younger sons marry before Yeshua?"

"Such a fine son and a successful carpentry shop. Surely there is a maiden in the village on whom he has cast an eye?"

"Now that James, Simon, and your oldest daughters are married, will Yeshua choose a wife?"

But with his warm laugh and obvious love for people, his kindness and compassion for them, the neighbors could only shrug. What fault could they find in him? Still, the questions persisted.

Returning home from another day's gossip at the local well, Mary entered the house and was surprised to find Yeshua repairing the door to the storage room. Then she saw Jude sitting in the corner of the yard again. She didn't have to ask who was responsible.

She sighed as she poured the water into the stone storage jar, and turned to watch Yeshua work. He looked up, and putting down his tools, went to her side, a smile on his face.

"You are concerned for something, Ima?"

She waved one hand in exasperation. "Every woman at the well has an opinion on who you should marry or why you haven't chosen a wife. "

His face grew somber. "You know I shall not marry, Ima."

She touched his cheek with her hand. "I know my son. I know, but I cannot explain to our neighbors."

She searched his face, her mind swirling with questions like the dust devils that sometimes came and stirred up the leaves in the streets, but she would not ask. She turned away and, picking up a bunch of leeks, laid them on a small wooden cutting board and began to chop them vigorously. Each day, week, and month that went by, season after season seemed to draw them closer to something she could not name. Thinking again of his birth so long ago, she knew who he was—but where was he going? To what end had he been born? She was aware he was still nearby, but went on chopping, finding solace in a familiar task.

For the last several years, Yeshua had taken to walking the hills in the evening after most of the family had retired for the night. Mary knew he was praying, and more and more preoccupied with his heavenly Father. Mary too, spent more time in prayer. In her quiet place on the roof, away from household demands, she beseeched Ha'Shem for her family, and for patience to wait on his will for his son.

❧

"It seems like only yesterday that I came as a bride to this house," she remarked to Yeshua one day after their evening meal.

He smiled at her and put a hand on hers. "We cannot stop time, Ima. The future always holds change." There was something in his voice that caused her to raise her eyebrows. Was he telling her more change was coming? He only smiled and rose from the low table. In a moment he'd gone out the gate for his solitary time in the hills.

She looked to see where Jude was and saw him also slip out the gate. Where did he go when he disappeared like that? Was he meeting with friends who shared his views of overthrowing the Romans? Yeshua had spoken to Jude about his friends, but he ignored the counsel of his oldest brother, almost to a point of defiance. Mary also spoke to him of her concerns. In a rare moment of affection, his face, usually sullen, softened.

"Do not worry about me, Ima. I just like to talk with those who share my thoughts."

She nodded, still not convinced. She was sure one day his rebellious nature would bring danger to her household. Was Jude becoming involved in the zealot movement? The zealots wanted to overthrow the Roman government by force and free Israel. She knew that the zealots were growing in number, and, to the dismay of her people, gaining the attention of Rome. They were being hunted down by the Roman soldiers and were always in danger, especially their leader, a certain Barabbas.

Mary gazed at her youngest son. If he was not careful he could bring danger to their family. The soldiers were ruthless with the zealots they caught, and sometimes whole families were arrested as accomplices. Many of the zealots were used as gruesome examples of Rome's cruel power and were crucified on a Roman cross. Mary shuddered and prayed silently for wisdom and protection for her son and their family.

⌒

James and Hodiah, living next door, came often to share the family meal. Hodiah proved to be a good cook, and a small paunch on James attested to her skills. Their boys were a joy to Mary as were Miriam's children. It was good to have the courtyard echo with the sounds of small children again. Mary loved to tell them stories from the Torah and saved small date treats for them when they had been especially attentive.

Now approaching her forty-fourth year, Mary could look around her family with joy, sometimes feeling a twinge that her Joseph was not there to share these years with her. It seemed so long ago that they traveled to Bethlehem, to Egypt, and then finally returned to Nazareth and their families. She told Jude and Rebecca about their father, to make him more real to them, but Rebecca grieved that she had been too young to know him. Mary kept the knowledge of the angels, the Magi, and all that had occurred in Bethlehem to herself, but thought on it often.

Yeshua had taken Joseph's place as a father figure to the family and she looked to him for everything. Mary remembered that when Rebecca was little, she loved to sit on Yeshua's lap in the evening and hear the stories he told. They were always about things around her that she could understand. Now she sat respectfully at his feet along with her cousins, still eager as a young child to hear his stories.

Mary sometimes wondered if Jude would have been as difficult had Joseph lived. Yeshua continued to be firm but patient with him, and Jude acknowledged his oldest brother's authority, but his rebellious nature, like a robber waiting for his prey, was never far from the surface.

Time slipped by like the wind that moved the leaves of the trees. She was aware of a change in the air and sensed the hour was near when Yeshua would leave her. Yeshua still worked with Joses, Simon, and James in the carpentry shop, but Mary sensed his restlessness. More and more she wondered, *for how long, Ha'Shem... for how long?* Knowing who he was, and how his birth came about, surely he was not sent to earth to just take care of her household. Many times the words were on her tongue to question him, yet each time she felt a check in her spirit and in her heart heard the words, *It is not his time, beloved woman.*

THIRTY-TWO

*J*oses's wedding in the month of Tammuz, after the wheat harvest, was a joyous occasion. Two women played the tambourine and one of the neighbor's sons played his flute. The table almost bowed with the food the women had prepared and brought to the wedding. Mary and Rebecca, working along with Hodiah, prepared honey-almond stuffed dates, saffron millet with raisins and walnuts, squash with capers and mint, and many loaves of round flat bread along with a garbanzo bean dip. The wedding guests laughed and danced, as James made sure the wine flowed freely.

Yeshua had taken James aside before the wedding and asked him to be master of the wedding feast. James had been surprised but pleased that Yeshua gave him the responsibility as host, but Mary noticed that Yeshua was giving over more responsibility to his brothers. It occurred to her that Yeshua also spent less time in the carpenter shop.

Mary realized other changes were due and gave Joses and Sarah the room her Joseph had added to the house when the two of them married. She could sleep in the main room of the house with Rebecca and Jude so that Joses and his new bride could have some privacy. Simon and Bithia had occupied the room until they moved to Mary's former home. The next year Mary and the local midwife held Bithia up over the birthing stool as the young couple was blessed with a baby boy, Shallum. Jerusha also gave birth to a son they named Johanon, and Mary was assured yet again of the Most High's diligent care over her family.

⌒

The following spring, astonishing news reached the family. Elizabeth and Zechariah's son John, whom Mary hadn't seen but a few times in Jerusalem at Passover, and at Yeshua's weaning ceremony, had grown to manhood and come out of the desert where it was rumored he'd been living with the Essenes, and was baptizing people in the Jordan River. Belonging to the Essenes was reason enough for gossip; the Essenes were a strict religious sect that owned property in all the major cities in Judah but lived in caves in the desert where they had their own rituals and ceremonies. Beyond that, however, John wore animal skins for clothes and, to Mary's astonishment, was reported to subsist on nothing but locust beans and wild honey. People were calling him a prophet. Mary wondered how Elizabeth and Zechariah were taking the actions of this strange son of theirs. Was this the reason John was born? She listened to the talk in the village and speculation as to whether he was just a holy man or a prophet. Her sons argued pro and con, James and Simon feeling he was not in his right mind, but Joses sided with Yeshua: it appeared that Adonai had called John for a reason.

"There has been no prophet in Israel since Malachi, over four hundred years. Surely the Father has heard our cries and John is the answer," Yeshua told them at the evening meal.

Soon it was rumored that hundreds, including Roman soldiers and tax collectors, were joining the people who streamed to the river to be baptized.

Yeshua considered all he heard and was thoughtful for several days. Finally, on the fourth day, he came to Mary.

"Ima, I must leave you to travel to the Jordan River. I would be baptized by John."

The moment she feared and yet hoped for had come. His Father was calling him and she could only wait and watch to see what Yeshua would do.

"When will you go?"

He smiled down at her, his face alight with anticipation, yet a touch of sadness. "I shall leave in the morning."

She sighed and put a hand on his cheek. "I will prepare food for your journey."

When James learned of the situation, he was irate. He stormed into the house and confronted Yeshua. "You are the head of the household, and shall you now wander off to follow this madman? John is our cousin, but I am not sure I wish to be associated with him. Surely his parents are shamed by now." He snorted, "Animal skins for clothing? Locust beans and wild honey?"

Yeshua put a hand on his brother's shoulder. "He is doing what he was born to do, James. Was his birth not miraculous to a couple late in years and our cousin Elizabeth considered barren?"

James shook off the hand and continued to glare at Yeshua. "He proclaims that the kingdom of God is near. He's baptizing people in the river. What good is pouring water over people's heads? Or telling them to repent of their sins? It is against the laws of Adonai. We are to bring a sacrifice for our sins. People flock to hear him, but not for his wisdom; he's a fanatic!"

"My brother, the time will come when what he is doing will become clear to all of you. Let us part in peace, for shall we rail against the Most High? Does the pot say to the potter how it is to be used? I feel the Father is calling me to go to the river and I must go. Will you see to our mother while I am gone?"

James' shoulders sagged like air let out of a bladder skin. He looked from Yeshua to his mother and sighed. "I will care for her."

Mary had been quiet, listening to the exchange. Now she moved forward and smiled at her second son. "Dear James. You are a blessing to me. I know I can depend on you."

He turned to Yeshua. "When will you return?"

"When Adonai leads me home again."

James stroked his beard thoughtfully, and finally, "If you feel this is what you must do, then I will not fight against the Most High. Safe journey, brother."

The two men waited quietly while Mary prepared a traveling bag with some bread, cheese, and a date cake. She filled a leather water bag and Yeshua placed it over his shoulder.

When he was ready, Mary and James followed Yeshua to the gate. Rebecca returned from the village well and looked curiously at the food sack and water bag Yeshua carried. Suddenly she realized he was leaving and clung to him, weeping. Yeshua put his sister gently from him. "I will return, little sister."

Mary embraced Yeshua and once more put a hand on his cheek. She looked up into his face and something passed between them. The miracle child placed in her womb so long ago had become a man, and he had a destiny to fulfill.

James returned to his house next door, but Mary stood at the gateway a long time, her hands clasped against her heart, watching the tall figure stride down the road until he was out of sight.

THIRTY-THREE

*M*ary stood quietly looking up at the sky. Somewhere in Judea or perhaps elsewhere, her eldest son walked. What could be keeping him? He went to be baptized by John. Did he become a follower of the baptizer? A mockingbird sang in the sycamore tree outside the wall and his song seemed to echo her melancholy mood. *Oh God Who Sees Me*, she prayed silently. *Watch over him and bring him home. You alone know his way and I do not. Forgive a mother's heart that yearns for her son. Yet he is your son also, loaned to me for this life.* She bowed her head. *I cannot know your purpose, yet as before, I am your willing servant. Grant me your peace to do your will.*

Even as the words were spoken in her heart, Mary felt the Presence surrounding her and filling her being with peace. The moment passed, but her heart was strengthened. She smiled to herself and began to gather eggs from the chickens. Nearby, Rebecca diligently swept the dirt courtyard, her face a picture of sadness, unaware of Mary's musings.

As she moved about the animals, Mary thought of the scene the night before. James had gathered the family and told them where their oldest brother had gone. There had been mixed reactions. Joses and Simon frowned and murmured between themselves, no doubt feeling the weight of responsibility along with James for the carpenter shop; Miriam, her practical daughter, shook her head in amazement as she spoke in animated whispers with her husband,

Aaron; Jerusha and Rebecca wept in distress. They had lost their father, would they now lose the only real father figure they had known? It was an emotional evening, draining Mary's strength. She remained quiet, letting each one have their say. It crossed her mind briefly to just tell them of his birth and who he was, but she felt uneasy in her spirit. Then Adonai spoke to her heart. *It is not yet time, beloved woman. You will know when the right moment comes. He will return.*

Comforted by her God, she weathered the family storm. Then it occurred to her that Jude did not venture a comment. He sat silently listening to his brothers and sisters with a strange look on his face. Mary frowned. It was hard to tell what was going on in the mind of her youngest son.

That very night, Jude had slipped out the gate and without a word to her or James, vanished. No one knew where he went. Mary could only pray he would not find himself in trouble.

To her relief, Jude returned a week later, strangely quiet. He endured a tongue lashing from James but helped in the carpenter shop without complaint. Yet he would not tell his brothers or Mary where he had been. Strange things were happening that she felt she had no control over. She could only lay her concerns at the feet of Adonai and wait.

❧

It was almost six weeks before Mary heard a familiar voice greeting her from the gate. She stopped kneading the bread and ran to embrace Yeshua and welcome him home at last. To her surprise, her elusive son, Jude, who had slipped out again two weeks before with no word, was with him.

As she embraced Yeshua, she realized that he was thinner and his beard had not been trimmed. "You have been gone so long, my son. Where have you been these long weeks?"

She turned to Jude and gave him a stern look. "And you, my son, will have to answer to James for your lack of help in the shop."

Yeshua greeted Sarah warmly, and seeing Bithia and Shallum who were visiting, picked up the baby to hold for a moment. Shallum reached up, touched his beard, and smiled.

Rebecca's face lit up with joy at the sight of the brother she adored.

Mary returned to her questions. "Did you stop to see your brothers?"

"They will have word soon enough. After our evening meal Jude and I will share with all of you."

Mary studied his face. There was a light in his eyes she had not seen before and a sense of power that seemed barely contained. What had happened to him while he was gone? Jude also seemed filled with suppressed joy. She looked from one to the other, bewildered. She could only nod her head, but her mind turned again with unspoken questions.

Rebecca and Sarah brought some cool water, figs, bread and fresh goat cheese. The two brothers ate hungrily and Mary, watching Yeshua, wondered how he had survived this long. When was the last time he had eaten?

Word spread quickly in their small town of the prodigal's return. The women of the family gathered at Mary's home. Yeshua embraced his sisters, who also appeared shocked at his appearance. Mary's heart rejoiced, hearing once again his contagious laugh as his small nieces and nephews gathered about him and vied to sit on his lap. They loved their uncle and couldn't seem to get close enough to him.

Then there were voices at the gate as James, Joses, and Simon burst into the courtyard, all talking at once. James stood back, his face like a thundercloud, and he turned to Jude. "These long absences while you roam about the country do not help your mother!" Joses and Simon had no such anger. They clapped Yeshua on the back, welcoming him home.

James spoke again, his voice edged with sarcasm as he addressed Yeshua. "I'm sure you have much to tell us as to where you have been for two months."

Yeshua put a hand on his shoulder. "I go where the Father leads, James. But I will tell you all you wish to know at our evening meal."

Simon inclined his head toward Jude. "He was gone for a week the day after you left for the Jordan River. When he returned, he didn't seem the same but would not talk about where he'd been, even though he endured a tongue-lashing from James."

"Jude will be all right, Simon. He has been with me." Yeshua smiled at Jude and something passed between them. There was a twinkle in his eyes. "I think his rebellious days are behind him."

Hearing the confidence in his tone, Mary raised her eyebrows. How could he sound so sure of that?

Miriam served a lamb and fresh fava bean stew she had hastily brought from home. Jerusha shared some squash with capers and mint; Hodiah, the wife of James, when summoned, brought some lentil, barley, and mustard green pottage; Bithia and Sarah put the morning's fresh bread and some goat cheese on the table. It was a feast worthy of a holy day.

Mary went to the storage room and got wine, which she and Miriam poured for the men.

Her heart soared as she listened to the familiar banter around the low table. It was like it had always been when Yeshua was home. Yet there was a sense of anticipation in the air. Something was coming and she didn't know whether to be afraid or rejoice.

Mary and her daughters served the meal and then stood back to wait nearby, listening. Mary especially watched her youngest son. There was something different about him. Jude seemed at peace. Her heart went out to him. All his life he fought against the family but mostly he fought against himself. What had touched his heart?

Simon, breaking off a piece of bread, spoke up first. "So tell us," he ventured, "where have you traveled all this time? Were you truly baptized by John?"

James leaned forward, his tone accusatory. "We'd like to know why you stayed away so long."

"Yes, what was it like?" Joses added.

Yeshua listened quietly, then turned to Jude who nodded his head for Yeshua to speak.

"First let me share good news of our youngest brother. He is to be married."

There was a sudden silence and then everyone began to talk at once. Mary moved to stand across from Jude. "You are to be married?"

Before Yeshua could answer, Jude spoke up. "I was in Cana, looking for Yeshua, and needed a place to spend the night. I met Abigail, daughter of Nathanael, at the local well. We liked each other right away. Her father agreed to allow me to stay in their small house by the sea. Then I found Yeshua the next day walking along the shore speaking to some of the fishermen. I asked him to speak to her father for me. She is of marriageable age and her father is a widower."

"Nathanael agreed to the marriage," Yeshua added. "The wedding will be in Cana in the spring, and we are all invited."

Mary almost wept with relief. This troublesome son of hers who had caused her so much anxiety and heartbreak over the years would be settling down with a wife at last.

Jude continued. "Abigail and I will make our home in Cana. I will do woodworking, the trade I've been taught, but I love the sea and so Nathanael will also be teaching me to fish."

Jude looked around at his family and then caught Mary's eyes. She smiled at him in understanding and he turned back to look at his brothers. "When I was gone the first time, I followed Yeshua to the Jordan. I wanted to see this strange cousin of ours for myself.

John was as he has been described, with a leather girdle, animal skins for clothing, and neither hair nor beard having seen a razor in a long time."

All eyes flickered over to Yeshua. He merely smiled, hearing the silent rebuke for his own appearance.

Jude went on. "Never have I heard words like John spoke. He railed at the Pharisees and told the tax collectors not to take more money than they were entitled to. He even told the soldiers to be content with their wages. And they listened! Even the priests and members of the Sanhedrin listened to his words! Then I saw Yeshua make his way through the crowd and they parted for him."

The family sat almost in shock. They had never seen Jude so animated. There was a light in his eyes that made them glow like the flame of a candle.

Yeshua remained silent next to Jude as he continued. "They spoke a moment and then John baptized Yeshua. When Yeshua rose from the water, a white dove came out of nowhere and briefly lit on his shoulder before flying away." He closed his eyes as if to listen. "Then we all heard a voice. It seemed to be all around us. It was the voice of Adonai, I'm sure of it. The voice said, 'This is my beloved son, in whom I am well pleased.'"

Jude turned and looked at Yeshua. "You are my older brother, but who are you that Adonai should speak thus?"

Everyone began speaking at once.

"Is Yeshua to be a prophet now?"

"Jude was imagining things."

"A voice from heaven. What will Jude come up with next?"

"Does this mean Yeshua is leaving us again?"

Yeshua finally quieted down the uproar. "I must do the will of Adonai. He has called me to teach our people. To tell them the good news, that the kingdom of heaven is at hand. I am to share this with all who will listen." He looked around at his family and finally at Mary.

"It is time, Ima."

Her heart raced and she fought tears as she nodded. This was what he came for then? In the back of her mind, she sensed he would be more than just a traveling preacher, but she, like the others, would have to wait and watch. In her heart it was like the gathering of the clouds and the stillness that came before the storm. Was she ready?

THIRTY-FOUR

*I*n the months since Yeshua left them again, Jude worked diligently in the shop without complaint, to the amazement of his family. Peace had settled on the household and Mary, hearing of Jude's zeal at the shop, thought perhaps he wanted to be as ready as possible for his new tasks in Cana.

The almond trees filled the hills around Nazareth with a profusion of pink blossoms as the spring rains came again. Mary loved the Feast of Purim celebrated at this time each year. She never tired of the story of Esther, the young Jewish girl who was chosen by the king of Persia to be his queen. Esther kept her Jewish heritage a secret as instructed by her uncle, Mordecai, who had raised her. A wicked counselor of the king, Haman, was angry that the Jew Mordecai did not bow down to him and persuaded the king to order the death of all the Jews of the land in retaliation. At the risk of her life, Queen Esther revealed herself to the king and was not only able to save her people from the terrible edict but also saw the destruction of the wicked Haman. Now every year the Jews rejoiced at Purim and gave gifts to one another in remembrance of Queen Esther's brave act.

The sound of singing in the fields was heard along with the swish of the scythes as the men of Nazareth harvested the flax. The women of the family prepared for Jude and Abigail's wedding. Finally, after the barley harvest was in, the family journeyed to Cana.

When they at last left Nazareth, Mary could scarcely contain her excitement. Not only for the wedding, but because she knew Yeshua would be there. He had promised.

⌒

Mary tapped her foot to the music of the flute and the lyre as two women waved tambourines and shook them to the beat of the music. Food was plentiful and she was enjoying herself. She looked around at her family with satisfaction. Hodiah was keeping a close watch on her daughters Amasa and Timnah; Miriam and Aaron's sons, Amasa and Reuel, were hovering over the date cakes to their mother's consternation. Jerusha sat quietly in a corner with her husband Nahor. She was heavy with their second child. Bithia kept a close eye on Shallum who had discovered his legs and wanted to be everywhere at once.

James had been named the master of the wedding and was overseeing the serving. Yeshua was talking to someone, one of his disciples. She still had a hard time believing that her son had disciples—men who vowed to follow him anywhere.

Strange stories trickled back to the family about miracles. People healed and restored.

Mary longed to go to where Yeshua was teaching to hear for herself, but she was under the authority of James and he wouldn't hear of it. "This will all die down eventually and we can get back to a normal life," he had said.

⌒

The rabbi had performed the ceremony under the *chuppah*, and as Mary watched Abigail walk slowly three times around the canopy, she marveled that Jude had selected such a lovely bride and that her father had accepted Jude as his son-in-law. It was obvious that the young couple were taken with each other and to Mary that boded well for their marriage. Dear Joseph, how happy he would have been for this day. An arrow of sadness pierced her heart. She still missed him.

The glass was smashed and at last the festivities began. With ribald comments from the men and good wishes from the women, Jude took his bride into her father's house where Nathanael had prepared a room for their wedding chamber.

Simon, designated the friend of the groom, waited by the door of the house for the proof of Abigail's virginity and in time displayed the bloody sheet to the waiting family. Mary breathed a sigh of relief, though she was not surprised. Some of the guests applauded, and everyone smiled. It was a good omen.

Some men were grouped around Yeshua, laughing at something and she noted one of the younger disciples, laughing heartily. What did Yeshua say his name was? Oh yes...John. As she glanced around at the guests, she became aware of James talking animatedly to one of the servants hired for the day. The servant shrugged and James's face registered alarm. Something was wrong. Mary caught her breath and went to investigate. They were out of wine, an embarrassment for Nathanael. She thought quickly. Who could help? She looked across the small courtyard to Yeshua, then hurried over, and put a hand on his arm, interrupting his conversation.

"They have no wine."

He turned to her, his eyes dancing and then his brow furrowed, as he understood what she was saying.

"Woman, what am I to do with you? My time has not yet come."

Woman—a term of respect but not Ima, *Mother*. It was a rebuke, although a gentle one.

She shuddered at her audacity. What did she expect him to do? Even so, she turned to the servants. "Do whatever he tells you to do."

Yeshua sighed. There were six large stone jars nearby that were to hold water for purification. Yeshua pointed to the jars. "Fill them with water."

There was something commanding in his tone. The servants glanced at each other and then hurried to fill the jars as quickly as possible. When the jars were full, Yeshua spoke to one of the servants. "Now dip some out and take it to the governor of the feast."

Rolling his eyes, the servant did so and beholding the dipper, turned startled eyes to Yeshua. Then he hurried to James. Mary held her breath and watched as her son tasted the proffered ladle. His eyes grew large. He stepped forward and announced to the gathering, "Most hosts put out the good wine first and, when the guests have drunk much, bring out the poorer wine. Nathanael, you have kept the best for last."

The faces of Yeshua's disciples registered amazement and awe. Mary realized that they had also seen the miracle. Would the servants tell what he had done? It was the first time she glimpsed his power—and she sensed his life would never be the same again.

There were smiles and nods from the guests but Mary's pride in what Yeshua had done was tempered by her guilt. How had she known he would do something? She had been presumptuous, and Yeshua rebuked her. She moved to the far side of the courtyard and nursed her embarrassment.

Presently she looked up and Yeshua stood before her. There was no condemnation in his eyes, which fairly twinkled with amusement. "Are you enjoying yourself, Ima?" She was forgiven.

THIRTY-FIVE

The festivities continued into the night, but, rather than extending for several days, ended with the morning for the men of Cana needed to tend their nets and fishing boats and then prepare for Passover. The month of Nisan had begun and in Nazareth the wheat would be ripening in the fields and the figs were plump and juicy on the trees. As soon as Passover had ended, the families would have to hurry home for the harvest.

As Mary and the family gathered their things, Yeshua spoke to them. "I have found a house in Capernaum. It is more central to my ministry. Come, you and my brothers. Join me for a time. There are still a few days before Passover."

James hesitated. The family with wives and children was large. "Can this house in Capernaum accommodate us all?"

Yeshua smiled. "It will."

James reluctantly agreed. "We will come but we must leave for Jerusalem in two days."

When the family reached Capernaum, Mary was surprised at the size of the house. Truly there was room in the courtyard, the roof, and inside the house, for all of them. Yeshua led her to a small room with a single bed, a table, and an oil lamp. "You will be comfortable here, Ima. I will join my brothers in the courtyard." Then she knew it was the room he stayed in when in the city.

She turned to face him. "I knew your ministry would grow. I welcomed it and yet feared it, not knowing where it is to lead you. Ha'Shem watches over you, but you will be in my prayers, always."

⟋⟍

With the women and children rested and refreshed in Capernaum, it made the journey back past Nazareth to Jerusalem easier for all of them. However, in Jerusalem the family had to split up among homes of relatives for there was not a house that could accommodate them all. James and his family stayed with Mary and Rebecca at the home of one of her cousins. Simon and Joses and their families went to the homes of their wives' relatives. Jude and Abigail stayed with Abigail's uncle. Mary was not sure where Yeshua and his disciples were staying, but she overheard one of them mention the garden of Gethsemane, a wooded area outside the city. She had seen the grove once, and thought it a beautiful place with the gnarled and ancient olive trees.

As, once more, Mary and her family waited for the roasted lamb, in the distance Mary could hear the choirs from the great Temple singing the *Hallel*. The choruses swelled as they echoed through the city. Mary's mind went back to the Passover long ago when Yeshua was twelve. How foolish she was to fear for him. He had not been lost, but only seeking to do, even then, his heavenly Father's will.

His Father's will. Was it just to be a rabbi and preach about the kingdom of heaven? She knew it was more than that. She could not deny the miracle of the wine in Cana and her heart told her it was only the beginning. She had glimpsed the power of God.

⟋⟍

James burst into the courtyard with Mary's cousin. His face was red and he looked behind him at the road outside before closing the gate. He carried the portion of the lamb that Mary and his family would share.

"Quickly, we must eat the lamb and the Passover meal as ordained, but be prepared to gather our things. We will not be staying for the rest of the week."

"You are leaving?" The cousin's tone was hopeful.

"James, what has happened?" Mary anxiously asked.

"Your son, and my brother, has gone mad. He made a whip of cords and began to drive all the moneychangers out of the Temple. He overturned tables, scattering money on the stones. The people picked some of it up before they were driven back by the Temple police!" He took a breath, his chest heaving with the effort of running back to the house.

"Ima, you cannot imagine the chaos. Animals running everywhere, doves fluttering as he opened their cages and set them free." James was almost in her face now. "And do you know what he had the gall to say? 'My Father's house shall be called a house of prayer, and you have made it a den of thieves!'"

"Did one of you try to stop him?" Mary put a hand to her heart to still its hammering.

"Stop him? Fight the Temple police? We are not mad also. We remained in the shadows and then fled the Temple and came here."

"Was he arrested by the Temple police?" Were her worst fears realized?

James waved a hand in frustration. "Arrested? No, of course not. He strode out of the Temple court like he was a king, with that ragged and worthless band of followers right behind him. No one stopped him. Why? Why did they not arrest him on the spot? At least in prison he is not wandering the countryside spreading his...gospel, as he calls it."

Mary caught her breath in relief. Yeshua was safe.

Knowing the children were hungry, the Passover meal was celebrated in near silence except for the expected prayers, and even then James kept looking over his shoulder, half expecting the Temple police at their door.

When the necessary ceremonies were observed, James turned to Mary. "We are not staying for the rest of Passover week. It is too dangerous. I've sent word to my brothers for the family to gather outside the gates of the city at first light. We will return to Nazareth as quickly as possible, and pray there are no repercussions against his family!"

Out of the corner of her eye, Mary saw her cousin look to heaven and nod with visible relief.

~

At dawn, the family reunited just outside the city and began the journey back to Nazareth. Mary was feeling her age and tired more easily. Her daughters walked by her side, glancing at her from time to time with concern. She welcomed the rest at the end of the day and let Rebecca bring supper to her. The grandchildren played games and the younger ones chased one another around the camp. Was it so long ago that her own children did the same? Now Yeshua was traveling the country with his disciples; Jude and Abigail lived in another city; her children had homes of their own. Her parents and Joseph's parents were gone, and Joseph, dear Joseph, had been lost to her so many years ago. Now she was the grandmother, the matriarch of the family. Where had the years gone?

Rebecca made a pallet for her mother and Mary was ready to lie down and get some sleep. They still had a two-day's journey ahead of them.

She closed her eyes and prayed silently. *Oh God Who Sees, watch over your son as he travels to do whatever you have called him to do. Keep him safe. I don't know where his road is leading, but you do. Help me to be grateful for the time I had him, and help me to trust in your plan for him.*

A small breeze came up and stirred the leaves in a nearby tree, disappearing as quickly as it came, but not before she felt a gentle touch on her cheek.

They had traveled as quickly as possible considering the children and only when everyone was weary from walking did they stop for the night. At first light James barely allowed them to eat something before they were packing up to get on the road again. Mary felt she had never traveled so long and been so weary. She wanted to shake James by his shoulders, but knew he was determined to preserve the safety of his family from an unknown danger. It was with great relief that they reached Nazareth and each family wearily dispersed to their homes.

⁓

Mary waited anxiously for any news of Yeshua. He was moving around the country, sharing his message that the kingdom of God was at hand. The stories of healing abounded and many in the village, including her sons, shook their heads in disbelief.

"Stories, embellished by travelers…."

"He's going to get himself arrested yet. It's a wonder the chief priests and elders put up with this."

"I'll believe it when I see an actual miracle myself."

And with surreptitious glances at Mary, "Did you hear of the chaos in Jerusalem? The man is mad, I tell you."

Mary listened but kept her thoughts to herself, wondering.

One day a traveler came into Nazareth and stood in the square. As people gathered around him for news, he blurted out, "John the Baptist has been arrested by Herod. It bodes evil for him. He has been thrown in the castle dungeon."

Mary's heart cried out within her. She thought of the beautiful baby boy she had helped bring into the world when she stayed with Elizabeth and Zechariah. He was certainly an unusual boy, who when he was grown, spent a great deal of his time in the desert.

And then the way he had appeared suddenly, strangely dressed, and crying out for the people to repent of their sins and baptizing those who did in the river. Mary shook her head.

She wondered what had happened to Elizabeth and Zechariah. Were they still alive? She had not seen them at Passover for several years. Did they know what John was doing? He, too, had been a miracle child. Was he born for this? Her mind turned with possibilities. Was Yeshua then destined for prison for angering the leaders? Surely that was not be the plan of the Most High. It couldn't be. She walked to a quiet hillside and wept as she cried out to the Father of her son.

THIRTY-SIX

To her delight and relief, Mary had word that Yeshua was coming back to Nazareth, and with his disciples. She heard that there were four of them now. She checked the storage room and put daughters-in-law Bithia and Sarah to work preparing vegetables. Hodiah, Jerusha, and Miriam came to help also. The women prepared date cakes and baked extra loaves of bread. James reluctantly brought wine from his storeroom, but only at Mary's request.

James shook his head. "He is welcome as a member of the family, but at the first sign of trouble, he must leave. There will be no discussion."

"I understand, my son. I'm sure there will be no trouble."

James only waved a hand in the air and stalked off.

Jerusha and Miriam brought fresh goat cheese and dilled cucumbers with olives and crumbled goat cheese. Mary toasted almonds, whole cumin, and sesame seeds. She added nigella seeds. Her guests would be able to dip their bread in olive oil and then in the nut mixture.

When at last Yeshua arrived at the gate, the men behind him one by one touched the *mezuzah* and entered. They looked weary and their manner was hesitant, as if unsure of their welcome. Then to her surprise, Jude and Abigail entered the courtyard. Mary glanced at Abigail's small rounded belly. Another grandchild. She beamed and embraced the girl.

Mary joyfully greeted Yeshua and basked in the warmth of his eyes as he looked down on her.

"Welcome home, my son. We have sorely missed you. You are well?"

"I am well. We cannot stay long, Ima, but I'm glad to be with you again."

The family greeted Yeshua and their youngest brother and his wife lovingly and even James seemed relieved that Yeshua appeared healthy and well.

Mary covertly perused her guests. As her other sons stood by her, Yeshua introduced his disciples. "You might remember Andrew and his brother, Peter. You met them at the wedding. They are fishermen, but now my trusted helpers, too."

Andrew had an open face and Mary felt he was a trustworthy man, a man who could be depended on. Peter, on the other hand, had almost a surly expression. With his wide shoulders and strong arms, Mary could picture him hauling in fishing nets. His bearing was one of subdued power.

"Also you met Nathanael and Philip at the wedding."

Each of the men nodded in turn and finally all of them reclined around two low tables that had been put together for the family and Yeshua's guests. As Mary and her daughters served the food, Mary wondered at the four men. Would there be more? Would he accomplish the purpose of Ha'Shem with this small handful of followers?

⌇

As the men ate, Jude looked around at his family. "I have a story to tell." To their surprise, he told an amazing story about a nobleman, well-known in Cana.

"He had an only son and the boy became deathly ill. The physicians shook their heads and word went around that the boy would not live through the day. Yeshua had come to Cana and stopped by to see Abigail and me. The nobleman actually came to our house seeking Yeshua and begging him to come and heal his son. To my amazement, Yeshua merely told the man to go his way, and that his son was well. The man took my brother at his word, squared his shoulders and thanked Yeshua before striding quickly back toward his home. Word came later that, when he reached his home, the boy was well."

There was silence at the table. The faces of the disciples showed no surprise, only reflected confidence as if this was something that happened all the time. Mary glanced at her daughters and their eyes were wide. Yeshua could do such a thing?

Yeshua looked up at her and as their eyes met, she heard the words in her heart: *This is what I have come for.*

Mary lit the Sabbath candles, passing her hands over the flame and reciting the blessing. "Blessed are you, Lord our God, King of the universe, Creator of the light of fire."

The sunset painted the sky orange and gold, its setting marking the beginning of the Sabbath. Mary looked around at her family gathered before her, and felt truly blessed to have all of them together at this holy time. The meal was a happy one; all the family talked at once and the disciples shared the places they had been in the last few months. Philip shared that they had even been in Samaria.

Joses interrupted. "Why would you spend any time in Samaria? We Jews don't have anything to do with Samaritans. Couldn't you travel around the area?"

Yeshua shook his head. "It was necessary. There was work for the Father there."

Philip continued. "There was a woman at the well of Jacob. We passed her on the way into Sychar to get food for the Master, but she didn't even look up at us. When we returned to the well, here was Yeshua talking to her. We wondered what he was saying and why he was talking to a foreign woman and one who looked of questionable reputation."

Andrew cut in, "She suddenly dropped her water pot and rushed back into the town and then to our amazement, she brought half the town back with her to the well!"

Peter surprised them by finally speaking up. "They invited us to come and stay in Sychar and provided homes to stay in. Yeshua healed all who came to him and taught them from the Torah for two days."

James turned to study his brother. "You healed all of their sick? How can you say you did this? Only God can heal."

Mary bit her lip to keep from crying out, "He is the son of God." When could she tell them? When would Adonai allow her to speak of his birth and mission? Yeshua glanced at her and smiled. "Yes, only God can heal. I only do the will of the Father. He chooses to heal those I lay hands on."

The pleasant atmosphere around the table suddenly shifted as Yeshua's brothers jumped to question, his disciples defended, and the brothers, disbelieving, only questioned the more.

Mary and her daughters could only watch in distress as the family gathering was filled with intense dissension. Finally, Yeshua held up his hand. "Let us not spend our short time together in disagreement. We shall leave after the Sabbath."

James waved a hand in frustration. "Perhaps, if you must persist in this so-called ministry, it is best you not return to Nazareth for a while. You have a house in Capernaum, minister there."

Yeshua looked at James with sadness in his eyes. "You are the head of the household now, James. I will abide by your wishes."

❧

The next morning when the sun rose on the Sabbath, Yeshua and his disciples accompanied Mary and the family to the synagogue. The atmosphere was still tense between Yeshua and James but no more was said. Simon, Joses, and Jude walked behind them, talking quietly among themselves. The women followed, moving slowly for the sake of Abigail's pregnancy.

Yeshua's reputation had preceded him, so, as was the custom with traveling rabbis, he was asked to read a portion of the Torah and speak. Mary, her heart full of love for her son, watched and listened with her daughters from behind the screen of the women's area.

Yeshua stood and was handed the scroll of the prophet Isaiah. He opened the scroll and, after finding the place he wanted, read, *"The Spirit of* ADONAI ELOHIM *is upon me, because* ADONAI *has anointed me to announce good news to the poor. He has sent me to heal the brokenhearted; to proclaim freedom to the captives, to let out into light those bound in the dark; to proclaim the year of the favor of* ADONAI."

He closed the book, gave it back to the attendant and sat down. The eyes of the entire congregation were fixed on him. They had known him all his life, had heard the rumors of his miracle-working, and were waiting to hear what he had to say.

"Today this Scripture is fulfilled in your hearing."

The congregation murmured approval. Mary heard a man in front of the screen say, "Is this not Joseph's son?"

But when he spoke again, the nods of approval stopped. There were frowns on the faces of the men, and the women near Mary glanced at her with eyebrows lifted.

"You will surely say this proverb to me, 'Physician, heal yourself! Whatever we have heard done in Capernaum, do also here in your country.'"

Yeshua looked around at the congregation. "Assuredly I say to you, no prophet is accepted in his own country. But I tell you truly, many widows were in Israel in the days of Elijah, when the heaven was shut up three years and six months, and there was a great famine throughout all the land; but to none of them was Elijah sent except to Zarephath, in the region of Sidon, to a woman who was a widow. And many lepers were in Israel at the time of Elisha the prophet, and none of them were cleansed except Naaman the Syrian."

Suddenly there were angry murmurs and the men began to shout out against him. To Mary's dismay, they rose up and grabbed Yeshua by the arms, rushing him out of the synagogue toward the brow of a hill. The women hurried out behind the men and Mary's heart pounded. What were they going to do to him? Then, to her horror, she saw that they were going to fling him over the cliff! She cried out, "No!" but no one paid any attention to her. Frantically she looked around for the disciples to help him but they stood back, helpless, horror and shock written on their faces.

She tried to push her way through the crowd along with his brothers, trying to reach him before the men could follow through with their intent, but to Mary's surprise, the uproar suddenly quieted. The men let go of him and stood back. Yeshua walked through the midst of them away from the hill and joined his disciples who quickly followed him away from the synagogue. Mary stood speechless. What had just happened? Why did the men stop? They seemed to be milling around looking at each other and scratching their heads. They didn't even seem to see him.

Mary and the family quickly returned home and found Yeshua and his disciples gathering their things.

"We must leave you, Ima. I don't wish to bring any trouble on your household."

He embraced her, nodded to the rest of the family, and within moments, he and his small band of disciples were headed down the street. Mary stood at the gate and was amazed to see that none of her neighbors had returned home yet. The street was silent.

Oh, Ha'Shem, thank you for saving him! This time she did not need to be told that it was not his time.

James, Simon, and Joses stood talking with Jude in low tones. Rebecca stood next to Mary. "Ima, what just happened? I don't understand."

Simon, overhearing her, murmured. "I don't think anyone understands. Why would he say what he did? Why did the men stop suddenly from their intended purpose of throwing him off the cliff?"

Joses shook his head. "It was as though he was invisible. He walked right past them and they looked at each other as if he wasn't even there."

Jerusha and Miriam had evidently returned to their homes, no doubt at the urging of their husbands. No one wished to speak with any of his or her neighbors. James quickly sent Hodiah home. She gathered the dishes she had brought and with a worried glance at Mary, hurried out of the courtyard. Sarah sat quietly in the corner of the courtyard with Bithia who held Shallum on her lap and looked anxiously at Simon. Finally, Sarah got up and began putting a few things on the table for the evening meal. There would be no cooking, as it was the Sabbath. Later they would cut up cheese and set out fruit and bread left over from the previous night for the evening meal.

Mary checked the stew from the night before. Because they had prepared so much for the guests, there was enough left over for the family who remained. She grieved that her son's visit had been cut short. She did not understand some of the things he said, but she believed in who he was. Their leaders did not support him in spite of the miracles. His words only seemed to cause them anger. It was a strange turn of events. What was coming next? She shook her head in bewilderment.

Mary went over to Bithia and took Shallum in her arms. The little boy seemed to sense that something was wrong and clung to her, his eyes wide, his thumb in his mouth.

James, Simon, and Joses sat on a rug under the sycamore tree but they were silent, each with his own thoughts. Mary felt that in spite of James's outburst, they didn't want to criticize a brother they loved so well. At last Simon and Bithia left for their own home with their son. For now the incident was over, but what would be the repercussions?

THIRTY-SEVEN

*J*ude seemed to have sources for tracking the travels and ensuing miracles of Yeshua and his disciples. He kept Mary and the family apprised whenever he was able to get to Nazareth. The list of miracles grew and stories abounded. Mary learned that Yeshua had added more disciples and that there were even women of means who helped support the ministry. Mary shook her head and increased her prayers for him in her private times.

"Everywhere Yeshua goes," Jude told her on one visit, "thousands flock to him. He has only to lay hands on the sick and they are healed. Once when I was in Capernaum I sought him but he was on one of the hillsides, speaking to the people. I stood with the crowd and was amazed at his teaching. I saw a man with leprosy who braved the revulsion of the people to fall down at Yeshua's feet. He begged Yeshua to heal him and cried out, 'If you are willing, you can make me clean.' How can a mere man cleanse a leper? Yeshua reached out and did the unthinkable. He touched the man!" Jude paused, remembering the scene. He turned to Mary. "And the man was cleansed from his leprosy that moment!" He shook his head. "Ima, where does he get his power? I cannot believe he has turned to sorcery."

Mary chose her words carefully. "Our God has chosen him, my son. His power comes from Ha'Shem."

"From Ha'Shem? I do not understand."

Mary reached out and touched his cheek. "Remember the words of the great prophet, Isaiah, *'Here is my servant, whom I support, my chosen one, in whom I take pleasure. I have put my Spirit on him; he will bring justice to the Goyim [Gentiles]. He will not cry or shout; no one will hear his voice in the streets. He will not snap off a broken reed or snuff out a smoldering wick. He will bring forth justice according to truth; he will not weaken or be crushed until he has established justice on the earth.'"*

Jude's brow furrowed. "He is a prophet then?"

"Perhaps, my son. I feel in my heart that we will all understand one day. When it is time." It was all she felt she could say.

"I hope it is soon. There is much murmuring among our leaders." He picked up his traveling bag. "I must return to Cana. I have been gone several days and Abigail will be worried."

"Give my love to her. Your son thrives?"

Jude grinned. "He eats well and thrives, Ima."

She smiled at him. "That is good. We will see you in Jerusalem at Passover."

Jude embraced Mary briefly and in a moment was on his way up the narrow street.

She sank down on a wooden bench and looked up at the sky. "Oh Ha'Shem, I long to tell my family who he really is. Yet I must not spoil your plan and the path you have chosen for him. Give me grace to be patient, give me wisdom, Oh Most High. I am your servant, always."

She watched the shadows breach the wall and begin to slip across the patio. Rebecca would soon be returning from the marketplace with Hodiah. She had enjoyed a surprise visit alone with her youngest son and that was a blessing.

~

She looked forward to Passover again this year, for she knew Yeshua would be there and her heart longed to see him.

When the family reached Jerusalem, they kept a low profile. James felt it was not wise to proclaim their relationship to this controversial rabbi. Beniah had died the previous year, so they stayed with his nephew who occupied the house. He was hospitable as all families were called to be at this time of the year, but Mary sensed reluctance on the part of both him and his wife. When the family did not discuss Yeshua, they seemed visibly relieved.

The whole city was talking about the man Yeshua had healed at the pool of Bethesda—a man who had been crippled for over thirty years. Yeshua had merely said to the man, "Stand up, take your bed, and walk," and the man had. The Sanhedrin was furious that Yeshua had done this on a Sabbath and everyone was expecting the rabbi to be arrested any day. When it did not happen, people shook their heads in amazement.

One of the disciples she had welcomed to Nazareth, Andrew, came to the house. "Dear lady, the Master has asked me to bring you to the house where he is staying. Will you come, alone?"

Her heart leaped at seeing her oldest son and she quickly nodded her head. Her other sons had gone to the Temple to present the lamb for their sacrifice. She told her daughters only that she would be back soon. Allowing no time for questions, she lifted her mantle over her head and slipped out, walking quickly at Andrew's side through the city. People were everywhere and the smell of lamb roasting over many fires around the city filled the air.

She looked up at the tall disciple. "You are not going to the Temple?"

He smiled. "We have already made our sacrifice, dear lady."

When they entered the house, her escort quickly left and Mary moved into the open arms of her son. "I have prayed so long. I don't understand what you are doing, yet I know you are in the will of the Most High." She stepped back. "Do you not wish to see the rest of the family, my son?"

"They do not believe in me, but there will come a time when they will know who I truly am."

"Can I not tell them? Every time it is on my tongue to speak, I feel the Lord restraining me. Surely they can know now."

"All things must come in my Father's time, Ima. You will know then why I have been sent."

His expression changed and for a moment he looked away, seeing something she could not see. A shadow of great sorrow crossed his face and a stab of fear pierced her heart. What did he mean?

When he looked back at her, his tone was gentle. "It will not be as you have imagined, Ima. You must trust the Father with what you cannot see."

For a short time they sat on a rug as she filled him in on the family news. Joses and Sarah had a son; Hodiah had given birth to a daughter; Simon and Bithia had a daughter; Sarah and Joses's first child was a son. Yeshua chuckled at her obvious delight in her small grandchildren.

"Miriam and Aaron are doing well. My household is busy and full. You already know Jude and Abigail had a son, evidently you've been to Cana recently." She lifted one eyebrow. "We miss you in Nazareth also."

He merely smiled and told her of the places he'd been and what had transpired. She listened, transfixed, heeding especially to the miracles, and hope rose in her heart.

"You are to take the throne of David and save our people from their sins. The angel told me long ago. Is that not true?"

He hesitated, but only for a moment. "All is in the Father's hands, Ima, and in the Father's time."

She studied his face, not sure of his meaning, but sensing he would say no more, she remained silent.

Finally Yeshua rose and assisted Mary to her feet. "You must return to the family." He turned to a young man who had entered a few minutes before. He looked at Yeshua with obvious devotion.

"John, will you escort my mother? I trust you to see to her safety."

The young man smiled at her, and as she remembered him from the wedding in Cana, something in her heart went out to him.

"I will treat her as my own mother, Master."

Mary embraced her son once more and took her leave, grateful for this precious time he had arranged for her.

John walked closely with her, acting as a buffer against the crowds that pressed in the streets. As they walked, Mary wondered to herself. Why is this disciple different from the others? It was obvious he and Yeshua had forged a strong bond between them. Perhaps that was why she was drawn to him.

She returned to the house and fortunately the men had not yet returned. Her daughters looked at John with questions in their eyes, but they would not ask where she had been. Rebecca was bolder. "Have you seen Yeshua?"

Mary removed her mantle. "Yes, I have seen him."

"Why would he not come here to see us?"

Mary hesitated. "Our time was short and he has much to do. There will be another time."

Yet why did she feel this heaviness? Was it the last time she would see him alone? He belonged to the people now. Things were changing faster than she wished. Sooner or later James would find out where she had been and she would have to endure his displeasure. He would also have questions. Yet even now, did she know the answers?

THIRTY-EIGHT

*M*ary turned from Rebecca and went to see how far her daughters had gotten with the preparations for the Passover meal. The *charoset* of finely chopped apples, walnuts, and cinnamon with sweet wine was mixed, the unleavened griddle bread laid out, the saffron millet was prepared with walnuts. The cups were ready for the wine and the pitcher of wine was placed nearby. She watched Jerusha place the salted water and parsley on the table. All they needed was the lamb to complete the meal. She wondered where Yeshua and his disciples were celebrating on this holy day. As she said no more about Yeshua, all the women understood that it was not to be discussed.

The men brought in the roasted lamb and the family enjoyed the Passover meal, renewing their covenant with their God.

When the week came to an end, they returned to Nazareth. Mary had heard no more from Yeshua. There was still danger in the city for him for the Sanhedrin let it be known that he needed to be stopped. Mary feared she would hear of his arrest any day. James, Joses, and Simon were anxious to get their families safely out of Jerusalem, hoping the fervor would die down.

"At least he has not led the rabble here," James murmured.

Simon glanced at Joses, who nodded. "We could not stop him. One day the leaders will."

On the way back to Nazareth, James approached her. From the thundercloud on his face she realized Hodiah had spoken to him about her visit with Yeshua. She sighed. Hodiah could not keep a secret, especially from her husband.

"You went to see Yeshua?" It was more an accusation than a question.

"Yes, he sent for me."

"Don't you know you could have been in danger? The Temple police could have arrested him and you also as a follower!"

Mary eyed her second son calmly. "Nothing happened. I wanted to see my oldest son, regardless of the controversy surrounding him."

"You should have asked my permission."

She put a gentle hand on his arm. "Dear James, you were not there, you were at the Temple and I didn't know when I would see your brother again."

James waved a hand in the air, his face close to hers. "He has rejected us. Why do you pursue him? He prefers to traipse around the country doing miracles, if indeed that part is even true. We must be careful, Ima. He angers the leaders wherever he goes, miracles or not." He thought a moment, frowning. "When he returns to Capernaum, we must go to him—Simon, Joses, and I—and see if we can talk to him. Surely he can see what he is doing to his family."

"I will go with you, but I fear it will do no good. He is on the path Ha'Shem has set for him, whatever that is."

James eyes became steely with his resolve. "We will see." He turned and walked away.

The month of Elul was just beginning, bringing the fierce heat of summer. It was a bad time to travel and those who ventured on the roads were careful to fill their water skins. It was also the month set aside for repentance and confessing one's sins against God. Mary insisted on going to Capernaum with James, Joses, and Simon. She had a suspicion that what James had in mind was for Yeshua to repent of his sins against his family and return home, properly chastised. She thought of her own motives for going with them...to be a shield between her sons.

"If he has gone mad," Simon was reasoning, "what good does it do to try to talk to him? We have work to do."

Joses frowned. "I agree. What good will it do? He persists in what he is doing. Let him continue. If we cannot stop him, the leaders will."

James had sent word to Jude, but Mary's youngest son had declined, citing as his reason too much work. Joses and Simon were finally convinced. It was perhaps best if Yeshua came home with them, they reasoned, moved by the persuasiveness of James. It would not bode well for the family if the Sanhedrin was stirred up, for there was an undercurrent of rebellion against the iron hand of Rome. How the Jews longed to be free from their oppressive rule. It was rumored that one of the disciples of Yeshua was a zealot. Mary suspected it was Judas Iscariot. The few times she had met him, her impression was that of a man who observed and used things for his own advantage. She wondered why Yeshua had made him their treasurer. It was a position of trust, but was the man really trustworthy?

In her heart, Mary knew Yeshua would not return to them, to the life he'd known before his ministry, but as she walked, part of her wanted to save him from the wrath of the Sanhedrin. The news that trickled to Nazareth was not good. The leaders accused him of ignoring the law, of healing on the Sabbath, and of other perceived crimes against the Torah. If they only knew who he was, she reasoned. He was God's son. She pondered those words in her heart and once again was overwhelmed with the weight of the magnificent burden the Most High had placed on her shoulders that night long ago.

The family arrived in Capernaum to find a crowd pressing around the house Yeshua shared with his disciples. The people were so thick the family could not make their way into the house where Yeshua was teaching. People pressed against each other and murmured among themselves. When James asked one man what was happening, the man replied, "The rabbi is teaching. This morning at the synagogue he healed a man with a withered hand and our leaders were angry that he healed on the Sabbath."

James nodded impatiently. "We are his family. We would speak with him. Can you get a message to him?"

The man shrugged and whispered a few words to a man in front of him who passed the message to someone in front of him, and finally to someone inside the house. Mary could hear the voice of her son, his tone firm with authority.

"When an unclean spirit comes out of a person, it travels through dry country seeking rest and does not find it. Then it says to itself, 'I will return to the house I left.' When it arrives it finds the house standing empty, swept clean and put in order. Then it goes and takes with it seven other spirits more evil than itself, and they come and live there—so that in the end, the person is worse off than he was before. This is how it will be for this wicked generation."

Mary frowned. What did he mean? Did the people listening understand his words? There was a pause and people looked back at Mary and her sons. Yeshua must have been told their message. She waited for Yeshua to come out to them.

Yeshua was silent for a moment and then she heard his next words clearly as he responded to the messenger.

"Who is my mother? Who are my brothers? Look! Here are my mother and my brothers! Whoever does what my Father in heaven wants, that person is my brother and sister and mother."

He was ignoring their request. She pulled her mantle closer about her face to hide her embarrassment. Had he disowned his family? Those in the crowd who claimed to believe in him were his family? She wanted to weep. She knew that he belonged to the world but now she wrestled with her thoughts.

"What did I say?" Joses grunted. "It has been a waste of time."

Mary stood looking at the door of the house, hoping that Yeshua would come out after all.

Joses and Simon stepped to her side. "Let us return home, Ima. You are weary. We will find a shady place to eat the food we brought and then when you are rested, we will leave."

James looked toward the house, his eyes smoldering with anger. He took longer to process Yeshua's response, but finally said, "He has chosen the people over his family. We can do nothing here. He is treading a dangerous path with the Sanhedrin, but that is his choice. We must return home, and we can only hope he does not involve his family in this ministry of his."

Mary let her sons lead her away but she moved in a daze. Her heart felt like a stone in her chest. All she could think of was that her oldest son had turned her away.

James left the family at the gate and returned to his home. Rebecca and Sarah hurried to Mary's side and greeted her warmly, "Ima, did you see Yeshua? Why is he not with you?" Rebecca still glanced at the gate hoping to see her favorite brother.

"Mother, it is good to have you home safely."

"Was the trip hard for you? How is Yeshua?"

Then they saw the faces of their husbands. "What is wrong?" Sarah stood before Joses, waiting for his answer.

"He would not see us."

Sarah started to speak but pursed her lips instead and returned to cutting up vegetables for the evening meal.

Finally Sarah went to the gate and talked quietly to Joses who shrugged and slowly shook his head. Then motioning to Simon, the two brothers left for the shop. They'd brought their mother home safely and there was work to do.

THIRTY-NINE

*M*ary sent the shuttle back and forth through the threads of her loom. As she concentrated, her thoughts again were on her oldest son. *Ha'Shem, where are you leading him? Why does he speak as he does? I know the crowds follow him wherever he goes, and you have enabled him to perform strange miracles that draw the people. Protect him, Adonai, let him not come to harm, yet I pray he will fulfill your will for him.* She bowed her head and yielded her anxious thoughts to the One who had cared for her for so long, and in her spirit heard the words: *He is fulfilling the purpose for which I sent him. Do not fear, beloved woman. You must trust me whatever the cost.*

"Your will be done," she murmured softly, yet the words *whatever the cost* played themselves over and over in her mind.

Suddenly Rebecca, who had gone for water, hurried into the courtyard. She was out of breath from running. "Ima! Yeshua is coming down the road, with his disciples!"

Yeshua was coming home again? Mary rose and rushed to the gate, peering down the road as a group of men came into view. She would recognize her son no matter how far away. Why was he here? She was torn between frustration at her treatment in Capernaum, and joy at seeing Yeshua again. It looked like he was bringing a group of disciples with him. She turned to her daughters.

"Sarah, quickly, see how much wine we have and bring the dried dates from the storeroom."

Sarah looked toward the gate. "Should I tell your sons he is here?"

Mary smiled. "I believe they will know soon enough. Rebecca, go next door and see if Hodiah has stew to share, and extra *challah* bread." Joses and Simon would come and welcome him or peacefully stay away, she reasoned, it was James's temper she was concerned about.

In a short time Yeshua and his disciples stood at the gate. His eyes were warm as he looked at Mary. "Peace be upon this house. May we enter, Ima?"

She opened the gate and was warmly embraced. With her hands on his arms she looked up into his face. He had aged during the two years of his ministry, but he looked strong and healthy. "Why did you not see us in Capernaum?" she burst out. "James was angry that you treated us so."

He sighed. "There were reasons, Ima. I know why you and my brothers came. Had you succeeded, you would have been interfering with the plan of my Father."

Suddenly she was ashamed for going along with James. She knew Yeshua was sent to her long ago for a reason, and he would accomplish what the Most High had sent him to do. Why had she listened to James?

"I've wanted to tell them who you are, my son. But each time I sought to do so the Spirit restrained me. If your brothers knew, they would be more supportive of your ministry."

Yeshua motioned for his followers to enter the courtyard. They did so, touching the *mezuzah* briefly and then finding places to sit and rest on the blankets she'd hurriedly put down on the packed earth. Yeshua turned back to her. "Only the Father knows the time, Ima. They must believe in me, not because of your words, but because they have seen the works of the Father."

She took a small breath and nodded her head in understanding. "Come, rest yourself and partake of our Sabbath meal." Then she remembered. "My son, it has been a year since the last time you came. The men sought to do you harm for your words in the synagogue. Are you safe?"

"We are safe. Word has gone out concerning my ministry and the works the Father has done through me. I will be teaching in the synagogue."

She nodded, but fear for his safety still pressed on her heart. However, she said no more. As she left him to oversee the preparation of food for them, she glanced at the small group of disciples. She recognized them and looked for John. He was sitting under the sycamore tree speaking quietly with the one named Andrew. When he felt her glance he looked up, and smiled at her. She would speak to him later. He would tell her of the miracles he'd seen Yeshua perform. She could count on that.

James barely touched the *mezuzah* as he entered the courtyard followed by Rebecca and Hodiah who carried a pot of lentil stew and a loaf of *challah* bread. Mary sighed with relief. They would have enough.

James frowned. "You have come home again, brother. Are you here to stay?" His tone belied his hospitable words.

"No, James. We will be leaving when the Sabbath ends. I have something to share with the people of Nazareth."

James waved a hand. "They almost killed you the last time you were here. Why would you risk your life and the lives of your... ah...disciples, to come here?" He spread one hand to include the family. "Do you wish to bring shame to all of us again?"

"The Father has sent me, and assured me I will not come to harm here."

James stood there staring at Yeshua, clearly exasperated. "Very well, in obedience to the Torah, you are our guest. I shall expect you to keep your word and leave as you have said, after *Shabbat*, and hopefully before there is more trouble."

Yeshua nodded, and when James had turned away, Mary saw a slight smile playing about Yeshua's lips. He caught her eye and raised his eyebrows.

Jerusha and Miriam did not appear with their families and Mary felt it was because of the incident the year before. Their husbands must have required them to celebrate the holy day at home.

The *shofar* sounded across the town of Nazareth, announcing the beginning of the Sabbath. The women placed the food on the table and the *challah* bread in front of James for Yeshua had deferred to him as the head of the family.

The candles were placed on the table in front of Mary and noting the nearness of sundown, Mary quickly lit them with a twig from the small brazier. She covered her head with her mantle and waving her hands over the candles, welcomed the Sabbath. Then she covered her eyes and began the familiar blessing: "Blessed are you, Lord our God, Sovereign of the universe who has sanctified us with his commandments and commanded us to light the candles of *Shabbat*."

As Mary prayed over the candles as she had done each Sabbath of her life, it was as if her heart could hear the prayer lifted up by the other women of Nazareth. Women all over Israel, and indeed wherever Jewish families were gathered, were speaking the same prayers. She imagined Ha'Shem looking down and seeing the lights of thousands of candles as his people rejoiced in the blessings of *Shabbat*.

Sarah and Hodiah gathered the children and the family walked to the synagogue for the brief evening service. Yeshua and his disciples were quiet during the service and while the men glanced at them from time to time, there was no incident.

Jerusha and Miriam greeted Yeshua briefly after a quick glance at their husbands, and with apologetic smiles for Mary, hurried to their homes. The rest of the family returned to the house to enjoy the evening meal.

Rebecca, now twenty-one and too old to throw herself at Yeshua as she did when she was young, instead hovered close by, making sure he had all he wanted of what food they had prepared.

When he smiled up at her, her plain face glowed with adoration, and when she radiated love like this, Mary felt she was almost pretty. She remembered speaking to James for the second time about finding a match for her, although because Rebecca was slow of mind along with being plain, Mary had not been surprised when even the matchmaker shrugged and lifted the palms of her hands in defeat.

Suddenly Mary's thoughts were interrupted as she heard Yeshua stating he would speak at *Shabbat* services the next day. She caught a look between James and Simon. Simon rolled his eyes and shrugged. There was a moment of silence until Joses finally asked the question Mary felt had been on all their minds, "So, brother, what news do you bring us of your travels?"

Mary and the women listened eagerly for before Yeshua could answer, John blurted, "I saw something I would not have believed a year ago. This was the second time I have been awed in this way by the power of Adonai. Jarius, the leader of one of the synagogues, came to the Master to beseech him to come and heal his young daughter who was dying. While we were on our way there, the man's servants came to tell him it was too late, the girl was dead. They didn't want him to trouble the Master. Yet Yeshua told him to have faith, to not be afraid and just trust Adonai. We continued to the man's house. The mourners were already there, weeping and wailing, and the mother of the child was likewise in tears. Yeshua asked them, 'Why all this commotion and weeping? The child isn't dead, she's just asleep.' The people became derisive, for they didn't believe him."

John glanced at Yeshua who gave him an imperceptible nod to continue.

"Yeshua took only myself, James, and Peter into the room with him, along with the parents. He took the child's hand, and he said to her, '*Talitha, koum!* Little girl, I say to you, get up!' At once the girl got up and began walking around; she was about twelve years old. Everyone was amazed, and the Master gave the parents and us strict orders to say nothing about this to anyone. It was obvious the child was hungry, so he then told the parents to give her something to eat."

When he finished, Mary looked at James for his reaction. James studied John closely, then he looked at his oldest brother. "You've told no one else about this? How then can you prove this happened?"

Peter spoke up, one of the few times he did that Mary could remember. He glowered at James. "We do not lie. It happened as John has told you. It was the mourners who spread the story, and the healer who had told the people she was dead." He continued to look directly at James as if daring him to contradict John again.

Joses was speechless, contemplating what he had just heard. Simon was bolder. "You are telling us that Yeshua, our oldest brother, who grew up with us, raised a dead girl to life?"

Peter nodded.

Simon scratched his head and looked up questioningly at his wife. Bithia had paused, her hand in midair as she was serving, to listen to the story, her eyes wide. She shrugged her shoulders and shook her head before continuing to serve.

James rose and beckoned to Hodiah. "Gather the children, we are returning home." Simon stayed a few moments longer. "I'm not sure how to understand what I have heard, but I wish you safe travels, brother." He inclined his head toward Bithia, who rose with their sleeping son in her arms and in a moment they too were gone. Yeshua looked after them, a sadness in his eyes that broke Mary's heart. When would her sons realize who he was?

When Rebecca too had gone to sleep, Mary saw to Yeshua and his disciples and noted they had made themselves comfortable for the night in various parts of the courtyard. The moon was rising as she slipped up to the rooftop to pray.

FORTY

*T*he morning of the Sabbath, Mary walked with the women as they went to the synagogue for the services. She remained calm outwardly, but prayed to herself for safety for Yeshua and that there would not be another incident like the one the year before. It had taken months for the talk to die down. She and her daughters couldn't go to the well without a barrage of questions. To her relief, Yeshua and his disciples sat quietly, only participating in the prayers of the service along with the other men in the congregation.

Watching through the lattice from the room for the women, she caught her breath as she realized the rabbi had nodded to Yeshua. Were they letting him speak again? Yeshua rose and strode to the front as the men in the back near the lattice began to murmur.

"He comes again. Perhaps Adonai has a word for us. I have heard of the miracles he has performed."

"Maybe we were a bit hasty before."

"Perhaps Ha'Shem has touched him to be a prophet. Should we fight against the Most High?"

On the murmurs went until the leader raised his hand for silence.

When Yeshua began to teach, Mary saw astonishment on the faces of the listeners, for he spoke as one who had much learning.

He opened the words of the Torah to them and talked about the kingdom of heaven.

Mary heard hushed comments again.

"Where does this man get all this wisdom?"

"What are all those miracles worked through him we've heard of?"

A tall man nearby asked in a whisper heard by all around him, "Is this not the carpenter's son? Is not his mother called Mary? And his brothers, James, Joses, Simon, and Jude?"

Another man nodded and asked, "And his sisters. Are they not all with us?"

Another harrumphed in disbelief. "How did he suddenly receive authority to do all this?"

Mary sighed. Yeshua had offended them again, but at least they were not shouting angrily at him as before.

Yeshua looked around at the congregation, his eyes filled with sadness. "The only place people don't respect a prophet is in his home town, among his own relatives, and in his own house." He stepped down from the platform and beckoned to three or four people who had brought sick relatives to the synagogue, perhaps hearing he would be there and hoping beyond hope for healing. His face full of compassion, he laid his hands on each one in turn and healed them of their infirmities. A woman near Mary suddenly moved from behind the women's screen and made her way to Yeshua. Mary knew her. She had fallen and broken an arm. It had not been set properly and had healed at an odd angle. She stood before Yeshua, ignoring the men behind her, who murmured at a woman leaving her place. He smiled at her and taking the crooked arm, closed his eyes for a moment. When he opened his eyes, he gently grasped the crooked arm and it straightened in his hands. Her face radiating joy, the woman praised Ha'Shem and raised her arm to show everyone. A hush fell over the congregation and when he had healed the last person, the people parted in awe as he walked out of the building with his disciples.

They returned to the house and this time Jerusha and Miriam came with their families. Obviously Aaron and Nahor were relieved there had been no repeat of the riot of last year.

The family gathered around the table for the midday meal and for the Sabbath prayers. The disciples talked quietly among themselves, glancing at the family surreptitiously. Prior to the meal, Yeshua gathered his small nieces and nephews around him and told them stories, his eyes twinkling. Mary's heart lifted to hear her son and grandchildren laughing together. His brothers watched also and spoke among themselves. *How torn they are,* Mary thought, *between responding to him as the brother they have always known and the rabbi he has become. He is now moving in realms they do not understand.*

Mary enjoyed the fellowship of her daughters but her heart went out to Rebecca who watched Yeshua, her face showing her longing to be at Yeshua's feet as her young cousins were. Mary went to her, putting a gentle hand on her shoulder.

"You see him so seldom, child. Go, enjoy his company."

With gladness Rebecca obeyed and her reward was a wonderful smile from the brother whom she looked to as a father.

As the three stars of evening appeared, Yeshua recognized James as now head of the household, and waited quietly. James intoned the first prayer of *Havdalah*. After the blessing, one cup of wine was filled so full, it overflowed onto the plate it was set on. The wine represented joy. "May the joy of *Shabbat* overflow your week." James then passed the cup so everyone could sip from the cup of joy.

James continued, "Blessed are you, Lord, our God, Sovereign of the universe who creates the fruit of the vine."

Then, holding up the small *besamin* box of cinnamon and bay leaves, "Blessed are you, Lord, our God, Sovereign of the universe, who creates the varieties of spices."

And turning to the specially braided *havdalah* candle, it was lit as James murmured, "Blessed are you, our God, Sovereign of the universe who creates the light of the fire."

James turned to Yeshua and with a lift of his chin, bid him continue with the final prayer.

Yeshua glanced around at his family and his eyes finally rested on his mother as he spoke the last prayer of the evening: "Blessed are you, Lord our God, Sovereign of the universe, who separates between sacred and secular, between light and darkness, between Israel and the nations, between the seventh day and the six days of labor. Blessed are you, Lord, who separates between sacred and secular."

The candle was returned to Yeshua, who turned it upside down at an angle, slowly extinguishing the flame in the wine on the plate where the cup of joy overflowed. As the flame sputtered out, Yeshua said, "May the light of *Shabbat* linger in your hearts throughout the coming week."

The *shofar* sounded, ending *Shabbat*. Before leaving, James studied the face of his older brother. "I do not understand what you are doing, but I pray you will come to no harm."

Mary realized it was difficult for James to say even that. His love for his elder brother warred within him, for a moment stronger than his frustration at a ministry he didn't understand.

Yeshua embraced him and his brothers in turn, and watched them go. Rebecca had waited eagerly for his individual attention and her face glowed when he turned to her.

"You are a great help to Ima, Rebecca. How fortunate she is to have you near her. You have been well?"

"Oh yes. I pray for you every day and ask Ha'Shem to watch over you. I wish I could go with you. I could help you and make sure you had a nice supper every night."

"Ah, that would be generous of you, dear sister, but what would Ima do without your help?"

Rebecca hung her head for a moment considering, and then nodded. "Ima needs me more?"

"Yes, Rebecca. Ima needs you more. You must never forget that you are one of Ha'Shem's chosen ones. You are dear to him."

She tilted her head and thought. "I belong to Ha'Shem," she murmured simply.

Yeshua drew her to himself and kissed her on the top of her head. "I will cherish your prayers."

Finally, she reluctantly bid him goodnight. As she turned toward the house and her bed, Mary heard the soft click of the gate and knew that Yeshua had slipped out to walk the hills and pray to his Father as he had done so many times before leaving home for his ministry.

She smiled as she listened to the soft snores of one or two of the disciples then once again climbed slowly up to the rooftop and knelt, letting the moonlight wash over her. A night bird sang his praise from the sycamore tree as she bowed her head and sought the comfort of Ha'Shem, lifting her cares before him in the darkness.

❧

Early in the morning, shortly after the sun rose, Mary, Sarah, and Rebecca quickly prepared fruit, some bread, and diluted wine for Yeshua and his disciples as they prepared to leave. Mary wrapped bread, cheese, and date cakes from the crock in the storeroom for their journey.

To Mary's surprise, James entered the courtyard and stood by the gate watching as the disciples thanked Mary for her hospitality and then left one by one.

Yeshua turned to Mary. "I bid you farewell, Ima. I do not know when we shall see each other again, perhaps at Passover in Jerusalem? He embraced her and Rebecca, then put a hand on the shoulder of his brother Joses who had risen early also, preparing to go to the carpenter shop. "Farewell, my brother. I will see you again."

"May the Most High watch over you, Yeshua." Joses responded, his voice breaking.

Yeshua paused by the gate as he and James regarded each other. James didn't speak, but Yeshua nodded as though he had, and following his ragged band of disciples, he walked out of Nazareth again.

James turned to Mary and shook his head. "I do not know what to believe, Ima. There is no doubt he can do miracles, but where did he suddenly get his power? How did he become this… this *prophet* or whatever he is?"

Mary felt the words on the tip of her tongue, yet still Adonai had not released her to speak. When would be the time? Instead, she put her hand on her son's arm. "I'm sure it will all be clear in Adonai's time, James."

He shook his head and Mary could almost feel the turmoil in his mind. With a sigh, James nodded to Joses. Together they departed for the carpentry shop, leaving questions hanging in the air.

FORTY-ONE

The town of Nazareth was shocked by the news. Word came to them that Herod, the bloody king, had beheaded John the Baptist. Mary, hearing the details, grieved in her spirit for Elizabeth and Zechariah. Had he accomplished all he was given to do? Fear rose in her heart for her eldest son. What would be his fate when he accomplished what Ha'Shem had given him to do? Would he end up like John, a victim of the corrupt society in which they lived? Surely not. She clung to the words of the angel that he would save their people from their sins and take the throne of David. Perhaps the people, seeing the miracles, would make him king instead of the merciless Herod, and he would vanquish their enemies once and for all. But would that not plunge their people into violence and war? The thoughts played in her mind over and over...my son...my son.

He is my son also, beloved woman. He does the work I sent him to do. Your trust must be in me and not in what you hope. Trust me.

Mary bowed her head. "I do trust you, Oh God Who Sees Me. Forgive me for seeking only my own desires. May your will be done."

A soft breeze brushed her cheek as it had many times through the years, like the touch of an angel's wing, and as before, she was strengthened and peace settled on her soul.

228 Diana Wallis Taylor

Yeshua rarely appeared in Nazareth after that visit—usually only at night, to visit Mary, leaving again the next day. Sometimes he brought a few disciples, and sometimes Mary was blessed by a visit with Jude. He could not allow it to be known that he was there lest people flock to Mary's home and disrupt the family, for the stories of his miracles continued to abound as travelers came to Nazareth and spread news of the things they had seen and heard. Mary and her family listened with amazement. The husband of a family returning from visiting family in Bethsaida spoke outside the synagogue one Sabbath.

"We were in a crowd of thousands listening to Yeshua speak near Bethsaida. People were spread out all over the hills, yet we could hear every word he spoke. We were there for hours and then people began to be restless and hungry. After conferring with his disciples, he asked the people to sit down on the grass in groups of fifty. He took what appeared to be a young boy's lunch of loaves and fish and blessed the small meal. Then he sent the basket out to the crowds. When the basket reached me, I was hesitant to take food lest there not be enough for those near me, but when I took out bread and some fish, to my amazement, the same amount reappeared in the basket! The basket kept making the rounds of each group and all were fed. The disciples picked up twelve baskets of what was left over!"

Mary listened and her heart swelled at this amazing story. Yeshua was truly serving his heavenly Father. Miriam and her husband Aaron stood next to Mary, and Aaron was shaking his head in amazement.

"So many stories of miracles have come to us. It is all so hard to believe." Aaron stroked his beard. "Yet I saw with my own eyes the people Yeshua healed when he came this last time."

Miriam nodded. "I knew the woman who had the broken arm. I had seen her at the well with her arm bent at an angle. I'm sure it pained her and made it hard to do her household tasks. After

Yeshua prayed for her, the arm was normal. We cannot deny the call from Ha'Shem for our brother to preach about the kingdom, yet I don't understand how he is able to heal. We have heard of blind eyes opened, the deaf hearing again, lepers cleansed, and that he has even raised one from the dead. How can he do these things? We never saw any evidence of these powers when he lived with us all those years."

Mary smiled at them. "Even a rabbi is not considered ready to teach until he is at least thirty. The Most High has chosen him for a great ministry. When he performs miracles, the people flock to him and he is able to share the message Ha'Shem has given him to share. We can rejoice that he was with us as long as he was." Once again, she wanted so much to say more, but knew it was not her place to share. She could only pray for the eyes of her family to be opened.

The rest of her family had been listening along with others from the village. James was tight-lipped and Joses and Simon said nothing. Finally, people began to disperse toward their homes. Joses picked up his son, and he and Sarah escorted Mary home. James lifted his chin and Mary knew he and Hodiah would join them along with the children. She glanced at Simon but he gave her a slight shake of the head. Bithia was in the early stages of pregnancy and Mary knew she was not feeling well. They would spend the Sabbath at home.

Stories of miracles and also the anger of the Sanhedrin trickled back to Nazareth as the fame of Yeshua spread. As she walked, Mary sighed inwardly. Why did he anger the leaders so much? Why did it matter if he healed someone on the Sabbath? They would help one of their donkeys out of a ditch on the Sabbath, and give their animals food and water. Why not the water of Ha'Shem and the gift of wholeness for those who suffered? She pondered these thoughts a great deal, yet found no answer.

FORTY-TWO

The fall came and with it the Feast of Tabernacles, one of the feasts requiring all Jewish men to travel to Jerusalem. It was the third year of his ministry and Yeshua had come quietly during the night seeking rest from the rigors of his travels. He and Mary had talked quietly into the night as he shared with her some of the events and miracles he had done through the Father. Because she knew who he truly was, he could be himself, just her oldest son, for a short time.

The dawn was breaking over the mountains and there was a slight nip to the air. Mary had quietly sent word to her daughters and Simon that he was there. Since Mary's family was so large and they frequently came together, the neighbors did not suspect the presence of her oldest son. It had been a time of family sharing and Mary could see Yeshua visibly relax, yet she sensed something different, a sense of sorrow that his eyes couldn't hide from her. Sometimes she saw him gaze in the direction of Jerusalem, his expression unreadable.

Yeshua was breaking fast with James and Joses. The conversation had been mundane with occasional laughter. Suddenly James addressed Yeshua as they ate together. "The Feast of Tabernacles approaches, brother, shall you depart from here to go to Judea? Your disciples need to see the works that you are doing. For no one does anything in secret while he himself seeks to be known openly. If you truly do these things, show yourself to the world."

Mary paused in her serving. She realized what James was asking Yeshua to do, even in sarcasm. Was it time for her son to let the world know who he truly was? She waited for Yeshua to answer.

Yeshua picked up a piece of bread and contemplated it a moment. Then he looked up at James, his expression thoughtful.

"My time has not yet come, but your time is always ready. The world cannot hate you, but it hates me because I testify of it that its works are evil. You go up to this feast. I am not yet going up to this feast for my time has not yet fully come."

James stared at him and flung one hand in the air. "Again you speak in riddles...your time? What time are you waiting for?"

Yeshua remained silent.

With a heavy sigh of frustration, James rose, and, nodding to Joses, he bent to gather their traveling bags. Simon waited at the gate to join them.

Mary approached them. "A good journey, my sons. I will pray for your safe return. Thank you for the shelter for our use." Her sons had brought branches and formed a shelter in their courtyard. As the Lord required, the family would occupy the shelter for eight days as they thanked Ha'Shem for his provision for them during the year.

Sarah began clearing the table and Yeshua rose. Shallum had been sitting next to Yeshua, obviously devoted to his uncle. Mary smiled at the little boy. "Would you see if there are any eggs this morning?"

Shallum nodded. He liked the chickens and being responsible for gathering the eggs for the day.

Mary walked with Yeshua to a corner of the courtyard under the sycamore tree. "You will not go to Jerusalem now?"

"I must not go openly at this time, Ima. It is best I go alone. I will be recognized soon enough. My disciples wait for me outside

Nazareth but we will travel by twos and threes so not to draw attention."

"My son, I fear the Jewish leaders. You anger them with your actions. Is it necessary to antagonize them?"

He smiled down at her. "I will come to no harm, Ima. I must finish the work of the Father."

"And then?"

"Let us not speak of unknown things, Ima. I covet your prayers for me. You know who I truly am and that is a comfort to me. Soon enough the world will know. But not until the Father's time."

He embraced her and kissed her on the forehead. "I do not know when we shall see each other again. Perhaps at Passover?"

"It is a long time until spring, but I shall be there at Passover, my son. I will look for you."

He nodded, and pulling the cowl of his mantle over his head to hide his face, he stepped through the gate and began walking quickly up the road.

Mary looked after him until he turned a corner and was out of sight. A feeling of unease came over her; was it a portent of something to come? Would he finally reveal himself at Passover? He had the will of people behind him, but was it enough to take on Rome?

FORTY-THREE

*J*oses entered the courtyard, dusty and tired from the long walk from Jerusalem. He put down his traveling bag and sat down on the wooden bench. He put his face in his hands and Sarah quickly brought some fruit and cheese for refreshments. Mary poured a cup of wine and handed it to him.

"It was a good festival in Jerusalem? And your brothers?" She sensed there was more on his mind and waited quietly for him to speak.

"James has gone to his house as has Simon. Jude sends his regards to you, and left us at the road to Cana." He pursed his lips and stared at her a moment. "As to your eldest son, who would not go with us when we left for Jerusalem, evidently he changed his mind."

"He came to Jerusalem?"

"At first people were asking where he was, especially members of the Sanhedrin. We were sure he hadn't come, since they are so anxious to stop him. But then, suddenly, there he was, sitting on the Temple steps, teaching the people!" Joses shook his head at the memory.

He grabbed a few grapes and popped them in his mouth and took a bite of the cheese, washing it down with the diluted wine. Then he waved the cheese in his hand at Mary. "He will be arrested, you know. You defend him, yet you know he angers the leaders. It is enough to teach the people but when he calls the leaders 'white-washed tombs full of dead men's bones', what does he expect?"

"Joses, what happened in Jerusalem?"

"The sun was up in and the morning air was crisp. We were singing, '*God is my salvation. I am confident and unafraid; for YAH ADONAI is my strength and my song, and he has become my salvation!*' The procession of priests entered the Temple court reciting the great *Hallel*. We were following the priest as he ascended to circle the altar seven times. Then suddenly, as the priest was making his appeal to God to provide water for the people, just as he was pouring out the water libation from the golden pitcher onto the altar, who should interrupt but my eldest brother, Yeshua, who stood up and proclaimed loudly, 'If anyone thirsts, let him come to me and drink. He who believes in me as the Scripture has said, out of his heart will flow rivers of living water.'

"Ima, did you hear that? He didn't tell the people to go to Ha'Shem. No, he stood there quoting the prophet Isaiah and told the people to come to *him*! He stood there proclaiming to be God! Ima, the humiliation of it! The priests were furious; the people exploded in an uproar, Jude was looking for a route of escape, and Simon and I were shaking. James was in shock."

Mary's heart pounded. "Was Yeshua arrested?"

Joses shook his head. "The Temple guards ran in his direction then stopped and retreated. Maybe they lost sight of him in all the confusion. We didn't wait around. We dragged James away and got out of there. We quickly left the city and came home."

His voice broke with sudden tears. "How can we ever come to Jerusalem again, or show our faces at the synagogue after this?"

Joses put down his food to embrace Shallum, who had run at the news his father was home. He pulled the boy onto his lap. He looked up at Mary and Sarah, his face showing bewilderment.

"Ima, Sarah, he healed a blind man, a man who had been blind since birth. He gave him new eyes. Do you understand what he did? He prayed for the man and the man grew new eyes! All the leaders could do was rant and rave that he had healed on the Sabbath and was a sinner!"

Sarah sat down next to her husband. "Did you say the man had no eyes and Yeshua gave him new eyes and he could see?"

"Yes, that is what happened. We were all witnesses."

Mary pondered this amazing deed by Yeshua. "And still they did not arrest him?"

Joses shook his head. "They fear the people, Ima. If they arrested him, the crowds would riot and bring the Roman soldiers to the Temple. Even at this latest incident at Sukkot, there was a ripple of voices from the crowd claiming him to be the Messiah. I've even heard murmurs that there is a movement to make Yeshua a king."

She considered his words. Was this then his time? Would he now take the throne of his father, David? She longed for answers, yet Ha'Shem was silent.

Sarah gave Mary a look of sympathy. No one in the family knew what to do about Yeshua and his fame grew by the day. She rose and began gathering the platters for the evening meal. Rebecca, who had listened to the conversation, frowned, and Mary could see she was puzzling over this news. In Rebecca's world, Yeshua could do no wrong. She would not see or believe the storm clouds that were gathering over him.

James and Simon did not appear with their families and Mary was relieved. She did not want to talk with James right now. It was enough that they had a quiet meal, and Joses and Sarah retired when Shallum was asleep.

Mary waited until Rebecca also slept, and then quietly made her way to the roof, her place of sanctuary where Ha'Shem met her in prayer. She knew better than to ask what would become of Yeshua and his ministry, but instead asked for strength to meet whatever the future held for her.

When you are weak, beloved woman, then I am strong. You must lean into my strength and know that there will be sorrow, but remember the words of the psalmist: joy will come in the morning. Let that sustain you for much is to come that you will not understand.

She bowed her head, lost in prayer for some time, until the hooting of an owl brought her back to the present. She rose and making her way down the steps in the dark, sank wearily onto her pallet and in moments drifted into a troubled sleep.

⌒

Mary and Rebecca walked slowly to the marketplace. The heavy heat of Elul was upon them, and, though it was early morning, the sun already beat down on the streets, a signal of the stifling day to come. Mary looked toward the fields that lay fallow, with grain stalks still bearing some sheaves. It was nearing the end of the Sh'mitah year, the seventh year of the Jewish cycle. No fields were to be reaped, nor grapes harvested. Gates to vineyards and the fields were open to the poor and widowed, for according to the Word of the Lord, the seventh year was a year to let the land rest. Mary's family, along with the other families of Nazareth, had reaped a good harvest the year before. Grain was stored, dates and olives were preserved, and wineskins were filled with the fruit of the vine as women trampled the grapes in winepresses. The sixth year had been a bountiful year as the Lord promised in the Torah, and all prepared for the Sh'mitah year.

Mary's thoughts turned to the coming day of Yom Teruah and Rosh HaShannah, the first day of the month of Tishri, and the beginning of the Jewish civil year. With Rosh HaShannah also came the beginning of the ten days of awe, when every Jew examined his life and confessed his sins to Ha'Shem. Each person was to search their heart for grievances held against God and one another, for acts of pettiness or unkindness committed and to offer prayers to Adonai for his mercy and forgiveness to Israel as a nation for yet another year. At the end of the ten days of awe came the holiest day of celebration, Yom Kippur…the Day of Atonement.

In Mary's mind she was a young girl again, sitting at the feet of her father as he explained all that occurred on that holiest of days. She could see his eyes alight and hear the timbre of his voice as he talked….

The High Priest leaves his home seven days before the holy day to study and review every detail of the prescribed ritual for no mistakes can be made. In case anything happens to him, they also prepare another priest to take his place.

But what could happen to him, Papa?

I will get to that, child, now you must listen.

On Yom Kippur, it is such a holy day that the priest changes his clothes and bathes several times. It is said he washes his hands and feet ten times. Then he must cast lots and choose between two goats—one to be offered as a sacrifice and the other to be driven into the Judean wilderness to die as a "scapegoat."

What is a scapegoat, Papa?

He carries the sins of the people away. Even the priest must sacrifice a young bull for his own sins and the sins of all the priests. When the High Priest enters the Holy of Holies for the first time, he is dressed in white linen.

The people stand outside, waiting, as he makes first an offering of incense, filling the room with aromatic smoke. When that is accepted, he enters a second time with the blood of the young bull. The third time he enters he takes the blood of the goat that had been sacrificed and sprinkles it on the altar. Then the High Priest lays his hands on the scapegoat and makes confession of the sins of the people. This is the only time he speaks the name of the Most High. Then the people part, making a pathway, as another priest, chosen for this task, leads the animal toward the desert.

What happens to the goat in the desert? Does he let it go?

No, child, the animal is taken to a deep ravine some twelve miles from Jerusalem and pushed over a steep cliff. When the news of the animal's death is relayed back to the High Priest, there are final ceremonies and the day ends with great rejoicing. The fast of Yom Kippur is broken and we can return to our homes with renewed assurance that God will dwell in fellowship with Israel for yet another year, abiding by the laws of God.

This Yom Kippur ushered in a year that had great meaning: it was the Year of Jubilee. Every forty-nine years on the Jewish calendar, one year was set aside by God to give freedom to his people. It was a year to let slaves go free, to return property to the original owners, to forgive debts that had been held. It was a year of renewal and joy. As Mary considered this gift of Jubilee, she thought of her son. Would this not be the year for him to rise up and fulfill the calling on his life? Would he not set his people free from the bondage of Rome? She wrapped her arms around herself and let the thoughts run rampant in her mind.

Oh Ha'Shem, could this be the year I birthed him for? Is this his time?

She waited for the presence of the One she had given her whole life to; the One for whom she had endured the dark time of the birth of his son. Surely he would confirm her thoughts and give her that hope. But this time, the heavens were silent.

FORTY-FOUR

*M*ary had only ever been in Jerusalem for the Passover, first with her parents and then with Joseph and their children. She had never traveled to it for Yom Kippur. As she thought back, her heart grieved for the loved ones who were no longer with her, even for Passover; Joseph's father, Jacob, then the sudden and unexpected death of Joseph; the fever that took her parents, and finally the death of her dear mother-in-law, Rachel. Mary had borne eight children, and now was blessed with three daughters-in-law, two sons-in-law, and almost fourteen grandchildren. The family gatherings were noisy and usually a joyous occasion, except when the subject of her eldest son came up.

While his brothers loved him, they still thought he was mad, and Mary felt that Yeshua embarrassed them. They could not reconcile the brother who had stepped up as head of the household at the age of sixteen when their father died to this strange rabbi some called a prophet who traveled the length and breadth of their land, and in some cases neighboring lands, to teach and preach his gospel that the kingdom of heaven was at hand.

A flock of birds flew overhead, calling to one another and breaking her reverie. She glanced at Rebecca, walking by her side, the one daughter who had not married. Rebecca seemed content to take care of her mother and help in the household. The village women tsked over Rebecca's unmarried state, but both the neighbors and Mary understood the limitations of her youngest daughter. Rebecca rarely complained and with childlike faith enjoyed each day as it dawned.

When they neared the well, some of the village women gathered there were talking. When they saw Mary they suddenly stopped. She knew she was the topic of conversation...again. Her daughter-in-law, Sarah, had already gotten their water for the day but Mary had a list of spices she needed to replace. Her intent was to nod at them and pass by, but they had seen her and in a moment she and Rebecca were surrounded.

A woman called Havilah seemed to be leading the group. "Mary, we see you so seldom these days. How is that son of yours, the one who is traveling all over the country, supposedly healing everyone?"

Mary sighed. "He is well. I have not seen him for a while."

Havilah persisted. "We were just wondering. How is it that he is able to do these so-called miracles we hear about? When he lived among us he did nothing miraculous. He was just a carpenter. How do you explain what he is doing?"

What should she say? She sent a silent prayer to Ha'Shem for wisdom. Finally, she looked at each of their faces in turn: some were sympathetic, some judgmental, some just showing curiosity.

"All down through the generations of our people, Ha'Shem has called out those he wanted to use for his purposes; our lawgiver, Moses, Daniel, Elijah, Jeremiah, and many others in the Tanakh. I have known the hand of Ha'Shem was upon Yeshua from the time he was a boy. It was only when the Most High called Yeshua at last to serve him that he began his ministry. I cannot explain how he does what he does any more than I can explain the wind."

Another woman spoke up. "I hear he fed thousands with a few loaves of bread and some fish. Does he call down food from heaven? When he's hungry, does bread rain upon him?" Some of the other women tittered behind their hands.

Rebecca, always ready to defend the brother she adored, started to speak up, but Mary felt enough was said and silenced her daughter with a hand on her arm. She sought for something positive to say, but just as she was about to speak, Dorcas, an older woman, well-respected in the village, joined them. Her eyes flashed as she spoke.

"What is this? Does not our neighbor Mary have enough on her mind? Do you not remember Reba, the woman who had the crooked arm? When Yeshua came to the synagogue that day, did he not pray for her and it became straight? If he is a prophet of the Most High, who are we to sit in judgment? If Ha'Shem has called Mary's son to serve him, let us not speak as foolish women lest we bring judgment on our own heads."

Mary could have hugged Dorcas. The other women hung their heads and, with brief apologies, changed the subject.

As Mary turned away to continue her errand, Dorcas caught up to her. "I do not know the path Ha'Shem has chosen for your son, Mary, but I believe in him, and pray for him. This must all be very hard on you and the family." Her eyes were filled with sympathy.

"Thank you, Dorcas, for your kind words. Yes, my sons and family love him as their elder brother, but I'm afraid my sons do not support this ministry of his."

"I remember your son when he was growing up. He was always kind and helpful to the other children. He became a kind and compassionate man. I'm sure you are very proud of him. No doubt Ha'Shem has indeed called him to be a prophet." Dorcas glanced at the chattering women. "Do not let them upset you, Mary. They must question what they do not understand."

The woman's kindness overwhelmed her and Mary felt tears close to the surface. She could only nod as Dorcas put a hand on her shoulder and then walked away.

"Ima, it was nice of her to defend Yeshua. I'm glad she spoke up for you."

"Yes, Rebecca, it was kind. It is good to have a friend, isn't it?"

They proceeded to the marketplace and Mary was able to purchase what she had come for. As they started home, Mary led them down a side street, away from the village well.

FORTY-FIVE

The feast of Hanukkah had come and gone, but Yeshua had not returned to Nazareth. Mary treasured every bit of news that she could glean of him. Travelers came through Nazareth, occasionally bringing news, and Jude came when he could, but work was keeping him busy in Cana. He sold the woodcarvings he did in his spare time, and also fished, using Nathanael's boat. Now that Nathanael had Jude to look out for his daughter, his father-in-law had joined the band of Yeshua's followers. As Yeshua moved through the countryside, preaching the gospel that the kingdom of heaven was at hand, Nathanael sent word home from time to time of their travels. Jude was able to then share with Mary where Yeshua had gone and some of the miracles he had performed.

Now she sat with Jude in her small courtyard, listening eagerly.

"He speaks in parables, Ima. The masses do not understand, but he explains to his disciples later."

"And his miracles? What has he done lately that you know of?"

Jude shook his head. "If I had not heard it from a trusted friend, I would not have believed it."

"Tell me, my son. I want to hear all you can share with me."

"Ima, he raised a man from the dead who had been in the tomb four days."

She put a hand to her heart and stared at him. "Dead four days? He would be decomposing by then."

"Let me start at the beginning. In the village of Bethany, there are two sisters, Mary and Martha, and a brother, Lazarus, who befriended Yeshua. He stays with them often when he comes to Jerusalem but wants to stay outside the city. Well, Lazarus became ill and word was that Yeshua was in the region of Perea. They sent a messenger to tell Yeshua to come quickly, that his friend Lazarus was gravely ill and needed him. For some reason, Yeshua delayed, and by the time he reached Bethany, his friend Lazarus was dead. The mourners were there and Mary and Martha were devastated that he didn't come in time." Jude's eyes lit up and he put a hand on Mary's arm.

"He told Mary and Martha that their brother would rise again, but Yeshua had taught them about the resurrection, and they believed he was speaking about the end of the age. Yeshua asked to see where they had laid Lazarus and the sisters took Yeshua to the tomb. When they got there, Yeshua asked the men to roll away the stone."

"He asked them to roll away the stone of a new burial? Did the men do that?"

"Yes, my friend said they were reluctant, but did as he asked. Then he looked up at the heavens and spoke out loud, 'Father I thank you that you have heard me. And I know that you always hear me, but because of the people who are standing by, I said this, that they may believe you sent me.'"

Mary held her breath. "And...?"

"Ima, he just cried out in a loud voice, 'Lazarus come forth!' and the man came out of the tomb, still wrapped in his grave clothes!"

Mary knew that only God could do such a thing. What could she say to her youngest son who sat there bewildered even now by what he'd shared?

"What do you believe about Yeshua, my son?"

Jude shrugged, his eyebrows knit together as he sought an answer. "That he has been chosen by God to be a prophet, and to share the good news that the kingdom of heaven is at hand."

"Do you believe a mere prophet could raise a man who had been dead four days?"

"He has this power, Ima, power to do miracles. Does this not come from God?"

"Did not your brother James say that only God could do the things Yeshua does?"

"Yes, but Yeshua is not God. It would insult Ha'Shem to allow him to call himself that. He grew up with us, worked with us. I have known him all my life. Ha'Shem inhabits the heavens, not the earth."

"My son, each man or woman must decide for themselves who he is. I cannot tell you. In time, I believe we will know, but Ha'Shem has not revealed it as yet." It was all she could say. Yeshua had told her his family must believe for themselves, not because she revealed to them all who he was. It was a hard task, but she had been obedient and kept that knowledge to herself. She could only pray the eyes of his family would be opened one day and Ha'Shem would release her to tell the story of his birth.

When Jude had gone, Mary at least knew that Yeshua had also traveled to Samaria, then back to Galilee, healing the sick and teaching the people. He'd gone to Perea and then Jericho and finally back to Bethany.

The Passover was drawing near once more, and Mary and her family made preparations to journey once again to Jerusalem. Mary loved Passover and the joyous ceremonies in the Holy City, but more than that, she hoped to see Yeshua. Jude had also told her that the Sadducees and the Pharisees hung around Yeshua like vultures, trying to find a way to trip him up or catch him in an act of fraud. It seems he angered them most by performing miracles of healing on *Shabbat*.

This time in Jerusalem, Mary spoke with James about leaving the family group to stay a day or two with her friend Susanna. Assured that she would rejoin the family at the Passover meal, James reluctantly gave permission. Nearly forty-nine now, Mary was feeling her years. As long as it was to Susanna's house and that she was not seeking Yeshua, James indulged her. Her daughters had lifted the task of preparing for Passover from her shoulders years before, and she was free to enjoy visiting an old friend, accompanied as ever by her devoted Rebecca.

Mary was surprised to find one of her son's followers staying with Susanna as well. The follower was called the Magdalene, but her name was Mary also. The Magdalene shared her story of being delivered by Yeshua from seven demons that had tormented her from childhood. She was devoted to Yeshua and followed his ministry.

"It is my joy to share in the material needs of the Master and his disciples, my lady. I have funds I receive from time to time from my uncle who runs the family boat-building business in Magdala." Mary found she liked this forthright woman—one of many who shared their financial means with Yeshua out of the fullness of their hearts.

John came to Susanna's home the evening they arrived to tell Mary that Yeshua would be entering Jerusalem the next day. "The entire city is in an uproar and the people are excited that he is coming again. Dear lady, he has healed and fed thousands. The city is preparing for the entrance of a king." John was exultant. "Now they will truly know who he is!"

Mary thanked him, but as he slipped away, rather than being elated at his news, she felt a sense of foreboding. Was he indeed coming at last as a king to claim the throne of David? What would the Romans do? What would the Sanhedrin do? It was a holy time, to celebrate the Passover as Moses had instructed them to do. Why did this heaviness fill her being? Could Yeshua still come to harm?

Susanna, along with Mary, the wife of Zebedee, mother of the disciples John and James, planned to watch with Mary and Rebecca from an upper window of the house that overlooked the main street of Jerusalem. The Magdalene would leave the house early in the morning. She wanted to go and walk with the other disciples behind Yeshua as he entered the city.

When Rebecca had gone to sleep, Mary returned to the main room of the house where Susanna had prepared a beverage and some dried fruit. Mary was eager to hear more news of her son from one who had followed him and seen his ministry firsthand.

Mary turned to the Magdalene. "You saw Lazarus raised from the dead?"

"Yes, dear lady, I was there. I saw him raised from the dead and restored to his sisters. There were many people there including members of the Sanhedrin and some of the priests. They could not deny this mighty miracle by the Master. Word came back to us later that they were plotting to kill Lazarus as well as the Master, saying the people were deceived. Yet I know that the only ones deceived were those leaders who chose to ignore what they saw with their own eyes."

Mary shook her head. "I fear something is going to happen. He cannot continue to anger the priests and leaders as he does."

"That is why we left Bethany and journeyed through Samaria and Galilee. The Master healed ten lepers but only one came back to thank him. He was a Samaritan. Yeshua also healed a blind man called Bartimaeus, a man blind from birth. The man kept crying out to Yeshua until the Master asked the blind man to be brought before him. Yeshua asked him, 'What do you want me to do for you?' The man replied, 'Lord, that I may receive my sight.' Yeshua didn't even lay hands on the man. He just said, 'Receive your sight; your faith has made you well.' Dear lady, the man could instantly see again!"

Mary marveled at this but held her peace. "Tell me more."

Magdalene thought. "Well, in Jericho, we ate at the home of a tax collector named Zacchaeus who became a follower of the Master. He vowed to restore any money he had taken fourfold!"

Mary smiled at that. "A tax collector offering to give back money he'd stolen in taxes? I would say that was a miracle."

The women smiled with her.

"Where is Yeshua now, Mary?"

The Magdalene looked wistful. "He is back with Lazarus and his sisters in Bethany. He will leave from there to enter the city tomorrow. Most of his followers stayed in the garden of Gethsemane; we could not all crowd into the house of his friends."

Susanna had been quietly listening. "I imagine it has been a wonderful thing to travel with Yeshua and see the miracles."

Magdalene nodded. "There were the teachings too. I wish you all could have heard him. He is like no other rabbi I have ever heard...such wisdom and knowledge. I learned much of the Torah from a friend many years ago when I was growing up. He tutored me at the request of my father because girls could not go to Hebrew school. Yet when I hear the Master speak, he makes the Torah come alive. He tells us the true meaning behind the laws of Moses. I have listened for hours and not been aware of the time passing."

Magdalene thought a moment. "I remember an amazing story John told me one day. He said they had left the Master to dismiss the crowds and were out on the Sea of Galilee. A storm rose and they feared for their lives. Suddenly, John saw a figure out on the water. The disciples were afraid that it was a spirit. Then one cried out, 'It is the Lord!' He was walking on the water!"

The women looked at each other. This was a strange tale to comprehend. Magdalene went on. "Peter, who always jumps ahead of himself, cried out, 'Lord, if it is you, bid me come to you on the water.' Yeshua told him, 'Come.' He climbed out of the boat and actually walked on the water, until he became fearful of the waves and started to sink. When he cried out to the Lord, Yeshua reached out and saved him and they both got in the boat."

Susanna frowned. "Are you sure John did not make up this tale?"

"No, John is the one disciple I would trust above all others. He was telling the truth."

The women were silent for a moment, considering what they had just heard, but Mary knew in her heart why he could do these things. They called her son *Lord*, and he was, but more than that, he was the son of God. Nothing would be impossible for him.

To change the tone of their conversation, Mary shared what it was like raising Yeshua, and how he had to become head of the house at only sixteen when his father died. "He had seven brothers and sisters to be responsible for along with me, his mother. Yet he never complained. He was patient with the other children and they adored him." She sighed. "It made it all the harder, especially for James, when he left and began his ministry. James had idolized him and I think he felt that Yeshua had deserted him, even though he was a grown man and married."

Mary had another thought. She turned to Magdalene. "Will you prepare the Passover for him? Do you know where he will eat the Passover meal?"

"He has not said, but I will prepare along with the other women. The men would not know what to do. The Master will let us know tomorrow where we are to meet."

Mary realized she was weary from her journey and much was happening the next day. She bade the other women good night and retired to her bed. She lay there a moment considering what Magdalene had told her. What would tomorrow hold? Would Yeshua reveal who he was at last? Her mind was too weary to contemplate all the repercussions, and she fell into a deep sleep.

FORTY-SIX

*M*ary rose early in the morning and bowed her head for her morning prayers. Then she asked Ha'Shem to watch over his son and guide him this day. She was apprehensive about what he was about to do; yet there was nothing she could do to stop him.

After a simple breakfast, the women took their places at the upper window of Susanna's house to watch for Yeshua.

It wasn't long before they heard singing and people shouting, praising God for the mighty works they had seen, and the disciples were crying out, "Blessed is the King who comes in the name of the LORD! Peace in heaven and glory in the highest!" The women looked at each other, worried. *King?*

Soon Yeshua came in sight, riding on a donkey's colt. People were flinging palm branches and cloaks in the path before him and dancing in the street just below the window where Mary and the other women watched the festive scene in amazement.

Rebecca waved from the window. "Look, Ima! There is Yeshua, and I see Mary Magdalene and Peter and John. I think Yeshua sees me!"

Mary saw Yeshua lift his head a brief moment. He knew they were there but didn't speak. The jubilant noise of the crowd was almost overwhelming. Hope once again rose in Mary's heart that Yeshua would at last fulfill the words the angel had spoken to her long ago.

Then one of the Pharisees cried out from a side street, "Teacher, rebuke your disciples!"

Yeshua called back, "I tell you that if these should keep silent, the stones would immediately cry out."

The Pharisee's face was red with anger as he angrily whispered with the men standing with him.

Suddenly Mary knew what she wanted to do.

"Take me to the Temple! That is where he is headed. I must speak with him one more time."

She put a cloak around her shoulders and pulled the mantle forward so her face was hidden. She didn't think anyone would know her; she was more worried about her sons seeing her.

As Mary, Rebecca, and Susanna made their way to the Temple through the throng of people, they had to take shelter in an archway as a flock of sheep dashed past, followed by several white doves. There was pandemonium in the Temple again and suddenly Mary knew what Yeshua was doing: driving the animals and moneychangers out of the Temple...again. She hesitated, but then insisted on continuing to the Temple courtyard where, to her surprise, Yeshua had settled himself to teach.

Mary motioned to Susanna and Rebecca to stand with her in the shadows behind one of the pillars of the Temple to listen.

The chief priests and elders were confronting him. "Tell us, by what authority are you doing these things? Or who is he who gave you this authority?"

Yeshua looked around at their self-righteous faces for a moment. "I also will ask you one thing, and answer me. The baptism of John...was it from heaven or from men?"

The leaders, near enough for Mary and the women to hear their whispers, conferred with each other, murmuring and waving their hands as they debated. "If we say from heaven, he will say, 'why then did you not believe him?' But if we say from men, all the people will stone us, for they are persuaded that John was a prophet."

One of the leaders faced Yeshua. "We do not know where it was from."

Yeshua gave a slight shake of his head. "Neither will I tell you by what authority I do these things."

It was the first time Mary had ever heard her son teach the people and she listened spellbound as he spoke again.

He talked about a man who planted a vineyard and then let it out to vinedressers. When it came time for the harvest, the vinedressers sent the owner's servants away empty-handed, beat others, and even cast one servant out of the vineyard. Then the owner sent his beloved son, thinking the vinedressers would respect him. Instead the wicked vinedressers killed the son to steal his inheritance.

"What will the owner of the vineyard do to those wicked vinedressers? He will come and destroy them and give the vineyard to others."

Yeshua looked around at the priests and leaders. "Is it not written, 'the stone which the builders rejected has become the chief cornerstone'? Whoever falls on that stone will be broken; but on whomever it falls, it will grind him to powder."

The anger of the leaders was like the buzzing of a hive of bees that had been disturbed. One started forward toward Yeshua, but the others drew him back.

Then Mary knew Yeshua had spoken this parable against them.

After a few words from the leaders, another man boldly stepped forward. The smug look on his face didn't bode well for Yeshua, but Yeshua watched him approach, his own demeanor calm.

"Teacher," the man began confidently, "We know that you say and teach rightly and you do not show personal favoritism, but teach the way of God in truth; is it lawful for us to pay taxes to Caesar or not?"

Mary leaned forward to hear his answer.

"Why do you test me? Show me a denarius." The man produced one from his sash.

"Whose image and inscription does it have?"

The man glanced at the coin. "Caesar's."

"Then render to Caesar the things that are Caesar's, and to God the things that are God's."

The man glanced back at those who had sent him and shrugged. One by one the Pharisees walked away.

Then a group of Sadducees moved forward. Mary knew that they did not believe in the resurrection as the Pharisees did, so she was surprised at their question.

"Teacher, Moses wrote to us that if a man's brother dies, having a wife, and he dies without children, his brother should take his wife and raise up offspring for his brother. Now there were seven brothers and the first took her to wife and died without children. The second brother took her as wife, but died childless, and in like manner, each of the brothers did likewise but none had any children. Last of all, the woman died. Therefore, in the resurrection, whose wife does she become? For all seven had her to wife."

Yeshua answered, "The sons of this age marry and are given in marriage, but those who are counted worthy to attain that age, and the resurrection from the dead, neither marry or are given in marriage. Nor can they die anymore, for they are equal to the angels and are sons of God, being sons of the resurrection. But even Moses showed in the burning bush passage that the dead are raised, for he called the Lord the God of Abraham, the God of Isaac, and the God of Jacob. For He is not the God of the dead, but of the living, for all live to him."

The Sadducees nodded, "Teacher, you have spoken well." And there were no more questions.

Mary had listened a long time and felt her weariness. She needed to rest. As she glanced up at Yeshua she felt his eyes upon her. He knew she was there and in her heart she heard, *Pray, Ima, for my time is at hand.*

FORTY-SEVEN

*D*ear lady, the Master wishes you to join us for the Passover meal. Will you come and help us prepare?" Magdalene stood before her waiting for her answer.

What would James say? Mary waited on that still voice within her. God Who Sees, what would you have me do?

Go with her.

She would talk with James later, but for now, she knew what she must do. Susanna and Rebecca came with her as they followed the Magdalene. Once again, the smell of lamb roasting over the many fires wafted throughout the city. They passed Gentile merchants selling fruit for the *charoset*, eggs, wine, and unleavened bread for those who had nowhere to bake it. The women hurried through the crowded streets to a building on the far side of the city. They climbed the stairs to an upper room and there found Peter and John looking a little uncomfortable, standing by the pile of ingredients for the Passover meal. When they saw the women and realized the Passover *seder* would be taken care of, they broke into smiles of relief.

Susanna looked around. "Do we have lamb?"

John nodded. "Our portion of the sacrifice." He lifted the linen cover on an earthen bowl. The lamb was still warm.

Magdalene frowned. "Where is Judas? Did he buy these things? He has the money bag."

Peter stood back, obviously uncomfortable, his dark eyes unreadable under bushy brows. "I don't know where he is, perhaps with the Master."

Magdalene made a dismissive sound and the women set to work; cutting the fruit for the *charoset*, preparing the bowl of salt water and the parsley, placing the bread and bottles of wine on the table as Rebecca distributed the wooden cups and platters. The women had to make do for containers to hold the special foods familiar to Mary from so many Passovers.

Peter and John stayed out of the way, and Peter made more trips to the top of the stairs to look for his companions than Mary could count. Finally, when all was in readiness, there was the sound of voices and heavy footsteps on the steps. Mary's heart lifted, for along with the other ten disciples Yeshua had called to himself, he was there. She saw his warm smile and relished his embrace.

"Thank you, Ima. It means much to me that you came."

She raised one eyebrow. "You know James will not be pleased with my not returning to the family for Passover."

He smiled again, but there was sadness in his face. "You must listen carefully, Ima, and pray for strength for the hours to come." He turned away and walked toward the table as Mary stood there, uncertain, as the seed of fear began to do its work in her heart.

When Yeshua and his twelve disciples took their places at the long table, Mary and Rebecca along with Susanna and Magdalene began to serve. When all had been placed where it was needed, the women retired to the back of the room to take part there.

Yeshua looked to his right and left, making eye contact with his disciples. "With fervent desire I have desired to eat this Passover *seder* with you before I suffer; for I say to you I will no longer eat of it until it is fulfilled in the kingdom of God."

Mary put a hand to her heart. What did he mean, *before I suffer?* What was he telling them? What did he want her to know?

Yeshua lifted the first cup of wine, gave thanks, and said, "Take this and divide it among yourselves; for I say to you, I will not drink of the fruit of the vine until the kingdom of God comes."

The disciples passed the cup, each taking a sip.

Then Yeshua took the unleavened bread and after offering thanks to the Father, broke the bread and said, "This is my body which is given for you; do this in remembrance of me."

At the end of the *seder*, he took the third cup, the cup of redemption, and lifted it, saying, "This is the new covenant in my blood, which is shed for you."

Yeshua rose from his place and laid aside his outer garment. He took a towel and wrapped it around himself. Then he poured water into a basin and began to wash the disciples' feet.

Mary was aghast. This was the task of the lowest of the servants. She almost rose from her seat, but Magdalene laid a hand on her arm and Mary pursed her lips. It was not up to her to intervene in what Yeshua did. She'd learned that at the wedding in Cana. She sat there, stunned, as Yeshua washed the feet of each of his disciples in turn. When he got to Peter, the big fisherman blustered and pulled back. "Lord, are you washing my feet?"

Yeshua answered, "What I am doing you do not understand now, but you will know after this."

Peter shook his head vehemently. "You shall never wash my feet!"

"If I do not wash you, you have no part with me."

Peter's eyes grew large and he thrust his feet forward. "Lord, not my feet only, but also my hands and my head!"

"He who is bathed needs only to wash his feet, but is completely clean. You are clean, but not all of you."

When he came to Judas, the man jerked his head back and stared at Yeshua. He said nothing while Yeshua washed his feet, but was clearly uncomfortable.

When Yeshua had washed their feet, taken his garments and sat down again, he said to them, "Do you know what I have done to you? You call me Teacher and Lord, and you say well for so I am. If then, your Lord and Teacher, have washed your feet, you also ought to wash one another's feet. For I have given you an example that you should do as I have done to you. Most assuredly, I say to you, a servant is not greater than his master; nor is he who is sent greater than he who sent him. If you know these things, blessed are you if you do them. I don't speak concerning all of you. I know whom I have chosen; but that the Scripture may be fulfilled, 'He who eats bread with me has lifted up his heel against me.' I tell you now, before it comes that when it does come to pass, you may believe that I am he. Most assuredly, I say to you, he who receives whomever I send receives me; and he who receives me receives he who sent me."

Mary watched her son's face and saw that he was deeply troubled. Finally he spoke again. "I say to you, one of you will betray me. And truly the son of Man goes as it has been determined, but woe to that man by whom he is betrayed!"

Mary felt panic rising in her heart. Betrayed? One of his trusted disciples would betray him...in what way? He had told his disciples they were to remember him by drinking wine, like a covenant in his blood, and eating the bread representing his body? She looked at Susanna and the Magdalene.

"What does he mean?" she whispered to Magdalene.

"I am not sure, my lady. These past weeks his step has been heavy and his countenance sorrowful. He has spoken of his death to us many times."

She glanced at Rebecca whose face only showed that she was glad to be there with Mary. The conversation was beyond her. Mary sighed. That was just as well, for there was no way she could explain to Rebecca what her beloved brother was saying.

Yeshua spoke again, "All of you will be made to stumble because of me this night, for it is written: 'I will strike the Shepherd, and the sheep of the flock will be scattered. But after I have been raised, I will go before you into Galilee.'"

Peter shook his head. "Even if all are made to stumble because of you, I will never be made to stumble."

Yeshua turned to his impetuous disciple, and his face was sorrowful. "Assuredly I say to you that this night, before the rooster crows with the dawn, you will deny me three times."

Peter was even more vehement. "Even if I have to die with you, I will not deny you!"

Mary frowned, the turmoil growing within her. He was to be a king, and save his people from their sins. How could he do that if he died? Surely they were misunderstanding him. Perhaps he meant they were to die to their own ambitions. Yet that did not fit with what he was saying. She vowed to speak with him later so he could enlighten her. Surely he would explain more clearly to his mother.

The disciples were in turmoil also. They heard his words on betrayal and were questioning among themselves as to who could do such a thing.

"Lord, is it I?" each one felt compelled to ask him. One of the disciples leaned over and whispered something to John who was on the Master's right. He nodded and asked, "Lord, who is it?"

"It is he to whom I shall give a piece of bread when I have dipped it."

He dipped a piece of bread in the sauce and quietly handed it to Judas. "Go quickly and do what you must do."

Judas looked stricken, but rose quickly and gathering his cloak around him, hurried from the room.

Mary watched the one disciple she had never grown to like, leave, and wondered what errand Yeshua had sent him on.

He to whom I give the bread after I have dipped it.

Yeshua gave the bread to Judas. He was the treasurer. Perhaps the group was in need of something. The other disciples paid no attention to Judas. The thought came again to Mary, *He to whom I give the bread....*

She put a hand to her mouth to keep from crying out, "Stop him!" but Yeshua looked at her and in his gaze she saw resignation and something else—determination.

Oh God Who Sees, give me grace to face whatever it is that you have called me to face. I am afraid for him and I need your strength.

Trust me, beloved woman, for after the darkness will come a great light.

FORTY-EIGHT

As the women began to clean up the remains of the Passover meal, the disciples rose and stood in a group, waiting for word from Yeshua as to what to do next.

Rebecca went to her brother and was embraced. He tilted her chin up with one finger. "Take care of Ima for me, will you?"

She nodded, tears in her eyes. "Will I see you again?"

"One day soon, dear sister."

Mary hurried up to Yeshua. "I do not understand, my son. What is happening?"

He put a gentle hand on her cheek and she covered it with her own as she searched his face.

"We must each do what the Father has called us to do. Your work ended when I began my ministry. You and my earthly father, Joseph, raised me to know the love of a family. I have loved each of you in turn. My work began a few years ago, and it is time for it to end also. I cannot explain to you what is to come, but in time you will understand. Return to the family, Ima; we will spend the night in the garden of Gethsemane. You shall see me tomorrow, but not as you wish to."

Before she could ask another question, he spoke a word to John and then strode out of the room and down the steps. The other disciples followed.

John approached her. "The Master asked me to see you and your daughter safely to your family. Magdalene is to return with Susanna for the night."

As the small group hurried through the streets, Mary pulled her cloak closer around her. On this familiar holiday, it should be a night to rejoice but she shivered involuntarily. Glancing at the shadows, she suddenly looked forward to being surrounded by her family. It was only James she did not want to face.

⁓

James rushed to meet her at the gate as her daughters and grandchildren surrounded her. The children cried, "Sabta, you are here!" Two of them took her hand to lead her into the courtyard of the cousin's home with James walking quickly by her side.

"Ima, we have searched for you. Simon went to Susanna's home and a servant told him you had gone. Where have you been? We have all been worried. Simon, Joseph, and Jude have been out searching for you."

She smiled at him, but before she could speak, Rebecca burst out, "We prepared Passover for Yeshua and his friends!"

James' eyes flashed but Mary cut off his words. "Dear James. I'm sorry to have troubled you so, but Ha'Shem sent me there. He told me to go and I obeyed."

He shrugged and lifted both hands in the air in exasperation. "It is good to obey Ha'Shem, Ima, but could you not have told us?"

"My son, I know you. You would have insisted I return to the family. Besides there was no time."

"My brothers will be here shortly. They will be glad to know you and Rebecca are safe."

Mary sank down on a stone bench as Sarah brought her a cup of goat's milk and some dates for refreshment. Her sons were all here and her grandchildren. Jerusha and Miriam were with their husbands' families and she wished there was a way to bring them also.

When she had rested a short while, her grandchildren gathered around her and she smiled at them. "Shall I tell you a story?"

"Yes!" they chorused.

Suddenly there was a commotion at the gate as Simon, Joses, and Jude burst into the courtyard, their faces reflecting relief when they saw her. James spread one hand.

"Ima was busy preparing Passover for our brother, Yeshua, and his disciples," James informed them, a note of sarcasm evident.

She rose quietly as they approached.

"You must not worry us like this, Ima," Joses was saying. "We feared for you in all the crowds."

"We only knew you left Susanna's home in a hurry. The servant didn't know where you had gone except you went with Magdalene." This from Simon.

As they crowded around her, embracing her in turn, Mary suddenly felt the warmth of Ha'Shem surround her. Sensing the presence of the One she had walked with and trusted for so long, she looked around at her family and knew she could share at last.

"All of you, sit down and get comfortable, I have a story to tell you."

They looked around at one another with raised eyebrows and murmured but did as she asked. When she had all of their attention, she began.

"Many years ago, there was a young girl in a small village in Judea. She was very happy, because she had become betrothed to the one young man in the village that she loved. It was during the time of Hanukkah, the Festival of Lights, and as she was saying her evening prayers, suddenly a great light shone around her and a magnificent being stood before her. She realized it was an angel and bowed her face to the ground. The angel told her not to be afraid, for she had found favor with God and she would conceive and bear a son who would take the throne of his father, David, and save his people from their sins. She did not know what to do with this news for she was a virgin and had not known a man. She asked the angel how this could be and he told her the power of the Most High would overshadow her and the child she would bear would be the son of God."

Joses murmured. "This is a strange story. We have not heard this before...."

Mary went on, "The angel told the young woman that her cousin, who was barren, had conceived a child in her old age, and the young woman was determined to visit this cousin and see for herself. The angel told her that nothing was impossible with God."

James frowned. "Isaiah? The prophet tells of a virgin who would conceive and bear a son."

"Yes, James," she responded. "That is true."

The grandchildren were fascinated. "What happened next, Sabta?"

"The young woman went to see the cousin and it was as she had been told. Her elderly cousin was with child, in her sixth month. The young woman also knew by then that a child grew within her own womb and that the angel's visit was not just a dream. After several months, the young woman returned to her village at last, but it was obvious to her betrothed that she was with child and her betrothed was very angry. He did not believe the story of the angel. He wanted to know who the man was that had fathered her child. He wanted to call off the wedding and decided to divorce her quietly, for he loved her and didn't want her to come to harm."

One of her granddaughters sniffed. "This is a sad story, Sabta."

"No child, it is a happy story, for that night an angel appeared to the young man and told him not to be afraid to take his betrothed as his wife. The angel told him that the child within her was God's child."

Jude was looking at her in a strange way, his mind seeming to turn with her words.

"The couple were happily married, but many people thought the child was the young man's and that they had not waited out their betrothal time. It was hard for him, but he rejoiced that he had been chosen to be the earthly father of God's son. Then one day, terrible news came to the village. There was to be a census. The emperor decreed that each man must return with his family to his city of origin and register. The young wife was nearly ready to give birth and yet she had to ride a donkey all the way to that town and there she gave birth. There were no rooms due to the number of travelers for the census but a good woman took pity on them and not only led them to her clean stable, but helped the young wife with the birth."

Jude was staring at her. "In what town was the child born, Ima?"

She returned his gaze. "Bethlehem."

Mary went on to tell of the shepherds, the Magi, and the young family having to flee to Egypt in the middle of the night to escape the wrath of Herod.

Tears ran down Rebecca's face and the faces of some of the grandchildren when Mary told of Herod's soldiers and the massacre of the little boys in Bethlehem.

One of the grandchildren, Timnah, asked, "Did they ever get to go back home, Sabta?"

"Yes, one night an angel told the young husband that Herod was dead. They returned to the village with the child Ha'Shem had given them, and had other children. God's child grew up in that family well loved by all around him. Only she and her husband and their parents knew their secret, for it was not something the village would believe."

Hodiah spoke up. "Is this young woman someone you know, Mother Mary?"

Mary took a deep breath. "Yes, daughter, I know her very well."

Rebecca frowned. "I don't know this story, Ima."

James interrupted. "It is only a story, Rebecca. Ima is very good at telling stories."

Rebecca persisted. "But I want to know her name."

Mary looked around at the faces of her family and knew that the burden had been lifted.

"Her name was Mary."

FORTY-NINE

*T*here was immediate silence in the courtyard, while in the distance the choirs of the Temple sang the *Hallel*.

Jude looked at his brothers. "Is this only a story, told to entertain us? I believe there is more to it." He turned back to Mary, who anticipated his question.

"Yes, my son. He had a name, given him by Ha'Shem."

"And it was…?"

She sighed. "The angel told me his name was to be…Yeshua."

Jude turned to his brothers. "Did I not tell you his power came from God? How else could the one we grew up with, who lived in our household, do these miraculous things?"

James leaned forward, his forearm on his knee. "Why then did he not do these things when he lived with us? Why did he wait until he left us to do these so-called miracles?"

Simon and Joses murmured among themselves and as Mary looked up, their wives watched her with raised eyebrows, shaking their heads slightly at this preposterous news.

Only Rebecca, in the simplicity of her mind, smiled and nodded. "I know who he is. He is my brother. I believe in him."

James faced her, the turmoil of his mind showing in his face. "Is this just a story, Ima?"

"I have never lied to you, James." She looked around at the others. "Any of you."

Her daughters began gathering the children to prepare them for the night and James finally murmured, "It is late. Surely you are tired from this day. We will talk more of this in the morning."

Mary's heart sank. They didn't believe her. She could only nod as she rose from the bench. She let Sarah and Rebecca lead her to the pallet they had prepared for her and lay down, listening to the rest of the family prepare for the night. An owl hooted softly from somewhere in the darkness and even the sounds from the city finally stilled. It was more than an hour that she lay there waiting for silence and then she rose quietly and made her way to a corner of the courtyard, away from the family. As she looked up, dark clouds gathered in the sky, obscuring the moon from time to time. Her heart was heavy with concern for Yeshua.

Pray, beloved one. Pray for him.

She knelt and bowed her head, lost in prayer as she beseeched the Most High for her son. She was still in prayer when the shadows of night began to give way to the faint light of the dawn, and she became aware that someone was tapping on the gate. Rising, she went to open it and found Magdalene and Susanna along with John.

Magdalene had been weeping. "Dear lady, they have arrested him. You must come with us."

"Arrested him? Who did this?"

John shook his head in disbelief. "The Sanhedrin. They sent the Temple guards to Gethsemane last night and arrested him. They carried clubs and swords as if they were after a hardened criminal. He was betrayed as he told us, but we didn't listen. Judas came into the garden and singled him out with a kiss."

Indignation rose up in her heart. "I heard what Yeshua said and that he was not going out for supplies. Yeshua plainly told you he was the betrayer!"

John flung up his hands. "We just didn't listen. They would have arrested all of us, but the Master persuaded them to let us go, that they had just come for him."

"Did he do anything? Defend himself? Did any of you defend him?"

John shook his head. "We had no weapons, dear lady. Only Peter had a sword and before Yeshua could stop him, he cut of the ear of one of the servants of the High Priest." He looked at Mary's face, almost in bewilderment. "In the midst of their arresting him, the Master reached out and healed the servant's ear!"

"But he didn't stop the arrest in some way?"

"No," said John. "He seemed almost to expect it and was submissive to them. They bound him and took him away."

"All of you who followed him, for years, merely let him be led away?"

"To our everlasting shame, we ran. Even now the disciples hide in the upper room, fearing arrest still."

Mary sighed, deeply. This was not as she had imagined. Why would Yeshua let himself be taken like a common criminal? She closed her eyes briefly and fought for courage. "Where is he now?"

Magdalene glanced at Susanna. "They took him to Caiaphas who condemned him and then they took him to Pilate."

Mary looked from one to the other. "Why would they take him to the governor? Why didn't the Sanhedrin deal with it?"

Magdalene spoke again. "That's what we thought, that the leaders would just have him flogged and let him go. But dear lady, they wanted the death penalty."

Mary's hand flew to her heart. "The death penalty? He's done nothing worthy of death."

John almost spat the words. "We cannot put anyone to death, the Romans took that right from us. Pilate had to order his death."

"And he did?"

"Not at first," said John. "I have done business with the High Priest and was able to get inside and follow this…this trumped-up trial. The Sanhedrin broke all of their own laws. No trial was to be at night. It was to take place before the Sanhedrin, in the daylight. Witnesses were to be brought. The accused had the right to present his or her case. They weren't interested in justice for the Master, only to get rid of him."

"Pilate could not find anything to put him to death for and told them so," John continued. "When they insisted, he sent them to Herod. When Herod also found him innocent of the charges and sent him back, Pilate still would not condemn him. He had him flogged and then asked the people if they wanted to release Yeshua or Barabbas, a murderer and a robber. Perhaps he thought they would choose Yeshua. Instead the leaders whipped up the crowd to call for Yeshua's death."

"I cannot believe that some of those same people who cheered him entering Jerusalem, flinging palm branches in his path, now cry out for his death," Magdalene almost sneered.

"Then how was he sentenced to death?" Mary looked from one to the other, fighting the panic that was filling her heart. He healed those who were sick and dying. Raised people from the dead. What can they accuse him of?

Susanna spoke up. "They threatened to go to Caesar. Pilate has made too many mistakes with our people. It was his office of governor against one man's death. He finally gave in to them."

John looked her in the eye, his face filled with anguish. "Yeshua will be crucified."

Mary felt her knees buckle and John caught her and held her up. "We are sorry to bring you this news, but felt you must know."

She pursed her lips, sending a silent prayer for Ha'Shem's strength. "When will this take place?"

"They are preparing him even now to carry his cross to Golgotha," said John.

"I will go."

She turned and found James standing behind her. Evidently he'd heard some of their whispered conversation. "What is this about my brother being arrested? You must not go, Ima. It could be dangerous for you. I grieve for my brother but he has brought this upon himself. We all knew he angered the religious leaders. They will probably flog him and let him go."

Mary seldom lost her temper but suddenly raw fury rose up in her being. She faced James, her eyes flashing. "You would keep me from any comfort I could offer my firstborn son? He is your brother and they have already flogged him. He is going to die, James. Do you not care?"

"Die? What are you saying?"

"He is to be crucified!"

James had never seen her like this, her anger almost forcing him a step backwards. Then he rubbed a hand across his brow. His eyes watered with unshed tears. "Ima. I have loved him all my life and looked up to him. But what can you do for him now? What can any of us do? Crucifixion is a brutal death. You would see this?"

"I will be there for him with all that is in my being. I am sorry, James, that your fear is greater than your honor."

She wrapped her cloak around her and in a moment followed John and the other two women. Her heart pounded as they hurried to the Via Dolorosa. *My son, my son. Oh Ha'Shem, how could you let them take him?*

FIFTY

*J*ohn guided the two women the best he could through the crowds and they finally stopped at a place close to the cobbled street to wait.

Mary peered up the street straining to see, and when a figure appeared, carrying a wooden beam, she caught her breath. Yet it wasn't Yeshua. A second man, also carrying a beam, followed him. Two Roman soldiers were driving them down the street, cracking their whips.

Then, another figure appeared and this time Mary cried out. He was barely recognizable. Blood streamed from the cuts made by the whip on his back and a crown of thorns had been fashioned and pressed down on his head so more blood streamed down his face. He staggered, weak from the beating and the loss of blood. She would have run to him but was restrained by Susanna and Magdalene.

"My lady, you must not...."

With strength born of anguish, she tore herself away from them and pushed through the people in front of her to kneel beside him, wiping his face with the corner of her mantle.

"My son, did it have to come to this? You have the power. You can save yourself."

He could barely speak. "Ima...do not weep for me. Weep for our people...I must do what I came to do...."

The Roman soldier driving him had been distracted by the crowd but now turned back and grabbed Mary's arm.

"Get away from him, now!" he snarled at her.

She looked up at the soldier with tears streaming down her cheeks. He was only a boy in a Roman uniform. She did not care who heard her pleading words.

"I am his mother. Can you not help him?"

The young soldier hesitated, his face softening for a brief moment. He glanced up at his fellow soldiers, but they were not looking his way. He still had hold of her arm, but this time he helped her up, murmuring, "I'm sorry, but you must step away."

John reached her and led her back to the sidelines, but to Mary's relief, as she looked back, the soldier ordered a tall, muscular black man out of the crowd. "You there. Carry his beam!"

The tall man did not show fear, he merely walked to where Yeshua knelt and, with his powerful arms, lifted the beam. When he had settled it on one shoulder, he held it in place with the other arm, then he reached down and slipped an arm around Yeshua, lifting and supporting him as they slowly made their way down the street.

Mary breathed her thanks to Ha'Shem.

The three of them made their way to Golgotha along with the crowd. Some of the women around Mary wept, but on other faces she saw eagerness to see this bloody event unfold.

As they stood as close as they were allowed, Mary watched them lay Yeshua down on the crossed beams. She closed her eyes as the soldiers hammered the nails into his hands and feet, hearing his cries of pain. Her body jolted with each blow of the hammer.

There was silence and she opened her eyes to the scene before her. All three men were nailed to crosses, and with howls of pain, they were lifted up and slammed into the holes in the ground as the bloodthirsty crowd waited for them to die in agony.

Susanna turned to Mary. "Do you wish to leave this place? There is nothing more we can do for him."

She shook her head. "I will remain by my son. I can wait with him. It is the least we can do in this terrible hour."

Her grief was raw, for her son who hung on a Roman cross, but also for her other sons, who should have been here with him. By now James will have told them, and their wives. She thought of Rebecca and how she would react to the news with no mother present to comfort her in the loss of one she idolized. It could not be helped. Mary was where she needed to be, and where she would remain.

Some of the religious leaders and priests made their way up the hill. They stood looking up at Yeshua.

"He saved others, let him save himself," one jeered.

"If you are the son of God, come down from the cross and we will believe in you!"

Observing the leaders, Magdalene shuddered. "Rightly did the Master call them white-washed tombs full of dead men's bones!"

Even one of the thieves, dying himself, railed at him, "If you are the Messiah, save yourself and us also."

The other thief moved his head with agony toward his fellow criminal. "We are suffering for our crimes but this man has done nothing." Then he looked at Yeshua. "Remember me, Lord, when you come into your kingdom."

Mary was startled to hear Yeshua respond. "Assuredly I say to you, this day you shall be with me in Paradise."

Never had Mary felt so little respect for the leaders of her people, standing there in their fine robes and looking self-righteous. They had done this to Yeshua. He was innocent and they arranged his death. Did not the Torah condemn false accusers of an innocent person? They should be punished with the same punishment they sought for Yeshua. If she had been given a sword at that moment she would have struck them down. Reason asserted itself and she bowed her head and asked forgiveness for her murderous thoughts. Was she not contemplating the very crime they were committing?

Her attention was drawn to the shouts of a group of soldiers behind the cross. They were throwing dice over something.

Magdalene gasped. "It is the robe I made for the Lord. They are gambling for it. May the Most High reward them for their deed!"

Mary stood with the comfort of Magdalene's arm around her shoulders. Here was a woman Yeshua had delivered of seven demons; a woman whose life had been a living nightmare for years. How she had suffered in her madness, until the day she ran into Yeshua and was freed from her tormentors. Magdalene was not afraid to stand with her, the mother of Yeshua. Instead she looked defiantly at those around her, her eyes blazing at the crowd's compliance with the subtle threats of the priests.

"They are fools, dear lady," murmured Magdalene. "They do not know what they are doing, the blind leading the blind."

Mary closed her eyes and drew her mantle closer, as if by so doing she could shut out the spectacle before her. She had friends standing by her. Gentle John, Susanna, and Magdalene, and a short time before, another disciple, Salome, had joined them. Yet she felt alone.

Her eyes were dry for she had wept until it seemed there were no tears left in her body. She was scarcely aware of the women on either side of her, holding her up and murmuring words of comfort.

A seed of bitterness rose up like bile in her throat. Is this what it all was for? She had waited through the years with a family life so normal it was easy to forget who her oldest son was. With fearful hope and yet dread, she had anticipated the day when he would fulfill the angel's words to take the throne of David. "Of his kingdom there would be no end," the angel said. She had wondered what it meant. She knew now that he had the power to lead a rebellion against Rome and prevail. Why did he enter Jerusalem as he did? How else would he be a king? The words seemed a mockery as she stood in the hot sun watching her son die.

Adonai, how can you ask this of me? I bore him for you, nursed him, and raised him, only for this?

The sky that had been clear, allowing the heat of the midday to beat down on them mercilessly, began to darken. Mary looked up. When had the clouds rolled in? This was not the time of year for rain.

The crowd suddenly quieted as Yeshua cried out, "My God, my God, why have you forsaken me?"

People began to murmur and Mary's heart cried within her. *Was he the son of God if God had forsaken him?*

The wind picked up, swirling the dust in their faces with a vengeance. Some of the crowd began to disperse, holding their mantles over their faces.

Come closer to me.

Mary focused her eyes on Yeshua. He had not spoken aloud but was asking her to come closer. Would the soldiers permit this? She looked at John, tears making rivulets in the dust of his cheeks, into his beard. Evidently he heard the same command, for he gently took her arm and drew her forward toward the cross.

The soldiers watched them, but did not interfere. Perhaps the young soldier had told the centurion in charge that she was the mother of the crucified man.

Though his eyes were glazed with pain and his voice husky from the dust, Yeshua looked down at his mother.

"Woman, behold your son." And then to John, "Behold your mother."

John bit his lip, struggling with his emotions. Unable to speak, he nodded his head in agreement.

Yeshua was asking John and not her son James to take care of her? She too nodded. She would do whatever he asked of her.

Then Yeshua cried out, "I thirst!"

The young soldier who had helped her dipped a sponge in a nearby stone jar of vinegar and placed the sponge on a hyssop branch. When Yeshua had tasted it, he spoke again, a final cry: "Father, into your hands I commend my spirit. It is finished."

Mary's fist came up to her mouth and her cry of "My son," was stifled as he bowed his head and his body slumped. Yeshua, son of Mary, and son of God, was dead. Then, all the grief and agony of Mary's soul poured out as her cries echoed from the hilltop.

FIFTY-ONE

The sky that had been threatening now deafened them with claps of thunder and lightning flashed again and again. All around her people cried out in fear and ran in every direction. The earth began to roll under their feet and John had to brace himself to hold Mary steady. Magdalene, Susanna, and Salome stumbled toward them and the four women held each other for several terrifying minutes before the earth was quiet again.

The centurion, who had fallen to his knees during the earthquake, struggled to stand up again, staring at the cross and the figure of Yeshua with a look of amazement on his face.

"Truly, this was the son of God."

The creaking of wooden wheels caught Mary's attention and she turned to see two soldiers making their way up the hill with the death cart. They murmured a few words to the centurion, and he nodded toward the crosses. One soldier checked the first thief and seeing him barely alive, broke his legs with the hammer to insure a speedy death. Then he came to Yeshua and studied the body a moment.

"He is already dead," John said quickly.

Before Mary could cry out, the soldier pulled his sword and thrust it into the body. Yeshua did not move as water and blood flowed from the wound. The soldier moved on to the other thief and broke his legs also. Unable to push themselves up to gasp for breath, the two thieves quickly expired. Assured that all the prisoners were now dead, a soldier put up a ladder and slipped a rope under the armpits of the first thief, tossing an end over the top of the cross to the other soldier. Then he climbed the ladder and, with a tool from the cart, pulled the nails out of the hands and feet. Using the rope, they lowered the body and tossed it unceremoniously on the cart.

Seeing the family gathered below Yeshua, they moved on to the other thief and took him down.

Mary gasped. Was this to be the final insult, to throw her son's body on a bloody cart and take it away?

She grabbed John's arm and cried, "Is there nothing we can do?"

He shook his head slowly, his eyes filled with anguish.

Just then, two men hurried up the hill toward the centurion. From their clothing it was obvious they were members of the Sanhedrin. The first man was carrying a large bundle wrapped in linen. The second man approached the centurion.

"I am Joseph of Arimathea. The body is to be released to me," he panted, showing a scroll to the officer.

Mary shook her head. What need did they have of her son's body? She started to move toward them but Magdalene caught her arm and whispered, "It is all right, dear lady. These men are followers. I know them."

The centurion glanced at the scroll and the seal and nodded his head. "Very well, take it and do it quickly."

The soldiers lowered the body of Yeshua from the cross and Mary, with tears streaming down her face, sank to the ground and lifted her arms. "Give him to me," she pleaded.

Joseph and Nicodemus, who had received the body, glanced at each other a moment, then John gently removed the crown of thorns as they laid the body of Yeshua across Mary's lap. She held him, keening and rocking with her grief.

She looked down at his face and saw where the soldiers had pulled out part of his beard, the cuts from the whip on his body staining her mantle. "My son, my son, what have they done to you?" she cried. She closed her eyes and in her mind's eye, saw a little boy looking up at her trustingly with a baby bird held gently in his hand. She remembered how fearful she'd felt when he clambered up the sycamore tree and tenderly placed the tiny creature back in its nest. When he'd climbed safely back down, she'd gathered him in her arms and kissed him.

"What a good boy you are, my son," she'd murmured.

A deep voice suddenly spoke softly in her ear. It was the Lord Nicodemus. "Dear woman, we have little time. We must get him to the tomb before Sabbath begins."

She nodded and forced herself to relinquish her son. Her arms dropped to her side as Joseph and Nicodemus lifted the body from her and gently but quickly bound it with fresh linen and the mixture of myrrh and aloe they had brought with them.

John helped her up. Mary could only stand and watch helplessly as these strangers prepared her son's body for burial. Because of who they were, Mary did not dare to interfere. Yet she had wanted to do this one last thing for her son.

Then Joseph turned to her. "I have a new tomb not far away; we can put him there." He glanced up. "We must hurry, the Sabbath is almost upon us."

The women and John followed the two leaders to a garden tomb. Nicodemus produced a *tallit* as the men entered the tomb to place the body inside. Joseph, Nicodemus, and John pushed the great stone in its track across the entrance. Then, murmuring words of sympathy to the small group, Joseph of Arimathea and Nicodemus hurried away.

Mary's voice broke as she turned to John. "Can we not see to him after the Sabbath? His burial was done in such haste. He must be prepared properly."

Susanna spoke up. "This has been a day of anguish. You must rest, Mary. We will come with you after the Sabbath to make sure all is done for him."

John stroked his beard and looked toward the city. "I will see you home, dear lady, and then I must find the others. I believe they are hiding in the upper room. They will want to know what happened."

He turned to the other women. "Come for her after the Sabbath."

As they turned to leave, a group of Roman soldiers appeared. Four of them rolled the stone away and glanced in the tomb, then with a nod to their captain, rolled the stone back in place. The captain stepped up and put an official seal on the stone, then, spotting the three women, waved a dismissive hand at them. "Go your way. No one is allowed near this tomb."

Mary looked at Magdalene in confusion. Soldiers were going to guard the tomb? Magdalene shook her head. "He is dead. What more can they do to him? That is the most foolish thing I have ever seen."

Mary could only nod, for weariness had wrapped around her like a cloak and grief had sapped her strength. She let the women lead her away.

FIFTY-TWO

When the first day of the new week dawned, Mary, Salome, Susanna, and Magdalene were up early.

They quickly bought additional spices to anoint the Lord's body and as they hurried toward the tomb, Susanna caught her breath.

"How are we going to get the stone moved?"

Salome and Magdalene shook their heads. They hadn't thought of that. When they reached the tomb they saw swords and a helmet and other items lying on the ground.

Magdalene frowned. "Where are the soldiers who were guarding the tomb?"

Then Mary gasped. "The stone has been rolled away!" She turned an anguished face to her companions. "Could the soldiers have taken his body?"

They rushed to enter the tomb and stopped, for two men in shining garments were standing inside. The women sank to their knees in fear and bowed their faces to the earth.

"Why do you seek the living among the dead?" one being asked, "He is not here, but is risen!" He turned to Magdalene. "Remember how he spoke to you when he was still in Galilee, saying 'the son of Man must be delivered into the hands of sinful men, and be crucified, and the third day rise again?'" Then they disappeared.

Magdalene gasped, "I remember his words, but then we saw him die." Her brows knit together in confusion.

Mary felt hope rise within her heart as she looked at the shelf where the body of Yeshua had been laid. The grave clothes were still there. Even the napkin and *tallit* that had covered his face was folded and placed to one side. She almost laughed out loud for the joy that sang through her being. As the new reality sank in, she knew without a doubt: he was not dead.

"Dear lady, go and tell the disciples what we have seen. I want to remain here for a short time." Magdalene turned back toward the tomb.

Mary and the other two women hurried across the city to the upper room where, from what John had said, they knew the disciples were hiding. They covered their faces and did not look around as they focused on their destination.

They climbed the steps and knocked three times, the signal they had been given. Andrew cautiously opened the door, his eyes full of fear as the three women entered the room. Mary was surprised to see her sons, James, Simon, Joses, and Jude, waiting for her.

James came forward and took her hands. "We came, Ima, but we were too late. We could not get through the crowds. We could only watch from a distance but could not tell what was happening. When the earthquake struck, we feared for you but could not get through. People were running away from Golgotha. One of the disciples recognized us and told us we might find you here."

Fear permeated the room. It was almost tangible in the faces of the men and women gathered there.

Simon spoke up. "Ima, people who had died were released from their tombs and were walking in the city, in their grave clothes!"

Jude turned to John. "I ran into a priest who was standing outside the Temple. He looked in shock and was murmuring, 'It is torn! It is torn!' I asked him what was torn, and he just shook his head and murmured, 'The great curtain, rent in two!'" Jude looked around at the group. "The curtain that separates the Holy from the Most Holy Place. It is over six inches thick!"

The group began to murmur among themselves as to what this could mean. James searched Mary's face, expecting perhaps to see deep grief. His look of sympathy turned to puzzlement. "What has happened? You do not grieve for our brother?".

Mary could hardly speak for the joy that flooded her soul. "He lives, James. He is not dead."

Just then Magdalene burst into the room, startling everyone. "I have seen him! I have seen the Lord. He spoke to me and said, 'Do not cling to me for I have not yet ascended to the Father.' He is alive!" Magdalene was almost dancing with her news.

Peter stepped forward. "You have been dreaming. You wish him to be alive, but he is dead. No one survives a Roman crucifixion!"

Magdalene faced them, her eyes flashing. "Has his mother told you of the great beings in the tomb, and of the grave clothes that lay there empty? Go and see for yourselves."

Peter's eyes widened as he and John looked at each other, then the two of them dashed for the stairs.

Mary, her sons, and the remaining disciples and followers waited for Peter and John to return. They gathered in small groups reviewing what they had seen and heard and speculating on what to do next. Some of the women still wept at the thought of the death of the Lord.

It wasn't long before they heard quick footsteps on the stairs and a rather abashed Peter and John stepped back into the room.

Peter faced Magdalene. "It is true, as you said. The tomb is empty. The grave clothes lay as you described, the *tallit* folded to one side. You say you saw him, but then where is he?" He spread his hands in frustration.

John came to Mary. "The body is truly gone." He too looked bewildered.

Two of the followers, Cleophas and Simon, got up. "We cannot wait to unravel this marvel; we have business in Emmaus. There is nothing we can do here." The men gathered their things and after a brief farewell, left.

James and Joses stood by Mary and she could see that James was trying to understand what he had heard.

"Ima, could not the soldiers have stolen the body? Perhaps you were dreaming, wanting him to be alive."

Mary sighed. "Dear James, consider what you have just said. If the soldiers had taken the body of your brother, would they have unwrapped the grave clothes first? Would they have folded the *tallit* and laid it aside?"

He shook his head. "Peter is right. If he is not dead, where is he?"

The day was drawing to a close and Mary was weary. Peter looked around the room and said, "Let us who are able find lodging for the night and gather again here tomorrow. Perhaps we will know more about our Lord's departure then."

It was agreed. Some gathered personal items and left the upper room. Those who had nowhere to go prepared to spend the night there. John turned to Mary. "Dear lady, you are welcome in my home, humble as it is. You are as my mother to me as our Lord has said."

Susanna and Magdalene merely nodded. They too had heard the words of the Lord as he entrusted his mother to John.

James raised his eyebrows and glanced back at his brothers for agreement. "You should come with us, Ima. We are your family."

Mary drew herself up and looked James fully in the eyes. "Yeshua entrusted me to John from the cross. I will do as he asked.

Come here again tomorrow, all of you, and we will decide what is best for me."

James blustered, but seeing the strength and determination in her face, finally nodded.

"We will return tomorrow to see if there is any more word on our brother. If not, you must come home to Nazareth with us."

"Tomorrow then."

When her sons had gone, she turned to John. "Shall we go?"

"My home is humble and I share it with my brother James and his wife, Huskim, but you are most welcome."

FIFTY-THREE

The home John shared temporarily with his brother, James, and sister-in-law was indeed humble. It was even smaller than Mary's own home in Nazareth. The three spoke into the night of what they had seen and heard, too overcome with sorrow and wonder to sleep. Mary shared with them the story of the angel and Yeshua's miraculous birth. She had shared the story with her family but not with any of the disciples, and they were astonished.

James sat silent for a moment. "I do not understand any of this. He told us many things, but perhaps we did not listen as well as we could have. If he is not in the tomb...." He was silent again.

When at last weariness overtook her, James and Huskim graciously gave Mary their more comfortable pallet for the night. Emotionally exhausted, she slept restlessly. The question that Peter had asked kept running through her mind, over and over: "Where is he?" If Yeshua had truly risen from the dead, would he not let his own mother know? Why this terrible silence?

⸌⸍

They ate a simple breakfast of fresh barley bread with olive oil and some dried figs. Barley bread was common among the poor, and Mary remembered how she'd had to resort to that at times to feed their large family. Fortunately, there was a goat, so Mary was offered a cup of fresh goat's milk with her meal.

She was anxious to return to the upper room to see if there was news of Yeshua, but forced herself to be patient until John was ready to go. James and Huskim would come with them.

When they reached the upper room, there was a chorus of voices. Everyone was gathered around Simon and Cleophas and talking at once. How did they manage to return from Emmaus so quickly? Something had happened. From the looks on some of the faces it was good news. When Andrew realized she was standing nearby, he touched Cleophas on the shoulder and inclined his head. "His mother is here."

Cleophas turned to Mary and her companions. "Dear lady, the most amazing thing has happened. Simon and I were walking along the road to Emmaus, discussing the events that had just happened and the death of our Lord, when a stranger appeared and joined us. He asked what we were discussing and we were surprised. He seemed to be the only stranger in Jerusalem who did not know the events that had just taken place. When he asked, 'What things?' I told him about the things concerning Yeshua of Nazareth, who was a prophet mighty in deed before God and all the people, and how the chief priest and our rulers delivered him to be condemned to death and crucified him. We told him we were hoping that it was he who was going to redeem Israel. Besides all this, today is the third day since it happened. We told him that certain women of our company, who had arrived early at the tomb to prepare his body, astonished us."

Simon broke in, "We said that when they did not find his body, they came to us, saying that they had seen a vision of angels who said he was alive. Two of the Lord's disciples, Peter and John, went to the tomb and found it as the women had said, but they did not see the Lord."

Cleophas shook his head slowly. "The stranger replied, 'O foolish ones, and slow of heart to believe in all that the prophets have spoken! Ought not the Messiah to have suffered these things and to enter into his glory?'"

Andrew stepped up. "Then he began talking about Moses and expounded to Cleophas and Simon all the things concerning the Messiah."

Cleophas nodded and continued. "When we drew near the village where we were going, he started to go farther, but we constrained him to stay with us, since the day was spent and night was approaching. He agreed to join us and when we sat down for the evening meal, he took the bread, blessed it and broke it, giving some to us." Cleophas looked at Mary and then around to the rest of the group, his eyes shining. "Our eyes were opened then and we knew who he was! As soon as we realized, he vanished from the table!"

Simon nodded. "Our hearts burned within us as he talked and opened the Scriptures to our understanding. We rose that very hour and came back to Jerusalem as fast as we could walk to share with all of you. The Lord has risen indeed, and appeared to us!"

Her sons, James, Joses, Simon, and Jude had just entered the room in time to hear the last part of Cleophas and Simon's narrative. James had a strange expression on his face and her other sons stood closely by, evidently agreeing with whatever he was going to say.

Suddenly there was a sound that made the entire group turn around. Mary's heart leaped within her. Yeshua was standing in the room with them, robed in white and smiling.

"Peace be unto you. Why are you troubled? There is much doubt arising in your hearts."

He spread his hands out. "Behold, my hands and my feet, that it is I myself. Handle me and see, for a spirit does not have flesh and bones as you see I have."

When they still hung back in shock and unbelief, he said, "Have you any food here?"

Magdalene slowly reached into a clay jar nearby and pulled out a piece of broiled fish. Another woman handed him some honeycomb.

Mary watched with clasped hands, joy spilling from every fiber of her being. "My Lord and my God," she breathed. The smile Yeshua gave her was radiant.

And so I am, Mary of Nazareth, blessed among women.

He took the fish and the honeycomb and ate them in their sight. Suddenly James and his brothers sank to their knees at his feet. Tears ran down their cheeks as they bowed their head to the ground.

"I did not believe," James murmured over and over, "Forgive me, Yeshua. Forgive me."

Her other sons said the same. Yeshua reached down and raised them to their feet. "Hear the words that I spoke to my disciples. I told them while I was still with them, that 'all things must be fulfilled which were written in the Torah of Moses and the Prophets and the Psalms concerning me.'"

As the entire group, their faces radiant at his appearance, slowly settled themselves on the floor to listen to his words, he began to explain, opening their understanding that they might comprehend the Scriptures.

"Thus it is written, and thus it was necessary for the Messiah to suffer and to rise from the dead on the third day, and that repentance and remission of sins should be preached in his name to all nations, beginning at Jerusalem. And you are witnesses of these things. Behold, I send the Promise of my Father upon you; but tarry in the city of Jerusalem until you are endued with power from on high."

Mary looked over at the faces of her other sons, faces filled with remorse. James turned to her, his eyes pleading for forgiveness and she returned his look with one of love. She had been given the words of the angel and the miraculous birth of Yeshua to prepare her for this time, but they only knew the big brother who had looked after them for so long. How difficult it was for them to believe that their elder brother was indeed the son of God. Then her own guilt assailed her. Had she not railed at Ha'Shem herself, not understanding that the resurrection would come?

After teaching them for several hours, Yeshua left them. Disconcerted by his absence, the disciples remained in the upper room, not sure when he would return or what to do.

Mary stayed with John as her sons found lodging with relatives in Jerusalem. Each day all would gather in the upper room for prayer and fellowship.

A week later, when all were gathered in prayer and Thomas had joined them, Yeshua suddenly appeared in the room. Thomas had been adamant that unless he saw the Lord for himself, he would not believe the women's story.

Mary looked over and saw Thomas standing at the top of the stairs, his eyes wide. He went to Yeshua and fell to his knees before him.

Yeshua smiled down tenderly at him, putting out his hand. "Reach your finger here, and look at my hands, and reach your hand here, and put it into my side. Do not be unbelieving, but believing."

Thomas bowed his head, "My Lord and my God."

"Ah, Thomas, because you have seen me, you have believed. Blessed are those who have not seen and yet have believed."

Yeshua looked around at his disciples. "Go to Galilee and I will meet you there." He turned to the rest of them. "I will see you again on the fortieth day." Then suddenly he was gone again.

Mary had realized in these past days that she must relinquish him as her son. His earthly ties were broken and he was her risen Lord. She had no preference above his other followers. He was indeed God, the visible likeness of Adonai. With the others she gave herself to prayer and fasting, seeking his will for these final years of her life. She was at peace at the home of John and James. Her family had reluctantly relinquished their claim to her in the light of Yeshua's words entrusting her to John.

Sometimes she felt the anguish of her son James, who had, in his unbelief, hurt her so and thus given Yeshua the impetus to entrust her care to John. Yet now her heart knew an inner peace and joy as she relished for this time the now peaceful company of her sons who joined her in the upper room to pray and wait for the Lord's instructions.

After the Lord was gone, Peter was deep in thought and finally stood up and faced his fellow disciples. "The Lord has told us to meet him in Galilee. We need to return to our families to provide for them. I am going fishing."

The others agreed and gathered their traveling bags. John turned to Mary. "James and Huskim will return with me to Galilee. You will come with us?"

James stepped forward and took her hands. "Let us all return to our families. I will not go against the wishes of the Lord, but surely you can come and visit your family. The children and grandchildren will be glad to see you."

Peace settled on her spirit. It was all right. "I will go with you."

Simon, Joses, and Jude gathered around her, their glad faces giving her assurance. She had been concerned for Rebecca who depended on her so. She knew of all her children, Rebecca would be the one feeling most abandoned.

Peter stopped at the doorway. "Shavu'ot is approaching. Since the Torah requires all able men of Israel to observe the holy day here in Jerusalem, let us return here in a month's time to prepare." He looked around and received nods of approval.

Little by little, the room which had been filled with the disciples and others began to empty. Mary's sons returned with her to the home of James and John, and she gathered what few things she felt she needed.

She felt her spirit lifting at the thought of returning to her home and family. She had the most wonderful news to share with them, and this time her sons would be able to back up her story.

FIFTY-FOUR

*I*t was a quiet afternoon as Mary and Rebecca walked the gentle hills of Nazareth, seeing the fruit trees blossoming and listening to the numerous birds calling to one another. Work in the fields had ended and the work in the vineyards had not yet begun. Each family traveling to Jerusalem would take two loaves of leavened bread made from their newly harvested wheat for an offering at Shavu'ot.

"Three times a year," Moses had commanded the children of Israel, "all your males shall appear before the Lord your God." It was a joyous celebration of the giving of the Torah, Ha'Shem's instructions to Israel. Thus the men of Mary's family had gone to Jerusalem for Passover, Chag Ha Matzot, the Feast of Unleavened Bread, and Shavu'ot, the Feast of Weeks. From all over Palestine, by the thousands, Jews of every nation came from every part of the known world. The roads were filled with travelers. Some stayed with relatives or in available lodging in the city, and multitudes encamped outside the city. Those who were not able to travel to the Holy City would celebrate at home with special services. It was time also, for Mary to return to Jerusalem with her sons.

It had been a wonderful time with her family. At Mary's suggestion, James had given his brothers a day and night with their families due to the long absence, but then sent word and gathered everyone; her sons and their wives, her daughters, their husbands and all the grandchildren. Unashamed at the tears that ran down his cheeks and into his beard, James had shared the miracle of the Lord's death and resurrection. This time it was not just Mary sharing the good news, but also the one brother who had been so skeptical and railed against Yeshua and Yeshua's actions. She looked around at the faces of her loved ones as puzzlement turned into joy at James' words. At last they understood why Yeshua had never married, why he'd begun his ministry teaching that "the kingdom of heaven was at hand." She suspected that Simon, Joses, and Jude had shared the news with their wives already and now, backed up by the words of James, there was no more doubt. As she listened to James speak, his face alight with the knowledge of his Lord, she felt a knowing in her spirit that this son would be instrumental in the furthering of the kingdom. She did not know how, but Ha'Shem whispered to her heart: *I have chosen him to serve me and he will be a leader of many.*

～

Mary's thoughts ran in many directions, but now she glanced at her daughter. Rebecca's face was alight with the pleasure of the world around her and a walk with her mother. She had been overjoyed at Mary's return and in tears had clung to her. "Ima, do not leave me again! Do not leave me!" And Mary knew that this time she would take Rebecca with her to Jerusalem.

They walked in the warm sunshine and the fields were quiet as it was the Sabbath and no work was to be done. They had this peaceful time together before they returned to her large family for their Sabbath meal.

"Tell me again of Yeshua, Ima. I am so happy he is alive again. I was sad for so many days until you came. I cried and cried. I didn't want him to die. He was good. The soldiers should not have hurt him. I wanted to take care of him and I could not be there."

"He knew your heart, Rebecca. Everything happened as Ha'Shem had planned. We did not understand at the time, but when he came to us in the upper room and showed us the nail prints in his hands and feet, and reminded us of the Scriptures that foretold all that he was to go through for us, we understood at last. He suffered that we might be able one day to go to the Father in heaven."

"He said he was the way...."

"Yes, the way, the truth and the life. He said that no man, or woman, comes to the Father but through him."

Understanding lit the girl's plain face. "He is like a door, then?"

Mary laughed. "Yes, dear one, he is like a door to heaven. He said, 'Whoever believes in me shall have eternal life.'"

"Then I shall see my brother again one day. I shall go to heaven and I shall see him. I believe in him."

They stopped for a moment, and Mary put a hand on Rebecca's cheek. "You have always believed in him, Rebecca, but now you know who he truly is, and instead of just believing in Yeshua as your brother, you now can believe in him as the son of Adonai and your Messiah."

"Yes!" Rebecca clapped her hands and with her eyes closed, tilted her face up to the sun.

Mary marveled. Would that all of her people could believe as simply as this special child Ha'Shem had given her. Though Rebecca was a grown woman, unmarried and slow of mind, she was always childlike and clear in the simplicity of her thinking. Mary sighed. Why do we make things so complicated? If Rebecca could grasp the Lord's message of salvation, could not all who heard it?

FIFTY-FIVE

*H*er daughters and grandchildren wept as Mary and her sons, along with Rebecca, prepared to leave for Jerusalem. Two of the younger children clung to her skirt.

"Will you return to us, Mother?" Hodiah asked, for James had decided that the women and children would remain in Nazareth.

"As the Lord leads, daughter. I do not know what awaits us in Jerusalem, only that I believe he will meet us there."

Mary, Rebecca, and her sons waved at the group gathered in the street outside her home, until they rounded a bend and she could no longer see them.

Her sons carried baskets of figs, pomegranates, olives, and dates as an offering to the Most High. There were two loaves of the leavened wheat bread for each family along with baskets of fruit as they fulfilled the words of Ha'Shem through the Lawgiver, Moses: *"For ADONAI your God is bringing you into a good land, a land with streams, springs and water welling up from the depths in valleys and on hillsides. It is a land of wheat and barley, grapevines, fig trees and pomegranates; a land of olive oil and honey."*

Farmers had tied the strands of a reed around the best of their crops as they ripened for harvest. One of the travelers led a white bull, his horns painted gold and garlands about his neck. There was a sense of joy, expectancy, and good will. As they traveled and others joined them along the road, some of the women came from their homes, adding the music of flutes and tambourines as they followed for a short while and then returned to their homes.

Mary had walked with Rebecca as far as she could and finally her sons put her on a donkey they had brought with them for her use. She didn't want them to think her feeble and had insisted on walking as far as she could. As the beast ambled along the road, she thought back to the journey to Bethlehem, when she'd been great with child, and felt each bump in the road as the donkey carried her to her destiny. Now, ensconced on a padded blanket, she was solemn again, for once more she was traveling toward the unknown, on the back of a donkey. Rebecca looked up at her from time to time as if reassuring herself that her mother was all right.

As they approached the Holy City, Mary was overwhelmed anew at the size of the great Temple that overlooked the city, its walls reflecting the morning sun. All around her the throngs streamed up the road and through the gates. Each traveler seemed to be carrying something; the men had a young goat or lamb, a sack of grain, or other bundle. The women balanced baskets of produce on their heads. The mood was joyful and strangers nodded to one another in greeting.

Outside the gates, numerous tradesmen had set up their tents in the Valley of the Cheesemakers. Here the mood was less jovial as buyers and sellers haggled over prices and shouted to be heard over the noise of the crowd. Various goods, fresh fruits, and vegetables were laid out on tables as slaves and servants shopped for their masters.

As they entered the city, the towers of the citadel adjoining Herod's palace were visible. Near the Temple Mount were the towers of the Antonia, the huge fortress named for Mark Anthony, the first King Herod's early patron. Now it was the headquarters of the Roman garrison, and the place where Pontius Pilate had sentenced Yeshua to death. Mary fought against the grief and anger that rose at the thought of what Pilate had done to her son, yet she remembered Yeshua's words, that it was the Father's plan and fulfilled Scripture. Her heart lifted. Yeshua was not dead. He was alive and had appeared to them all. Now there was nothing to be sorrowful about.

As agreed, Mary, Rebecca, James, Simon, Joses, and Jude returned to the house and the upper room where they had celebrated the Passover with Yeshua and where he had appeared to them after his resurrection. It was ten days before Shavu'ot.

The other apostles and Peter had already arrived and Mary was puzzled to see that he seemed strangely subdued. Others joined them, including the Magdalene, Susanna, and Salome. The women embraced and exchanged greetings and news of their families.

Rebecca, who tired easily, had nodded off, and Mary covered her shoulders with her mantle. Then she turned to Magdalene. "Your family is well?"

"My uncle and dear ones are well. It was good to see them." She looked over at Peter and the disciples who were talking quietly among themselves. "Where do we go from here? We have all returned, but will we see the Lord again?"

"I do not have the answer to that, but I do believe there is more he wants us to know. We can only wait and pray."

Mary's sons greeted the men. John had been talking with his brother James and, seeing her enter, came quickly to greet her.

"Welcome, dear lady, it is good to see you again. You enjoyed the visit with your family?"

"I did, John. And your father, Zebedee, he is well?"

John grinned. "He is well and still fishing. He was glad for our help for a time." He shook his head and his eyes were filled with wonder. "The Lord appeared to us as we were fishing and even prepared a breakfast of fish and bread on the beach. I do not understand how he does this, but we were blessed to see him again."

"That is good news, John. I long to see him again also." She sighed. "I am torn, John. I want to be obedient to our Lord's direction, yet I am getting older and my heart lies in my home in Nazareth."

"We shall seek the Lord's will together. He will show us what we are to do."

"Yes, John, thank you. We will pray."

As John turned to talk with another disciple, Mary looked after him. The Lord had given her into his care but she sensed he and the other apostles would not stay in Jerusalem. Where then should she go? Should she travel with them? Her heart longed for her family and grandchildren, that they would know Ha'Shem's plan for them. She had much to share. She sought a quiet corner and bowed her head, seeking the One who could answer her questions.

FIFTY-SIX

*I*t was a good thing the room was large, for there appeared to Mary to be over a hundred people gathered together. How blessed she felt to see all four of her sons interacting with other believers. She had hoped and prayed for this day and her joy bubbled over.

The women worked together to make sure all were fed. When the meals had been taken care of, the entire group settled themselves and began to pray, some in whispers and some silently. Disciples and friends came and went, bringing more food for the group.

The time seemed to pass quickly as the story of the Lord's death and resurrection was shared again and again. No one seemed to get tired of hearing it. Mary watched with pleasure as her sons listened to stories from the other disciples of the miracles Yeshua did, and what it was like to travel with the Lord for the past years. Her sons, in turn, shared what it was like growing up with the Lord and not knowing who he was.

The disciples had given themselves to prayer but many were restless and, like Mary, wondering what to do next.

At that moment, without a sound, the Lord stood in their midst. "Peace be with you."

Some of the disciples were in the upper room for the first time and looked upon him with awe and some with fear.

"Have you any food here?"

"Yes, Lord," Susanna took some fish out of a nearby basket and a piece of honeycomb. As he ate it before them, they marveled.

At his request, the group settled down around the room to listen as he began to open their hearts to the Scriptures. "These are the words which I spoke to you while I was still with you, that all things must be fulfilled which were written in the Law of Moses and the Prophets and the Psalms concerning me."

As he talked, Mary listened intently. This was the Father's plan all along. How foolish she had been to consider him an earthly king. He did not come to overthrow the Romans. By setting his people free, he meant freedom in him. They would know the truth and the truth would set them free. One day Mary would join her son in heaven in a resurrected body as she saw him here. How her parents, Heli and Anna, and Joseph's parents, Jacob and Rachel, would have rejoiced to see this day. How difficult it must have been to know who and what their first grandson was, and yet to remain silent that he might have a normal upbringing in a Jewish family with his brothers and sisters.

When Yeshua seemed to have finished his teaching, Mary approached him, seeing again the wounds in his hands and feet. "My Lord," she murmured as her eyes perused his dear face. "What would you have us do?" And Mary realized she was really asking for herself.

He smiled tenderly at her. "You will know when the time comes." Then he turned once again to the believers.

"Thus it is written," he said, looking around at the gathering, "and you are my witnesses of these things. Soon I will send the Promise of my Father upon you; but tarry here in the city of Jerusalem until you are endued with power from on high."

Mary knit her brows, puzzled...power from on high? What power was this? She sat down again with the other women and glanced at Rebecca, who watched her beloved brother, her face full of awe.

Yeshua continued teaching them through the night and, in the morning hours as the sun was rising and a rooster crowed over the city, Yeshua asked them to follow him to the Mount of Olives. Mary grasped Rebecca's hand and the women huddled close together as they stepped outside. Wouldn't a crowd such as this attract the attention of the Roman soldiers? They followed him toward the Kidron Valley and the grove of ancient olive trees, hardly speaking in the grey light of dawn, hardly speaking as they followed their Lord.

Mary and the other women looked around in amazement that the street, usually crowded with pilgrims, even early in the morning, was strangely void of people. When they reached their destination, Yeshua waited until they were all gathered before him. Then he admonished them once again to wait in Jerusalem for the Promise of the Father. As they listened and watched intently, he turned and raised his hands, the nail prints clearly visible. His garments glowed with a white iridescence as he pronounced a blessing on the group. There were muted cries and gasps of breath as to the amazement of all, he began to rise into the air and disappeared into the clouds.

Mary put her arms around Rebecca as the girl wept. "He is gone. Yeshua is gone." They clung to each other as along with the others, they stared up at the sky.

Suddenly, two beings in white appeared before them. Mary remembered the angels that had appeared to them at the tomb and the angel that had appeared to her so long ago to tell her she would bear God's son. She and the others listened respectfully as the angels spoke.

Their voices were deep and Mary felt the sound resonate through her body. "Why do you stand still gazing up at the clouds? This same Yeshua, who was taken up from you into heaven will so come in like manner as you saw him go into heaven."

Then, with a flash of light, the angels, too, were gone.

The entire group broke into words of praise and thanksgiving. How privileged they all were to be able to see and hear this moment!

Like pictures moving through her mind, the years passed in review. Was it nearly thirty-four years ago that the angel appeared to her and told her of the overwhelming task she was to be given? When Yeshua was born in that stable, he was so beautiful. She remembered his open eyes looking up at her, so unusual for a newborn. He grew quickly, a toddler playing in the sand; a little boy who climbed the sycamore tree to put the baby bird back in its nest; a child playing with his brothers and sisters. She thought of how he surprised the rabbi by knowing the Torah so well in Hebrew school; his disappearance in Jerusalem, only to be found in the Temple astonishing the elders with his knowledge; how he'd grown up to be a fine young man, able even at sixteen to become the head of the household at the death of Joseph. How proud Joseph was of Yeshua and how honored he felt to be his earthly father.

She knew she was forgiven for railing at her God at the brutal death he bore for all of them. She had felt her heart torn from her body as she watched him die. She hadn't understood until the resurrection. Yet now, she and every believer had access to the Father because of him.

Mary couldn't speak. Joy infused her, knowing at last: this is why he came into the world—and into their lives.

FIFTY-SEVEN

*M*ary took Rebecca's hand as they went with the group back to the upper room. Yeshua had told them to wait. But where would they wait? She and the women looked to the disciples who gathered in a small group and conferred.

It was determined that for now, they would return to the upper room. When they had done so and settled down, Peter addressed the group. "Men and brethren, this Scripture had to be fulfilled, which the Holy Spirit spoke before by the mouth of David concerning Judas, who became a guide for those who arrested Yeshua; for he was numbered with us and obtained part of this ministry. Judas betrayed the Lord and has hanged himself in remorse for his evil deed."

He shook his head sadly. "If only we had known who the traitor was, we could have stopped him."

Magdalene spoke quietly but firmly. "Had we stopped him, we would have stopped the Lord's plan according to the Scriptures. Didn't the Master tell us what he would go through? He told us over and over and we did not listen."

Peter glowered at her, a woman, speaking up among the men, but only for a moment, then, with a nod, he acknowledged the truth of what she said.

Mary's thoughts went back to that moment she saw Yeshua hand the sop of bread to Judas and just as Judas was leaving, remembered the sense of horror as she suddenly understood what

Judas was going to do. She'd stood up, thinking to do something, but Yeshua, knowing her intent, had stopped her with a look. Now she knew he'd known what Judas was going to do and allowed him to do it to fulfill Scripture. She pushed the disturbing thoughts aside and listened to Peter as he continued.

"For it is written in the book of Psalms: 'Let his dwelling place be desolate, and let no one live in it.' And, 'Let another take his office.'

"Therefore, of these men who have accompanied us all the time that the Lord Yeshua went in and out among us, beginning from the baptism of John to that day when he was taken up from us, one of these must become a witness with us of his resurrection."

The group nodded in agreement and murmured among themselves as to which man should be chosen.

"It is time to replace Judas with one of the disciples who has traveled with us the entire time of the Master's ministry," Peter went on. "Let us choose two worthy men and cast lots that the Lord may choose between them."

Mary wondered if it was possible that one of her other sons might be chosen, since they were the Lord's brothers, but she knew that they were as yet new believers. They had not been with Yeshua during his earthly ministry. After much discussion among the eleven, Justus and Matthias were selected. The group bowed their heads and sought the Lord's guidance, lots were cast, and Matthias was numbered with the eleven apostles.

To Mary's surprise, James rose and faced the group. There was no trace of his former arrogance, but a new strength permeated his words. "The Lord has asked us to wait for the coming of the Spirit. We do not know at this time what that means, but I propose that during the day we meet in the Temple to pray. We can return here in the evening and those that have homes here in Jerusalem can return there at night."

As James and Peter eyed each other warily, Mary wondered if there would be a conflict between them for leadership. Peter seemed in charge of the group, but she knew her second son. She'd seen him on the journey from Nazareth, chin in hand and deep in thought many times. He had something on his mind.

As people began leave for the night, and those that were staying began to settle down, James approached Mary. He knelt at her feet, tears in his eyes. "Ima, forgive me for the sorrow I caused you. I didn't understand. Even when you told your story, we were all doubtful of the truth. It seemed so unbelievable."

Seeing James before Mary, Simon, Joses, and Jude also rose and approached her.

Simon pursed his lips, blinking back the tears in his eyes. "It was hard to believe. I've known him all my life, just as my older brother. It puzzled me why he never married like the rest of us."

"I, too, wondered, Ima," added Joses. "He was so compassionate and strong; content with himself. There was always that air of authority about him. He took care of all of us and loved us. I believed only that he had dedicated his life to Adonai."

Lastly, Jude came, not stopping the tears that ran down his cheeks into his beard. "I followed him, saw some of the miracles, the ones I shared with you, Ima, yet…." He brushed a rough hand across his eyes. "I thought I knew something, but I didn't know anything. I couldn't imagine where his power came from. Only perhaps that Adonai had chosen him, like he chose Elijah and Isaiah and the prophets of old. Forgive me, Ima." He too knelt before her.

She reached out and put a hand on the tearstained cheek of her youngest son, who rushed through life, like the disciple Peter, impetuous and determined. Then she smiled at the other three. "Dear ones, I knew that one day you would know the truth. He has forgiven you long ago, and so have I. It is enough that I am here in this place with other believers to share the knowledge of our Lord.

And you, my sons, are miraculously here with me. It fills my heart with great joy."

She rose and embraced each of them in turn and gave a sigh of contentment, sensing the peace that was settling over the room. John came to Mary's side and the brothers stepped back, acknowledging his place as guardian over their mother as the Lord had commanded.

"You have your sons at last, dear lady," he said, acknowledging them with a glance.

"Yes, John."

"Let me see you home."

⌒

The next morning, at dawn, the believers met in the Temple in the area of Solomon's Porch where the Lord had taught so many times, to pray and discuss the Torah and the references to the Messiah. The women went and prayed in the court of the women. In the evening, they returned to the upper room. Mary looked around and wondered if it was big enough for the growing group of believers. In the last hours, the room was nearly filled to capacity. She estimated over a hundred men and women including the twelve called by Yeshua.

Mary, content at the home of John for now, was at peace to come these last two days to Solomon's Porch to gather with the other believers. Her worship poured from a grateful heart. She enjoyed the company of the other women, along with Magdalene, Susanna, and Salome, the mother of James and John.

A sense of expectancy began to permeate the group. The holy day of Shavu'ot was near when they would celebrate the Feast of Weeks.

Mary marveled as she thought of what Yeshua had said to them. Believers would do the acts that Yeshua had done during his ministry on earth? It was a wondrous and exciting thought.

They would now be his hands and feet on the earth. As she looked around at those gathered together, she could see the wonder of it on other faces as the group prayed and discussed the Scriptures.

Then, being the ninth day since Yeshua had left them, Peter stood up and addressed the group.

"Tomorrow is the Feast of Weeks. Tonight the men will go to the Temple to pray and study the Torah until first light. Let the rest of you join us in the Temple at our usual place of meeting at dawn."

He thought a moment, "We have not seen any soldiers here, for which we can be thankful, but I suggest that tonight we continue to go in small groups, lest we call attention to ourselves. The city is filled with pilgrims for our holy day and we should go unnoticed by the Temple guards."

The men agreed, and bidding goodbye to the women of their families, began to walk out the door in twos and threes. Mary stood and watched her sons as they left the upper room, nodding a brief farewell to them. Then, when the men had left, the women straightened the room and looked over the food, putting away what could be used the next day. Susanna and Salome returned to their homes, while Mary, Rebecca, and Magdalene along with the other women who remained, settled down for the night, to pray and prepare for their holy day. Mary, torn between her family and staying in Jerusalem with John and his family, laid her cares before her God, her heart open and obedient to his will for her.

FIFTY-EIGHT

*I*t was still dark, in the stillness before dawn, when Mary woke Rebecca and, along with Magdalene and the other women, they made their way toward the Temple. When they reached the place of prayer in Solomon's Porch, they found the disciples gathered. A sense of great expectancy filled Mary. This morning they did not all greet each other, but each one knelt or sat quietly, praying. Some had brought rugs, but others, including Mary, sat on one of the stone benches. Then, a scroll of the book of Ruth was obtained and the disciples took turns reading it aloud to the believers.

The sun rose slowly over the walls of the Temple, bathing the stones in a golden light. As the second hour of the day passed, all were involved in prayer and supplication to the Lord. They gave praise along with thanksgiving for what they had seen and heard.

Suddenly there came a sound from heaven, the sound of a mighty rushing wind, yet not a garment moved or fluttered. It filled the place where they were gathered and to Mary's amazement, tongues of fire hovered over the heads of each of the believers. She felt an enormous burst of power and realized this was the anointing the Lord had asked them to wait for. She stood and lifted her hands, joy filling her being as she began to praise her God in a language that was not her own Hebrew. She marveled at the glorious words that poured from her mouth along with the crescendo of voices from those around her who were also experiencing this wondrous move of the Spirit.

All around her, Mary heard a multitude of voices and languages she didn't understand, but there was no fear, for she knew this was of God. As the disciples worshipped, tears running down their cheeks and some nearly dancing with joy, men from other parts of the Temple began to gather, drawn by the strange sound and the amazing scene before them. Some stared at the believers in confusion.

Mary heard a man in the crowd nearby cry out, "Are these not all Galileans? How is it that we are hearing each in our own language, Parthians, Medes and Elamites, those dwelling in Mesopotamia, Judea and Cappadocia, Pontus and Asia, Phrygia and Pamphylia, Egypt and the parts of Libya adjoining Cyrene?"

Another man added, "We are visitors from Rome, proselytes, Jews from Crete and Arabia—we hear them speaking in our own tongues the wonderful works of God."

Another asked, "What could this all mean?"

Someone called out, "They are full of new wine!" and everyone laughed.

Suddenly, Peter stepped up on one of the benches near the gathered assembly and cried out, "Men of Judea and all who dwell in Jerusalem, let this be known to you, and heed my words. For these are not drunk as you suppose, since it is only the third hour of the day. But this is what was spoken by the prophet Joel:

'Adonai says:
"In the Last Days, I will pour out from my Spirit upon everyone.
Your sons and daughters will prophesy,
Your young men will see visions,
Your old men will dream dreams.
Even on my slaves, both men and women,
Will I pour out from my Spirit in those days;
And they will prophesy.
I will perform miracles in the sky above

And signs on the earth below —
Blood, fire and thick smoke.
The sun will become dark
And the moon blood
Before the great and fearful Day of ADONAI *comes.*
And then, whoever calls on the name of ADONAI *will be*
saved.'"

"Men of Israel, hear these words: Yeshua of Nazareth, a Man attested of God to you by miracles, wonders, and signs which Adonai did through him in your midst, as you yourselves also know—him being delivered by the determined purpose and foreknowledge of Adonai, you have taken by lawless hands, have crucified, and put to death; whom God raised up, having loosed the pains of death, because it was not possible that he should be held by it."

The people's attention was riveted on Peter and Mary marveled at the words that came from the mouth of this formerly so rough fisherman, for he spoke to them with power.

"David says, concerning him: *'I saw* ADONAI *always before me, for he is at my right hand, so that I will not be shaken. For this reason, my heart was glad; and my tongue rejoiced; and now my body too will live on in the certain hope that you will not abandon me to Sh'ol or let your Holy One see decay. You have made known to me the ways of life; you will fill me with joy by your presence.'*

"Men and brethren, let me speak freely to you of the patriarch David, that he is both dead and buried and his tomb is with us to this day. Therefore, being a prophet, and knowing that God had sworn with an oath to him that of the fruit of his body, according to the flesh, he would raise up the Messiah to sit on his throne, he, foreseeing this, spoke concerning the resurrection of the Messiah, that his soul was not left in Hades, nor did his flesh see corruption. This Yeshua God has raised up of which we are all witnesses.

Therefore being exalted to the right hand of God, and having received from the Father the promise of the Holy Spirit, he poured out this which you now see and hear. For David did not ascend into the heavens, but he says himself, *ADONAI said to my Lord, "Sit at my right hand until I make your enemies a footstool for your feet."*

"Therefore, let all the house of Israel know assuredly that God has made this Yeshua, whom you crucified, both Lord and Messiah."

Mary had listened with her sons and the other disciples in amazement at the speech from a man who seldom spoke any more than was necessary.

The men listening turned to one another and then to Peter and the other apostles, asking, "What then shall we do?"

Peter replied, "Repent and let every one of you be baptized in the name of Yeshua the Messiah for the remission of sins; and you shall receive the gift of the Holy Spirit. For the promise is to you and to your children and to all who afar off, as many as the Lord our God will call."

As Peter continued to exhort them, those who gladly received his words stepped forward by the hundreds to be baptized. The cleansing pools were nearby and the apostles labored the rest of the day baptizing the new believers.

Mary, Rebecca, and the other women were baptized with the rest and as Mary came up out of the water, she felt cleansed and refreshed in her soul. Those that were baptized stood and prayed for those who were lined up for their turn. It was the day to celebrate First Fruits, and here were the first fruits of the Lord's ministry.

Those on the perimeter looked on in fear at this manifestation of the Spirit and even the chief priests and leaders did not interfere, for the presence of Adonai filled the Temple.

FIFTY-NINE

As the women gathered together in a corner of Solomon's Porch, Mary turned to Magdalene. "What will you do now?"

Magdalene smiled. "My uncle is here for Shavu'ot and I believe the Lord is telling me to return with him to Magdala. I have work to do there to share what I have seen and heard."

Mary nodded, "May his grace go with you. We will meet again one day, if not here in the Holy City, then in the world to come."

The women embraced and Magdalene returned to the upper room to gather her things and meet with her uncle.

Rebecca turned to Mary. "Ima, I would like to return to Nazareth with Uncle Joses and Uncle Simon. I miss my chickens, and my baby lambs and tending my herb garden. It will be all right for Yeshua has told me so."

Surprised at the boldness of the child she had taken care of for so long, Mary could only gather Rebecca in her arms. "If Yeshua told you to go, you will be all right. You will be with your family that loves you."

Simon and Joses walked over to where they stood, their faces still glowing with the presence of the Lord and the gift they had been given. One tear ran down Rebecca's cheek as she watched her uncles embrace Mary.

"We will be back in Jerusalem and we will see each other again," Simon said, more to Mary than Rebecca.

Mary watched the three of them leave the Temple area and turned to see Jude standing nearby.

"What will you do, my son?" she asked.

"I am returning to Cana, to my home and Abigail. I will share all that has happened to me this day, and all I have seen."

When he had embraced her and gone, she looked into the crowd for James. When she finally saw him coming toward her, she waited, sensing the power of the Holy Spirit enveloping her again and sensed it had something to do with James.

"Ima," he said, reaching her side. "What will you do now? Will you stay with John?"

"For now, my son, until the Lord shows me a different path." She searched his face. "You will not be returning to Nazareth?"

"Only for a short time to gather my family. We will return here to Jerusalem. This new body of believers will need direction and organization. Peter and the other disciples have work to do here with so many new believers. I believe the Lord has given me this task."

"It suits you, James. I will remain with John as that was the Lord's wish. I want to gather the women and teach them the ways of the Lord."

"Then we will see each other from time to time, Ima. I am glad of that."

The crowds began to thin out as all who believed had been baptized. It was time for all to return to their homes and share what they had learned.

Mary stood quietly praying, uncertain of what she should do next. Then John was at her side. "Dear lady, let us return home where you may rest. We have had a glorious day and it is only the beginning. My brother James and I may eventually be traveling with Peter and the other apostles according to the admonition of the Lord to go out and share the gospel with others. First we need to teach the new believers and organize them into a *kehilot*, a new congregation. Your son has some good ideas for organizing into home groups. We have agreed to gather tomorrow as each of us seeks the Lord for direction."

For a brief moment, Mary felt bereft. She was nearly fifty years old and had seen much. Those she had been with for so long, including her family, were scattering in new directions. If one day John and his brother James left, it would only be she and Hodiah. Yet the wife of James was a godly woman and they got along well. Mary would not be alone. Together they could minister to the women who became new believers.

She took the arm of John and they walked slowly out of the Temple. This time the crowds, in respect for an older woman, parted for them.

Mary mused as they walked over the path her life had taken. From the moment so many years ago when she had been chosen of God for a fearful yet amazing task, she had done all that was asked of her. Now, facing an uncertain future, she would go forth in the power of the Holy Spirit, equipped to once again do whatever the Lord asked of her, until the day she saw him again in the life to come.

AUTHOR'S NOTE

I didn't plan on writing a book on Mary, the mother of Jesus. One only needs to browse Amazon to discover the myriad of books already written on her, this woman who looms larger than life on history's stage. But I had been contemplating the Bible and looking for inspiration for another novel when God made it very clear that Mary was to be the subject of my next book.

I felt that I was to keep one thing front and center as I wrote: Mary's humanity. She was only about fourteen years old when suddenly entrusted with the earthly son of the Most High God. What a terrible and magnificent burden for a poor, young Jewish girl, living in an insignificant Judean village!

Despite having read the story many, many times over the years, there were logistical difficulties I had never considered, as well as vast amounts of speculation surrounding Jesus' time on earth. These were the specific questions and speculations that I sought to answer in this book:

+ At such a young age, how did Mary get permission from her father to travel over one hundred and twenty miles to Juttah, where Elizabeth lived, which was past Jerusalem and Hebron? It was five days from Nazareth to Jerusalem alone. And how did she get there?

+ Living in a small house, how would Mary hide from her mother the fact that her time of the month did not come? How could she explain the angel's visitation in a way her parents could believe? Was that her reason for immediate haste to get to Elizabeth's?

+ Who helped Mary with the birth? Angels? Joseph?

+ The Scriptures say the star led the Magi, or astrologers, to Jerusalem, where they inquired of Herod and learned the prophecy from Micah stating that the "King of the Jews" was to be found in Bethlehem. How did they find the "house and the young child"? Was the star still shining over Bethlehem?

+ When were Mary's four other sons and at least two sisters born? The Scriptures name the sons—James, Joseph, Simon and Jude—but only mention "all his sisters" (plural).

+ How would I show my readers that Mary and Joseph were a typical young Jewish family, living in a small village in the hills of Judea?

+ Caught up in normal family life, was it easy for Jesus' family and his mother to forget who he was?

+ How and when did Joseph die? He is not mentioned again after Jesus' twelfth year.

+ What was Jesus' life in Nazareth like as the eldest son of the family? The son in a Jewish family was expected to take a bride by the time he was twenty—thirty at the latest. How did he and his family explain why he did not marry?

+ From the Scriptures, we learn that Christ came to earth to show us the Father, to take part in our humanity, and to proclaim the good news that the kingdom of heaven was at hand. His mission was not to marry and raise a family as has been suggested by certain writers. I firmly believe the following:

  1. Jesus was God incarnate. He was Jewish since his mother was Jewish, but his blood came from his Father, the almighty God. The blood of a child comes from the father's gene.

  2. Jesus was not to be joined to an earthly woman, for the angels of the Old Testament who left the heavenly realm

and did just that, produced the mixed race of giants and were condemned. They are being held (according to Scripture) in chains for the final judgment.

3. Mary Magdalene became a disciple out of gratitude, after Jesus had freed her from seven demons. The Scriptures do not say anywhere that she was a prostitute! She was just another grateful disciple who had been healed.

+ What was Jesus' mother, Mary, doing during the ministry of her son?

+ How did his family react to the ministry of Jesus? The Scriptures tell us that they did not believe in him until after the resurrection.

+ How could Mary face the cross, knowing the prophecy that had been given her in the angel's annunciation and the prophecy of others? What were her emotions when she saw her son dying, along with the promises she thought were made about him?

This book was a challenge—not only to retell a familiar story in a believable way, but to possibly answer the questions and speculations that I and many other readers have had. Perhaps this book stirred up questions you didn't even know you had!

Either way, let me assure you that much prayer went into this retelling, as I felt led by the Holy Spirit to write this version of the greatest story ever told. I hope it has been a blessing to you, as it was to me.

—*Diana Wallis Taylor*

ACKNOWLEDGMENTS

First, to Christine Whitaker at Whitaker House, who had a vision for *Mary, Chosen of God* and allowed me the privilege of writing this book. To Dr. Vicki Hesterman, who carefully went through the manuscript for errors and edits before it was sent to Whitaker House. To my knowledgeable Jewish friend Kimberly Farrar for her insights and suggestions to clarify references to Jewish customs and ceremonies. To Judith Dinsmore, who carefully edited the manuscript for Whitaker House and whose suggestions and encouragement enhanced the final copy. To my San Diego Christian Writer's Guild critique group for their insights and suggestions on difficult chapters: Martha Gorris, Ann Larson, Mary Kay Moody, Felicia Cameron, Sandi Esch, and Jean Mader (our grammar grandma). And finally, to my readers, who have encouraged me with their comments through the years and even sent in suggestions for titles. To all of you, I am enormously grateful and extend my profound thanks.

ABOUT THE AUTHOR

*D*iana Wallis Taylor was first published at the age of twelve, when she sold a poem to a church newsletter. Today, she has an extensive portfolio of published works, including a collection of poetry; an Easter cantata, written with a musical collaborator; contributions to various magazines and compilations; seven novels, including *Martha, Mary Magdalene, Claudia Wife of Pontius Pilate, Ruth Mother of Kings, Shadows on the Mountain, House of the Forest* and *Smoke Before the Wind* as well as a book on Halloween. Diana lives in San Diego with her husband, Frank. They have six grown children and nine grandchildren. Readers can learn more by visiting her website, www.dianawallistaylor.com.